She needed sleep badly

Tala Newsome knew that Dr. Pete Jacobi and his father had probably forgotten all about her. They were engrossed in their task—saving the life of the lion.

She leaned her head back against the bars and closed her eyes. She felt the gentlest caress on the top of her head. She blinked and yawned. The two men were still hard at work halfway across the big room.

There it was again. A fairy's breath that ruffled her hair slightly. She rubbed her hand over her head and felt the bars behind her. Must be her imagination. She relaxed again, and a moment later felt a tug on her hair. She reached behind her and felt…

She stifled a scream, jumped up and spun around. An elephant's trunk extended through the bars behind her. She froze as it slid gently over her face, down her cheek, then patted her shoulder as if to console her.

She gulped, moved back four paces and realized that she was looking into the faces of three large gray lumps clustered on the other side of the bars. Three elephants stood shoulder to shoulder, swinging their trunks gently back and forth.

"Hello, girls." Tala heard the affection in Pete's voice. "Just let me finish here and I'll introduce you."

Dear Reader,

What would you do if your truck nearly struck a wounded
African lion on a country road at two in the morning? Not
in deepest Africa, mind you, but in the Tennessee hills.
I'd probably lock the doors and do a fast U-turn, but the
heroine of *Safe at Home* has a stronger spirit. By morning
she's not only nursing the lion, but baby-sitting a trio of
opinionated elephants, as well.

All because she needs help from a grumpy veterinarian who
prefers animals to human beings.

Dr. Pete Jacobi doesn't want Tala Newsome around his
elephant sanctuary. She disturbs his mind and reawakens
his heart to feelings he's denied.

If that isn't bad enough, widowed Tala comes complete
with a son, a nearly adolescent daughter, an outrageous
grandmother-in-law and a tough mother-in-law—none of
whom intend to let some scruffy vet within a mile of Tala.
Pete can't cope with himself, much less an entire family.

Tala's not coping very well, either. She's broke, unable to
understand her kids, trying to live up to her in-laws and
fulfill her promise to her dead husband. Falling in love
with Pete Jacobi is the *last* complication she needs.

But love doesn't give a hoot about timing....

I hope you enjoy Pete and Tala's story—and, of course, the
elephants—Sophie, Sweetie Pie and Belle.

Carolyn McSparren

SAFE AT HOME
Carolyn
McSparren

HARLEQUIN®

TORONTO • NEW YORK • LONDON
AMSTERDAM • PARIS • SYDNEY • HAMBURG
STOCKHOLM • ATHENS • TOKYO • MILAN • MADRID
PRAGUE • WARSAW • BUDAPEST • AUCKLAND

ISBN 0-373-70892-0

SAFE AT HOME

Visit us at www.romance.net

Printed in U.S.A.

For the wonderful people at Y.E.A.R., the Yoknapatawpha Exotic Animal Refuge, for bringing me nose to nose with lions and tigers (pretty scary), and for The Elephant Sanctuary who told me about the logistics of keeping elephants. Any errors are mine, not theirs.

For Bruce Bowling, a veterinarian who puts up with 4:00 a.m. emergency calls.

Last but not least, for the nationwide large animal sanctuary system that provides a peaceful retirement for some of mankind's rejects.

CHAPTER ONE

SOMETHING TRIGGERED the alarm on the front gate. Pete Jacobi jerked awake, narrowed his eyes at the lighted alarm clock beside his bed. Two-thirteen in the morning. He'd been asleep less than three hours.

He groaned and raised his head. Icy rain still thrummed against his bedroom window. The powerful halogen motion detectors mounted under the eaves and by the front gate shattered the droplets into prisms.

If that was some local teenager trying to sneak in to test his nerve against the elephants, he'd picked the wrong weather for it. The girls were undoubtedly snoring contentedly in their enclosure. Or would have been until the noise woke them. They'd be pretty grumpy if any spotty adolescent kid from Hollendale tried to hoo-raw them tonight.

During the summer the girls often roamed the east Tennessee hills of the sanctuary most of the night, but they didn't like really cold weather. Although when the trees started to ice up, and Pete tried to insist that they wear their earmuffs, they'd pay little attention to him. If they wanted them off, off they'd come.

He swung out of bed, jerked on the jeans he'd

thrown on the floor, thrust his bare feet into the muddy rubber boots he'd dropped beside them. "Damn!" he snarled as his cold toes met the even colder rubber.

The lights and alarms should have spooked any normal intruder home to Hollendale by now. Pete shut off the alarm and heard in its place the insistent burping of the intercom he'd installed at the gate a couple of months earlier. Someone was still out there. He hit the talk switch. "Yeah?"

The voice that answered him was female and full of concern. "Please, you've got to help her! She's bleeding."

He jerked fully awake. "I'm a vet, not a doctor."

"I *need* a vet. I've got to get her inside. She's so cold already, I'm afraid she'll die on the way to town. I think somebody shot her."

He ran his hand over his hair and blinked to clear his eyes. "Okay, okay, lady. Relax. I'll come open the gate." He yanked his wet poncho from the hook beside the door and pulled it on over his shoulders. It felt as though he'd jumped into a vat of raw oysters. He took a deep breath, pulled open the office door and sprinted for the high-wire gates. His feet slipped and threw globs of mud onto his legs at every step.

She was hanging on to the far side of the gate with both hands. The moment she saw him, she turned and climbed into the front seat of a small pickup truck and slammed the door.

He clicked the padlock loose and began to pull the tall wire gates open. "Tomorrow I'm ordering an electric gate opener,'' he snarled into the teeth of the wind. He wouldn't, of course. Any extra money went to feed his girls, not to make his life easier.

The moment he'd shoved the left-hand gate open far enough for her to squeeze the pickup through, she floored the thing. He'd been intending to climb into the passenger seat beside her. Instead, her tires threw up a wall of icy muck that hit him square in the face. He yelped.

''Thanks a bunch!'' he called after her as he closed the gate and hooked the open padlock over the hasp. He wiped his face with one hand and strode back to the office. She'd slammed on her brakes and now stood beside the bed of the truck. She was wearing a dark parka with the hood pulled forward over her face. He could tell nothing about her except that she was maybe five foot six and slim.

''Help me. I can't move her.''

He leaned over the back of the truck expecting to see whatever dog or possum or coon she'd run over with her car. His mouth fell open. He turned to the woman. ''Is she yours?''

''No. I found her on the road. She's so still. She's not dead, is she?''

He reached a tentative hand next to the animal's rib cage. He felt a flutter. ''She's alive, but I don't know for how long.'' Without glancing at the woman, he said, ''Go around the side of the building to the parking area and in through the small door. Inside you'll find a button that raises the overhead door. I'll drive her in.''

He realized as the woman started away that if she

disappeared at this moment he would have no idea what she looked like or who she was.

He spun the tires getting the truck started, then moved it toward the growing oblong of light as the door lifted. He drove into the cavernous room, turned off the engine and stepped out of the truck. "Okay, close the door," he said. "Sleet's getting in."

She punched the button again, and the door began to lower. He jabbed at the intercom button on the telephone mounted on the wall beside him.

"There's no time to call anybody," she said urgently.

He waved her away. After a moment, a sleepy voice answered.

"Dad?" he said. "Throw on some clothes and get over here fast. Bullet wound. No, the elephants are fine." Pete glanced at the truck. "You are not going to believe this. Some crazy woman's just dragged in a half-grown female African lion."

"OKAY, BOY, what's all this about a lioness?" Mace Jacobi slammed the door to the parking area behind him, shucked his parka and gloves and walked over to the pickup truck.

"Take a look," Pete said. He'd hung his poncho beside the side door and slipped into a sweatshirt. He knelt on the lowered tailgate. "Can you believe this?"

Mace peered over his son's shoulder. "Well, I'll be damned!" He turned to the woman who hung over the side of the truck. Her fingers gently caressed the golden pelt of the animal. "She yours?"

"No. I almost ran over her on the road. At first I thought she was a big yellow dog, but the tail was too long, and she didn't move like a dog. Then she turned and looked at me and her eyes went red in the headlights and…" She took a deep breath. "She just keeled over. I jammed on the brakes and slid all over the road. Almost wound up going over the side of Bryson's Hollow."

"Bryson's Hollow?" Pete asked. "What's a lone woman doing driving the Hollow road this time of night?"

"I live down there. Please, there's no time for this. Can you help her?"

"Got to get her out of this truck and onto the examining table," Pete said. "Can't do it alone. Don't know how you managed it."

"I carry a big piece of plywood in the back of my truck. I dragged her onto it and used my trailer winch to haul her up."

"Madam," Mace said formally, "I take my hat off to you."

"She could have bitten your head off," Pete said. "Come on, Dad, she can't weigh more than a couple of hundred pounds."

"More or less. Madam, please be so good as to position your truck so that the rear end backs up to that steel table over there. No sense in carrying her farther than we have to."

Five minutes later, Pete and Mace Jacobi had the unconscious cat on the steel table. She was limp, but the heavy bones and sinews of her body looked like steel cables under her fur.

"What can I do?" the woman asked.

"You've done your part," Pete answered. "Dad, better get a full syringe of ACE ready in case she starts to come around. She's going to be pretty pissed off when she does."

"*If* she does," Mace said as he slid his stethoscope onto the animal's rib cage.

Pete gently probed the blood-matted pelt on her shoulder. "Doesn't seemed to have nicked any major vessels, and it's so damned hog-killing cold, the bleeding's pretty much stopped. Somebody shot her all right. No obvious exit wound. Bullet must still be in there."

"I'll get the X ray." Pete turned and nearly fell over the woman. "Why don't you go sit down back there out of the way and let us work."

She backed off as Pete rolled a heavy piece of steel equipment out of a cabinet in the corner by the office door.

"Listen, I can't keep calling you lady. You got a name?"

"Newsome. Tala Newsome."

Tala? Odd name. He wasn't certain he'd heard her correctly. But Newsome he recognized. The Newsomes owned most of the county and half the businesses in Hollendale. Irene Newsome was on the county council Mace had dealt with when he built the sanctuary.

Tala Newsome shoved back the hood of her parka and began to unzip it. Her long black braid was soaked and hair stuck to her cheeks in pencil-thin tendrils. Her nose was red, her cheeks and lips denim blue. And her eyes...

He stopped in midstride as her eyes hit him like a cannon shot. Then his father's voice jerked him back to the present.

"Don't stand there, boy. She's starting to warm up. Don't need her jumping up and tearing our heads off."

TALA SANK into a wooden kitchen chair propped against the metal bars that closed off the back section of the enormous room. The moment she sat down she realized how tired she was and how badly her shoulders ached.

Even without the lioness, the drive out to the farmhouse in Bryson's Hollow was no picnic. After midnight with winter sleet pelting the road, it was downright treacherous. Nights like this she wished she still lived in town with Irene, Vertie and the kids.

But she couldn't—not permanently. She'd tried staying in the big old Newsome mansion after Adam died, but as wonderful as Vertie and Irene were, she'd felt as if by leaving the farmhouse she'd somehow broken her last connection to her dead husband. She needed to be in Bryson's Hollow for now. Maybe someday she could move on, but not now, not yet. Not with so much unfinished business and so many promises to keep.

Besides, if she'd stayed with the Newsomes tonight, she'd never have found the lion.

She blinked her eyes, shook her head to clear it, and watched the two men working in the circle of light over the steel table. The rest of the storeroom, or hospital, or whatever it was, lay in shadow.

The younger one, Pete, was doing the surgery. She'd known he was here, of course. The whole town knew about the elephant sanctuary, but she'd never seen him, not even at the grocery store.

He had a good face, a strong jaw and crinkles at the corners of his eyes. At the moment they looked more like frown lines than laugh lines, but he might have a nice smile if he ever bothered to use it.

Of course, who wouldn't be grouchy being dragged out of bed at two in the morning in a sleet storm?

His father wasn't grouchy, though. He'd been woken up as well, but he'd spoken kindly to Tala. He was almost courtly, and he'd taken time to smooth his iron-gray hair and beard. But then, Tala hadn't given Dr. Pete Jacobi time to do much except throw on his clothes.

He looked a great deal like his father, only bigger. Much bigger. Like a professional football player. Or a big, brown grizzly. And when he'd stripped off that wet poncho, he had real muscles, and lots of chest hair. Broad shoulders…kind of a hunk…

In the semidarkness where she sat, she felt her eyelids grow heavy and jerked awake.

She ought to open the overhead door and drive back out into the night. She'd done all she could do for the cat, and she'd worked a double shift at the Food Farm tonight.

She needed sleep badly. She could simply unhook the padlock on the front gate and close it after her.

The younger Dr. Jacobi hadn't actually locked the thing, merely hooked it over the hasp. The men probably wouldn't even notice she'd gone.

Except that the minute that door began to lift, the wind and rain would whip in again. And one of them would have to leave what he was doing to close it behind her.

Excuses. What she really wanted—needed—was to stay until they finished, until they could tell her whether or not the cat would live. She couldn't bear the thought that it might die.

She'd been through too much death.

She leaned her head back against the bars behind her and closed her eyes. In an instant Adam's face swam up from her subconscious. Didn't often happen nowadays. She'd almost forgotten what having a husband was like, the sound of his laughter, the warmth of his arms around her...

She felt the gentlest caress on the top of her head as though someone had picked up a hank of hair between thumb and index finger. She blinked her eyes and yawned. The two men still worked halfway across the big room.

There it was again. A fairy's breath that ruffled her hair slightly. She rubbed her hand over her head and felt the bars behind her. Imagination. Too little sleep. Too much excitement. She relaxed again, and a moment later felt a tug on her hair. She reached behind her and felt...

She stifled a scream, jumped up and spun around. An elephant's trunk extended through the bars behind her. She froze. It slid gently over her face, down her cheek, then patted her shoulder, almost as though consoling her.

She gulped, moved slowly back four paces, and realized that she was looking into the faces of three large gray lumps clustered on the other side of the bars. There were six concerned eyes, not two.

The elephants stood shoulder to shoulder, swinging their trunks gently back and forth. She hadn't heard them approach—not a single footfall or shuffle on the concrete floor of what must be their cage. Where had they come from? Dark as it was, she could swear they hadn't been there earlier when she sat down.

She felt a sough of wind against her face. Around the corner of the enclosure in deep darkness she saw some kind of heavy plastic sway slightly. It looked like the barrier at a car wash. She fought down a giggle. She'd seen dog doors and cat doors, but never an elephant door.

The center elephant, by far the largest, with skin as heavily wrinkled as a hundred-year-old crone, reached out to her again. This time Tala put her palm up so that she could feel its soft breath on her fingertips. She reached out her other hand and stroked the long gray nose tentatively.

She felt her eyes begin to well with tears.

"Got the blasted thing!" Pete Jacobi shouted. Tala jumped, the elephants snuffled and swung away. The moment was over.

She turned to the light. Pete held up a round object in a pair of steel forceps. "Looks heavy—.357 Magnum at a guess. Came from a fair distance, otherwise there'd be more damage and one hell of an exit wound. Good thing it wasn't a rifle. What nut would go after a lion with a handgun?''

''For that matter,'' Mace answered, his head bent, his gloved hands busy with the wound, ''who'd have a lion around here to go after in the first place?''

Pete turned to look at Tala and smiled. She felt her heart turn over. His eyes really did crinkle at the corners, and he had a nice, wide mouth. She started to smile back when she realized he was looking past her.

''Hello, girls,'' he said. ''Not real thrilled at the sleet?''

She heard an answering snuffle and stomp. ''Let me get this wound closed and I'll introduce you,'' he said. Whether he planned to introduce her to the elephants or the elephants to her, she wasn't entirely certain. She suspected his priorities were elephants first, human beings second.

Tala knew no more than anyone in Hollendale knew about the two veterinarians. She'd seen Mace buying groceries at the Food Farm, but she'd never actually met him, although Irene liked him.

Apparently the younger one seldom went outside the sanctuary, and when he did, he pointedly ignored any effort to make friends. A real sourpuss, her mother-in-law had called him.

But watching his fingers as he worked over the big cat, Tala knew she'd been right to stop here, instead of driving the lion into town to Dr. Wiskowski's clinic. The way this vet smiled at his girls proved he wasn't a sourpuss with animals.

"Have you thought what we're going to do with her?" Mace asked his son. "We're certainly not set up for big cats, and she's got to be under constant supervision."

"One thing at a time, Dad." Pete's hands made gestures over the cat's shoulder. "While I'm closing, better give her a massive shot of antibiotics," he said.

"Right." Mace went to a drug cabinet along the wall, pulled a small key off a hook beside it, opened the cabinet and rooted among the bottles and jars. He held one up and squinted at it over the tops of his bifocals. "This ought to do." Then he pulled a large syringe from a drawer under the cabinet and filled it with milky liquid from the bottle. He returned the remaining medication, carefully locked the cabinet again and hung the key beside it.

Mace held up a small piece of the lioness's fur and slid the needle sideways into her neck. She didn't stir.

"Shouldn't she be waking up?" Tala asked.

"Bite your tongue," Mace said.

"The longer she's out of it, the safer for everybody," Pete added. "I'd prefer not to give her anything to put her under again if I can help it. Her heartbeat's a little weak. Big cats can lose a fair amount of blood without too much danger, but we have no way of knowing how much she bled before you found her, and it's not as though we've got a handy donor to give her a transfusion."

Mace peered down at the animal. "Neat. Couldn't have done better myself. Okay, now what?"

"I've still got that old dog kennel you used for the beagles," Pete said. "Won't hold her if she decides to climb out over the top, but with that shoulder, I don't think she'll feel much like moving for a couple of days. We can hook it together in a few minutes, put down some blankets and a water dish and close up the room."

"And pray she doesn't wake up and destroy the place."

Pete glanced at Tala. "You have any idea what you were getting into?"

"No. But I probably would have done it anyway," she said. "Only I don't know how I'll pay you..."

"Don't sweat it," Mace said, smiling at her over the tops of his glasses. "Don't often get a chance these days to work on a big cat. Kind of miss it."

"We'll work something out," Pete said.

Mace turned to his son. "Come on, boy, let's find those kennel panels."

"Can I help?" Tala asked.

"Nope. Climb into your truck and shut the doors in case she wakes up before we get back. Leave the windows up."

"She wouldn't hurt me."

"Yeah. Right," Pete said, and looked down at the cat. "Let's get her on the ground before we leave. Don't want her coming to and falling off the table onto the concrete."

"Get a blanket. We can lay her on that and then slide her onto it when we get the cage set up," Mace said.

Thirty minutes later all three of them grabbed the

blanket and slid the cat into the kennel. It was six feet high and built of sturdy steel cyclone fencing, but it had no cover, nor was it anchored to the concrete. One good bash by a large furry body could send it crashing to the floor.

At the moment, however, the cat slept. Pete filled a plastic bucket with water, set it in the corner of the pen and securely fastened the door to the enclosure behind him. "Keep your fingers crossed," he said.

"You better get on home," Mace told Tala kindly. "It's nearly four in the morning. Your folks'll be worried about you. Want to call them before you leave?"

"No one will miss me," she said, and realized how pitiful she sounded. "I mean, I live alone at the moment." She fought a yawn. She was suddenly desperately tired, so tired her knees started to give way.

She felt a sinewy arm around her waist, and grasped Pete's shoulder.

"Hey! Don't pass out now!" he snapped.

"She's out on her feet," Mace said. "No way can you drive home, my dear. Not along the Hollow road." He turned to his son. "She'd better bed down here for a few hours."

"Here?"

She pulled away from him. "I'll be fine."

"No, Dad's right. You're punchy. You've got no business driving as far as the gate." Pete walked off toward the door at the front of the room. "Come on. You can have the sofa. I'd give you the bed, but I've messed it up already, and you fit on the sofa better than I would."

"I couldn't—I've—you've…"

"I won't attack you."

"Better take him up on it," Mace said, and kneaded her shoulder gently. "I'll fix you one of my special caffeine bombs in the morning. That'll keep you awake until Christmas."

She glanced at the lioness. "Do you think maybe she might wake up before I have to leave?"

"Maybe."

That decided her. She nodded.

"You go on," Mace said. "I'll back your truck out and leave it outside by the front door with the keys in it. Don't want claw marks on it if she gets out."

"Right," Pete said.

"Oh, and Pete, if you do somehow manage to sleep in, I'll feed the girls in the morning and check on our patient. I'll wake you if I need you," Mace said.

Pete hunkered down a moment beside the cat, whose great pink tongue lolled between long, white teeth. "She'll probably wake us up early. If she starts mouthing off inside these metal walls, it's gonna sound like the hallelujah chorus."

Mace yawned and opened the door of Tala's truck. "Whatever happens to her now, my dear, take it from me, you did a fine job."

Pete shepherded her through the door in the far wall that led down a short hall to his quarters.

"What a sweet man," she said when the door closed behind them.

"Tell that to the vet students he's terrorized over the years."

"Vet students?"

"Yeah. He taught veterinary medicine for twenty-five years. Lived and breathed it. Now he's retired, he's terrorizing me." Pete opened a closet door and pulled out blankets, bedding and a pillow. "Now, we have to get you out of those wet clothes."

"I just want a flat place to lie down before I fall down," she said, looking around. The small living room obviously also served both as office and kitchen.

The gray tweed couch was plenty long enough, but from the looks of it, was nearly as old as the doctor himself. At this point, however, lumpy mattresses were the least of her concerns.

"You can have one of my old sweatshirts." Pete looked her up and down. "Probably come down to your knees. And I keep fresh toothbrushes in the guest bathroom."

For unexpected female overnight guests, no doubt. The ones who did *not* sleep on the couch. Although if he was as gracious to them as he'd been to her, she doubted he'd have many takers. "You're very kind."

He seemed to withdraw instantly from her small compliment. He tossed the bedding onto the sofa, disappeared into his bedroom, and a moment later tossed a gray sweatshirt on top of the pile. "Here. The guest bathroom's down the hall. You passed it on the way in. Fresh towels under the sink."

"Thank you."

"G'night," he said and shut his bedroom door. Not quite a slam, but close.

She made up her bed, stripped off her wet clothes in the bathroom and slipped on the sweatshirt. It had shrunk so short it barely covered her crotch, but was so big through the chest and so long in the arms that she probably resembled one of his "girls." She waved a gray arm at the mirror like a trunk and considered trumpeting, but thought better of it. She didn't think he'd be amused.

She tried to wring some of the water out of her long braid, pulled off the rubber band that held it and loosened her hair with her fingers. Come morning it would look as though rats had taken up residence, but at least it would be dry.

She realized she had left her purse with her comb inside her truck. It could darned well stay there. She'd retrieve it tomorrow morning.

She crawled onto the couch, snuggled down and listened to the rain drum on the windows.

She'd get up early and drive to the Newsome mansion in time to have breakfast with Vertie, Irene and the kids. She could hardly wait to tell them her wild story. Surely even thirteen-year-old Rachel couldn't act blasé about a real live lion. Eight-year-old Cody would probably beg to skip school and drive right back to the sanctuary to see for himself. Her children thought she was pretty boring. If this didn't make her at least a little interesting, nothing would.

She heard something more like a cough than a roar from that big room. Tala was up and through the door before she gave a thought to what might be waiting for her on the other side.

The lioness eased herself up on her good right paw and raised her head as she let out another half roar.

Tala dropped to her knees beside the kennel and laid a tentative hand flat against the wire mesh, ready to snatch it away. Instead, the cat butted her forehead against the mesh, for all the world like a house cat. "Hello, baby," Tala crooned as she worked her fingers through the mesh to scratch behind the lioness's ears. The animal rewarded her with a low thrumming sound.

"Are you nuts?" Pete Jacobi said from behind her.

"Look, she's awake," Tala said softly.

The lioness sat up and bared her teeth at Pete.

"Get out of there!" He grabbed her arm and hauled her to her feet, then practically dragged her back through the door. Suddenly he seemed to realize he was holding a barefoot woman wearing nothing but a pair of lace underpants and his old sweatshirt. He dropped his hands and backed off, although she could have sworn that the look he gave her legs was appreciative.

A moment later he was his old grim self. "Woman, don't you go through that door again under any circumstances. You hear me? The next time she could be sitting on top of the file cabinet waiting to bite your head off."

"But—"

"Listen," he said as though she were about three years old. "That is a lion in there. An *L-I-O-N*. It is not some big old pussycat. It is a carnivorous wild animal, and it's hurt. It doesn't know why it's hurt or who hurt it, and it will not differentiate between the good guys and the bad. You, lady, are not its rescuer, you are *breakfast*. Are we clear on that?''

''But—''

''Are we clear?''

She nodded.

''Now go to bed and let me get a couple of hours' sleep. And if she roars again, stick your head under the pillow and ignore her.''

But Tala found herself straining to hear another of those chuffing sounds.

After about five minutes of quiet, she began to drift off. The last face to swim into her consciousness was not Adam's, but Pete Jacobi's, his fierce amber eyes glowing out of a craggy face that seemed to morph into the face of a male lion with a heavy mane in place of his unruly hair. The face opened its mouth, but instead of that momentary smile she'd seen when he looked at the elephants, she saw only very long and very sharp teeth. *The better to eat you with, my dear,* she thought as sleep finally claimed her.

CHAPTER TWO

PETE JACOBI WAS HALFWAY through his morning shower before he remembered the woman asleep on the sofa. He must be in a bad way if he'd forgotten even for an instant the sight of those great legs sticking out from under his baggy old shirt. Very sexy. Much sexier than if she'd been naked.

Well, maybe not. Might be interesting to compare. He grinned at his reflection and arched an eyebrow at himself. Yeah.

Once she stopped looking like a drowned possum she'd turned into a good-looking woman. But too thin. Still, she either had gumption—or no brains at all.

He dressed as quietly at he could and opened the bedroom door. He half expected her to be up and gone. He hoped she wasn't. It would be nice if she stayed long enough for a cup of coffee and for him to check out his perceptions about her from last night. He wanted to see whether those big dark eyes were as stunning as he remembered.

From his door he saw one very shapely leg and bare foot sticking out from under a pile of quilts on the couch, and a cloud of long, heavy black hair spread over the other end of the quilt and falling almost to the floor. Somewhere between the two, the owner of hair and leg slept on.

Her right hand lay draped over the arm of the couch. The hand was thin and almost too fine-boned. Her nails were short and unvarnished, but well kept. He realized with a pang that he hadn't noticed whether she wore a wedding ring or not, and suddenly hoped that she didn't.

Pete shook his head, surprised at himself for his interest in her. He tiptoed past the couch and opened the door to the back room silently, then slipped through.

The lioness lay on her right side with her bandaged shoulder up. Her eyes rolled back in her head and her mouth gaped. Her tongue lolled from the corner of her mouth.

For a panicky moment he was afraid she wasn't breathing, then he saw the slow rise and fall of her rib cage.

"Morning, son," said a voice behind him. "Gave her another shot for pain. She has been sleeping the sleep of the innocent and pure of heart for some time. Where's your lady friend?"

"Doing the same, although *she* might not be so pure and innocent if she's driving country roads alone at two in the morning."

Mace Jacobi grinned and waggled his eyebrows. "What's that old song about preferring the sadder but wiser girl? Especially one as good-looking as that."

"Too scrawny. I didn't know there was a Newsome daughter."

"There isn't. Irene Newsome lost her only child more than a year ago. He was something fairly high up in the Fish and Wildlife. Supposedly shot by a poacher. Had a wife and a couple of kids. That's probably his widow you've got on your couch." Mace slapped a couple of white-wrapped packages on the steel table, looked at them over his bifocals and began to unwrap them. "I haven't had time to feed the girls yet."

"No problem. I'll do it." Pete hooked a bale of alfalfa and carried it toward the elephant enclosure. The girls waited impatiently, trunks swinging, their beady black eyes expectant. "What are you doing, Dad?" he asked on his way by.

"I started thawing a couple of deer-neck roasts last night. Thought I'd carve 'em up for Tala's baby over there. She's going to be mighty hungry when she wakes up."

"If she wakes up."

Mace peered at him over his glasses. "Oh, she'll wake up, all right. You did a good job. Every bit as good as I was at your age."

Pete broke the wires on the alfalfa and tossed fat green flakes through the bars for his girls. "Good morning, girls," he said with affection. They looked down their trunks at him. Once again he was aware of how differently they responded to Mace. They were much warmer toward his father. Pete seemed to have lost his "trunkside manner."

"Oh, I'm so sorry. I didn't mean to sleep so long," came a soft voice from behind him. Amazingly, his girls raised their heads in unison and lifted their trunks toward the voice. They never greeted *him* like that.

He'd long since realized that elephants were a whole lot more perceptive than human beings. The girls were aware of his fondness for them, but no matter how well he fed, scrubbed, pampered and babied them, they still treated him with a kind of offhand exasperation. Maybe they sensed his unhappiness—his guilt over past mistakes. Maybe one day they'd decide he'd made the grade and grant him their complete trust and affection.

"You were exhausted, m'dear," said Mace without looking up from the meat cleaver in his hands. "As soon as I get this done, we'll go over to my trailer and I'll make us all a good hot breakfast. The coffee's already on."

"Oh, I couldn't. I've already—"

"Nonsense," Mace rumbled. "My pancakes are legendary." He peered over his glasses at her. "You could use some honey and maple syrup."

Tala went to the lioness's cage and hunkered down. "How is she?" she whispered.

"As well as can be expected," Pete answered. "Dad doped her up again for the pain."

She put her left hand against the wire mesh and caressed the lioness gently. "Sweet Baby," she said. The lioness rumbled softly.

She wore no wedding ring. Pete was surprised at the relief he felt. Then as he leaned forward he saw that she wore a gold chain around her neck. Two gold bands, one larger and wider than the other, hung on the chain. Her wedding ring? Her dead husband's? He sighed.

Not that he was looking for a relationship. Not after Val. His heart lurched at the memory of Val, and his never-ending guilt.

Her fingers toyed gently with the pelt on the lioness's head. Pete took a deep breath at the thought of those fingers curling in the heavy mat of hair on his chest. He set his jaw, furious with himself that he'd allowed even that momentary distraction.

After a moment, Tala stood up easily and gracefully, something not many women could do from that kind of position.

Pete realized he was staring. No, glaring was more like it. She was too thin, all right, but definitely stood out in the right places. She'd plaited her dark hair into a single braid that hung down her back almost to her waist. The overhead light cut shadows under her strong cheekbones. Showed the circles under her eyes as well, unfortunately.

She smiled at him tentatively. "I folded the bedclothes and the shirt and put them on the foot of your bed," she said.

He rumbled something at her. He couldn't tear his gaze from her eyes. He'd never seen eyes that dark or that wide on a human being. They tilted at the corners, and even without makeup her lashes swept her cheeks.

"Last night you said you'd introduce me," she said and walked over to him. She moved like a dancer. Maybe she'd been a dancer at one time. Could be that was the reason she was so thin.

"Sure." Why did he always sound so abrupt when he spoke to her? "Sophie is on the right, the one in back is Sweetiepie, and the big one is Belle."

"She's the one that patted my head with her trunk last night and nearly scared me witless," Tala said, smiling over his shoulder.

He gaped at her. "She touched you?"

"Through the bars. Very gently. I knew you had elephants, of course, but I didn't know how many, and I hadn't seen them before. I was half-asleep in that old kitchen chair pushed right up against them. I didn't realize it was their cage."

He bristled. "They're not caged. Not any longer."

"I loved it." She leaned against the bars. "They are beautiful, aren't they?"

"Should have seen them when they got here," he said. "Skin and bones."

Mace looked up over the tops of his glasses. "The bars are to keep them from investigating—actually I mean destroying—this room. Elephants are endlessly curious. Unfortunately, they are also incredibly destructive while they're about it."

"But last night, Belle touched me so gently."

"She wasn't interested in seeing the inside of your brain," Pete said. "But if she decided to see the inside of that cabinet over there—" he pointed toward the drug cabinet "—she would just as carefully knock it over and stomp it until the doors popped off to check out what's inside."

"Oh." Tala glanced at the girls, who were keeping one eye on her while they bundled hay into their mouths. "Would you do that?" she asked Sophie.

As if in answer, Sophie dipped her head and curled her trunk.

Tala laughed.

Pete jumped. Her laugh was low, but it seemed to glitter in the chill air. Suddenly he felt as though he'd happily stick on a false nose and do pratfalls over floppy clown shoes if he could hear her laugh again. Too long without a woman, he decided, that was all it was. Too much Mace, too many elephants, not enough human companionship.

A low growl came from the lioness's enclosure. Tala looked at her quickly. "Oh, I'm so sorry, I didn't mean to wake the baby."

Suddenly she was all mouse again, anxious and subdued.

"The scent of meat woke her, not you. Ah, m'dear," Mace said over his shoulder, "might we be ready for a bite of breakfast?" He smiled over at Tala. "I'd say you've been christened Baby." The lioness stared at him with narrow, yellow eyes.

"Watch it, Mace," Pete said. "A hungry cat is a dangerous cat. Your dictum, remember? First time I went to work at the zoo."

"This particular baby, however, is missing both her front claws and her top left incisor," Mace said. "She could still kill me, but she'd have to work at it."

"What?" Tala asked. She looked from the older man to the younger. "You didn't tell me that."

"No reason to," Pete told her. "Didn't make much difference last night. But it means she's been somebody's pet—inasmuch as a lion can ever be a pet.''

"But people will still try," Mace said, neatly arranging bits of meat and bone in a steel bucket. The lioness rumbled in anticipation.

"Surely they know better," Tala said. "I mean, look at the size of her, and you say she's still young."

Pete shrugged. "They watch a National Geographic special or an episode of *Nova* and see a bunch of cute lion cubs playing around on-screen and they think how great it would be to have something like that. So they pick up the phone and order one."

"Order one? Like a pizza?"

"Not quite that simple, but even now that the government has cracked down on importing exotic animals, there are plenty of places where you can buy a lion cub born in the States and have it brought to you, if you've got the money, that is."

"But it's illegal to own exotic animals, isn't it?" she said. "In Tennessee, I mean."

"Sure is," Pete agreed, forking another flake of hay toward Belle. "Some people think they're above the law. Of course, in some places lions are used to police marijuana patches and other illegal operations. Scarier than dogs."

"My word," she exclaimed. "You mean she might have been guarding something up by the Hollow? What about the deer? How could you keep her from roaming to hunt?"

"Maybe you couldn't. Maybe she got out and her owner shot her when he couldn't get her back."

"I can't believe that. I grew up in the Hollow, and I wander all over it in the summertime. There's not enough flat land to grow a decent crop of collard greens, much less marijuana."

"All the easier to hide the plants in, m'dear," Mace said. "You'd be surprised what some people will get up to in the name of money. Still, I wouldn't think anyone would have declawed her or defanged her for use as a guard. More likely she was a pet that got too big and was dumped too far from home to find her way back."

"And then shot?"

"Possibly by someone who thought she was a cougar," Pete said. "She's the right color."

"But they're protected," Tala said. "And terribly rare. My husband was a warden and spent a good deal of time in the woods, but even he'd never seen one. I certainly haven't. As we said, Tennessee has awfully strict laws about exotic and protected animals. People were surprised you were able to get permission to bring in your elephants."

"You should have seen the hoops I had to jump through," Pete said. "And the girls aren't going to eat the neighbor's poodle—or the neighbor's kid, come to that."

"No. But they might stomp him, mightn't they?" Tala asked.

"Highly unlikely. I only take female Indian elephants. They can be a nuisance and certainly get cranky sometimes, but now that they can move around the place freely, they enjoy life—possibly for the first time since they stopped nursing on their mothers. And I've gone to great pains with the twelve-foot fences to ensure they don't go rampaging through the soybean fields around here.''

Mace held the steel bucket out to Pete. "Here. Feed the lioness.''

Pete felt Tala's breath on his shoulder as he turned away from her and walked over to the lioness's enclosure. The cat raised her body on her right paw and tried to stand. She made a deep trilling sound in the back of her throat, then let out a full-throated roar that shook the steel walls.

"Hold on,'' Pete said. He set the bucket down in front of the door to the enclosure, opened it a few inches and used the end of his pitchfork to shove the bucket inside. Then he quickly closed and locked the door.

The cat instantly swiped at the bucket with her muzzle and knocked it over so that its contents spilled on the concrete in front of her blanket. She collapsed in front of it and began to eat noisily.

Pete stood and felt Tala's hand on his arm. Her fingers felt warm and gentle.

"She's hungry. That's a good sign, isn't it?''

"Yes, it's a good sign.''

"What happens now?'' Tala asked.

"Damned if I know. We could be in big trouble just having her here. I need to call the Fish and Wildlife people. Find out what they want to do with her. You know anybody over there I could talk to?''

"I guess so. But please, don't call yet. I know they'll drag her off. Maybe they'll shoot her!'' Tala's dark eyes were enormous.

"Look, she obviously belongs to somebody. Illegally, but maybe somebody's looking for her."

"The same somebody who's already tried to shoot her! The one who bought that cute little cub a couple of years ago. You can't abandon her."

Maybe he'd been wrong about her being a wimp, Pete thought. Plenty of fight in her now.

"I can't risk the sanctuary either." He gestured toward the girls, who were watching the interchange avidly, as though they understood every word.

"She needs sanctuary, too. Just because she's not an elephant…"

"I am not licensed as a big-cat sanctuary."

"Somebody must be."

He took a deep breath. "Dammit, I can't take on new problems. I have my hands full with three elephants. Do you have any idea how much it costs to feed even one cat that big?"

"How much?" Tala asked.

"What?"

"How much does it cost to feed a big cat?"

Pete glanced over at his father, who had leaned his rear end against the end of the examining table, crossed his ankles, and was regarding them as though they were playing mixed doubles at Wimbledon. "Dad?"

"Nebraska Zoo Food charges ten bucks per ten-pound feed. Normally she should have one a day, but skinny as she is, and with her wound, I'd say two a day plus extra vitamins would be more like it."

"That's a dollar a pound, two thousand dollars a

ton. Plus shipping and handling?'' She looked at Mace.

Mace shook his head. "No tax either. Animal food is not taxable."

"I know that. We used to raise pigs." She turned back to Pete. "You haven't told me how much the surgery and drugs and things are going to cost."

Pete had already decided not to charge for his services. But he needed to convince her that keeping the lioness was not an option. "At least a thousand dollars," he said, and stared Mace down as though daring the other man to contradict him. "Even if we were to keep her until she's well, we'd have to construct a decent enclosure for her. And she's got to be kept clean, medicated. It's a hell of a job."

"We...I...have an account at the co-op in town. They have heavy-duty construction fencing and steel posts."

"Somebody'd still have to build it. And that would mean letting them know we've got a lion on our hands. Besides, that doesn't solve the problem of what to do with her in the long run."

"Don't you know any sanctuaries for big cats?" Tala asked, desperation in her voice.

Pete's annoyance evaporated. "Yeah. There's a network of sanctuaries across the country. We're all familiar with each other, whether we have elephants or big cats, or apes—whatever needs rescuing."

"Then please keep her till you can find her a decent home!"

"You realize you're asking me to break the law

and costing me a bunch of money I need for the girls.''

''I can't do anything about the law except to say that if anything happens I promise to take all the blame and get my mother-in-law to go to bat for you as well. She's on the county council. As to the money—I've got a little saved up, and we can charge the stuff at the co-op, and maybe we can make some arrangement for me to work off the rest. I can pour cement and dig postholes.'' She looked around the room. ''You could use some help. I'm a hard worker, and I'm quick with figures.''

''If I need any help, which I don't,'' Pete said, ''and can't afford if I did, I'd want a man capable of shoveling elephant dung, not—''

''A skinny half-pint woman?'' Tala asked. ''Look, I've been digging and shoveling all my life. I can drive a tractor and use a front-loader with the best of them. I may be skinny, but I'm tough.'' She shoved her sleeve up and made a fist at him.

He had to admit her arms were sinewy.

''I was born and raised on a dirt farm,'' she continued. ''Work doesn't scare me. Besides that, I can type eighty words a minute, I can keep books, I can scrub floors, and I know how to use a computer.''

''Whoa!'' Pete said.

''Honey,'' Mace said gently from behind her back, ''where were you coming from last night when you found Baby over there?''

''From work. I work the four-to-midnight shift as the assistant manager of the Food Farm.''

''Uh-huh. So you're already commuting to town

for an eight-hour day—or night. And Bryson's Hollow is farmland, so you're probably working a farm, at least part of the year. If you're Irene Newsome's daughter-in-law, I know you're also a mother, without a husband to take up the slack. You plan to sleep sometime in the next century?''

Tala's face flushed dark brick red. ''We let the whole farm go fallow, so I'm not working the land. It never was much good for crops anyway—too hilly. Even Mr. and Mrs. Bryson gave up and moved to Florida a few years ago, although I don't think they can bring themselves to sell the land their family settled in the 1700s. I can work a second job easy. I don't need much sleep so long as I can spend the weekend with my kids—that's not negotiable.''

''During the week?''

''They're staying in town with their grandmother and great-grandmother.''

''Your kids aren't with you?'' Pete asked. He heard the disapproval in his voice. From the way her head snapped around and her chin went up, he knew she'd heard it, too.

''My boy is eight, makes honor roll, and already plays Pop Warner football in the fall and baseball in the spring. And my daughter is thirteen and into cheerleading and gymnastics. I can't get them to all their practices and games and still work every night.'' She shrugged. ''Besides, Rachel hates the country, especially since…'' She took a deep breath. ''Her daddy died.''

''Still…''

"That's the way it works out best for us, Dr. Jacobi."

"I'm sure it is the best possible solution for the moment," Mace said, darting an annoyed glance at his son. "But nobody can work all the time. A young woman should not be driving home by herself in a sleet storm after one o'clock in the morning. How much do they pay you at that Farm place?"

"Eight dollars an hour," Tala whispered.

Pete closed his eyes. Not much. He wondered why she wasn't getting some sort of pension from her husband's death. At least she should have social security for the kids, food stamps, maybe ADC. She ought to be able to keep her children at home. But not if she had to leave them alone from before four in the afternoon until two in the morning.

"Fine. Then you come to work for us, and we'll match your salary plus ten percent," Mace said.

Pete gaped at him. "Mace, the money we've got is for the next elephant. We can't afford—"

"Oh, yes, we can. I can, that is. Actually, m'dear, you're cheap at the price. We expect you to get out enough fund-raising letters on that computer to more than pay your way."

"Wait a minute, Dad. We can barely afford health insurance for ourselves, much less for an entire family."

"Oh, that's all right," Tala smiled at him. "We still have Adam's insurance. The kids are covered until they're eighteen, and I'm covered until I go on Medicare."

Mace walked over and took both her hands. "You

would make an old man very happy indeed if you'd take our job and quit working until all hours of the morning. I promise you the hours here will give you much more time for after-school activities with your children.''

Inwardly, Pete groaned. He did not need or want anyone underfoot, certainly not this woman who gave him urges he'd been quashing. He didn't have time for urges.

Suddenly, all three elephants lifted their trunks and trumpeted. Everyone jumped. Tala looked up at them and laughed that glorious glittery laugh once more. ''They know, don't they?'' she said to Mace.

''Of course, m'dear, they know everything.'' Mace dropped his arm across Tala's shoulders. ''And obviously they approve. Now, it's time for my world-famous pancakes. We have to put some meat on those bones. Coming, Pete?''

Pete watched as Mace helped Tala on with her parka and ushered her out into the frigid, but blessedly sunny, morning. Instantly, the girls swung away from their bars and walked purposefully toward the door to their enclosure that led out to the pastures beyond. They were going outside to meet Tala at close quarters.

He closed his eyes. What he felt was envy. She had a quality that endeared her to animals and people alike. Mace was no pushover, yet here he was simpering away like Maurice Chevalier.

And here Pete was once more—odd man out, even when it came to his very own elephants.

"Blast it, they'll scare her half to death," he swore and trotted out the door.

"Ah, GLORIOUS MORNING," Mace Jacobi said, linking Tala's arm through his. "The roads should be completely dry in another hour."

Tala started to reply, then noticed that the girls had silently meandered up behind her. How could they be so huge yet move so quietly?

She turned and caught her breath. Without bars, and in direct sunlight, she realized how monumental they were. She shaded her eyes with her hands, stared up at them and gulped. Mace patted her arm.

"Just checking you out, m'dear," he said, and walked on. "They've already said they approve."

Tala squared her shoulders and followed him, expecting any moment to feel the thud of a trunk on the top of her head. When they reached the steps of Mace's trailer, however, she turned to see that the girls hadn't moved, but were swaying back and forth in unison like overweight chorus girls. She smiled and waved at them, then followed Mace inside.

"Let me take your coat," he said. "And how do you like your coffee?"

"Black, please."

"You should have cream and sugar, but we'll make up for that. The pancake batter is already in the refrigerator. I simply have to pour and flip. Please sit down. It's cramped, I know, but I don't normally have company, certainly not so beautiful nor so early."

How could anyone be afraid of this man? Tala

thought. He was as courtly as a knight, unlike his grumpy son. Her breath quickened as the face of that son rose up unbidden behind her eyes. He was nearly as big as the elephants, and a good deal scarier. "I don't think Dr. Jacobi wants me here," she said as she reached for the cup of steaming coffee Mace handed to her.

"*I* am Dr. Jacobi, and I *do* want you here. Besides, don't let Pete fool you. We can well afford it. We desperately need the help. I'm not making that up."

Suddenly he sounded formidable indeed. This must be the man who terrified vet students. "I don't want to cause trouble," she said in a small voice.

"Nonsense! You are just what my stubborn son needs. He's turning into a hermit, and an ill-tempered one at that. Been too long since he had to deal with human beings. Animals don't talk back, although the girls give a very close approximation when they're pissed."

"Why not?" she asked. "Human beings, I mean."

He glanced at her. "Long story, and not mine to tell. Ask him when you know him a little better."

The door opened at that moment, and the object of their conversation ducked to avoid smacking his head on the lintel. Suddenly the trailer seemed tiny.

Tala squeezed into her corner. Adam hadn't been but a couple of inches taller than she, and slightly built, although muscular. She'd always felt comfortable with him, with his even temperament. The children took after him physically—slight, well-co-ordinated and athletic. Temperamentally they were more like Tala's Cherokee grandmother, especially Rachel, who was anything but calm.

This man looked as though he could wrestle one of those elephants to the ground if he had to. And he seemed to have the nasty temperament of her granddaddy's Jersey bull. What was his problem, for heaven's sake?

She moved over even more to give him as much room as she could, and held her body as tight as possible. She heard the sizzle of pancake batter hitting hot fat and smelled the luscious aroma of pancakes—with something else. "Do you add vanilla?" she asked Mace.

"Ah, the girl has a good nose."

"Not an asset around here," Pete said. "There are times when the odors of wet hay, wet elephant and wet elephant droppings can peel paint."

He was obviously trying to discourage her. "No worse than chickens," she said. "Or pigs. And piles probably not much larger than a full-grown cow's. I've cleaned up after all of those. And then, of course, there are babies. After two kids' worth of dirty diapers, bad smells don't bother me much."

"That, m'dear, is something about which my son knows nothing whatsoever," Mace said as he flipped the first saucer-size pancake expertly onto a plate.

Tala glanced at Pete. For some reason his father's remark seemed to annoy him a lot more than it should have. Was this another bone of contention between them? Pete hadn't made Mace a grandfather?

"Here you go, m'dear," Mace said, and sat a short

stack of steaming pancakes in front of her, followed in quick succession by a small collection of jugs and jars, and a butter dish. "Maple syrup, plain syrup, honey, blackberry syrup. Take your pick." He beamed at her.

"This is too much. Dr. Jacobi, wouldn't you like to take this one?"

"That's about a quarter of what Pete puts away. His are coming up, and mine thereafter. The only problem with pancakes is that they require baby-sitting."

Tala stopped in midpour. "Oh, God, can I use your phone?"

"Of course." Mace looked puzzled. Pete stood and pressed his big body against the far wall so that she could squeeze through.

"Phone's in my bedroom," Mace said. "It's set on intercom at the moment. Just punch one of the buttons. You'll get a dial tone."

"Thank you. I'm sorry."

"I'll keep your pancakes hot for you."

Mace's bedroom was as spartan as a monk's cell and spotlessly clean. She picked up the telephone and punched a button, then dialed. The phone was answered on the first ring. "Irene?" she asked.

"Good Lord, Tala! Where on earth have you been? I've been calling your house since seven this morning. Ten more minutes and I was going to send Sheriff Craig to find out if you'd gone over the side of a cliff in the ice."

"I'm so sorry, Irene. I meant to check in earlier."

"Your phone out of order? I swear, Tala, Vertie and I have been frantic what with the sleet and all."

"And the children?"

"Oh, I didn't tell them I couldn't reach you. They've had enough to worry about. The school finally decided to operate today. Two flakes, and they usually slam the doors. Wasn't a bit like that when I was growing up. We went to school rain, sleet or snow."

Tala relaxed. At least Rachel and Cody weren't worried about her. Since Adam's death, Rachel acted as though she never gave her mother a thought, but Cody worried constantly. Maybe Rachel worried as well, but she'd never let Tala know.

In the background she heard, "Has Miss Tala deigned to call at last? Give me that phone!"

A moment later Tala grinned at Vertie's tone. "Why on earth do you think God gave us the telephone if not to keep in touch with our loved ones?"

"I've already apologized to Irene," Tala said.

"Won't do. My daughter-in-law forgives folks too easily. Apologize to *me* this instant, or I will drive myself out there personally and snatch you bald-headed, young lady."

"Yes'm. I apologize."

"Well?"

"Well what?"

"You drove off into the sleet at midnight and disappeared off the face of the earth. Is your phone dead? Did you have an accident?"

"No. I'm fine. I meant to come by this morning and have breakfast with all of you, but I slept a whole lot later than I planned. I'll come by this afternoon on my way to work and tell you about it. If that's all right,'' she added.

"All right? It's an order.''

After the usual pleasantries and a good deal of fending off questions, Tala hung up the phone. She was so lucky to have in-laws she adored and who adored her.

She felt her eyes well with tears. If not for Irene and Vertie, she'd never have survived Adam's death. Couldn't survive now, for that matter. But she had to aim for independence. As Tala had told the Jacobis, she was not afraid of hard work. And she was definitely not the type to turn into a white-gloved young matron drinking tea and eating sugar cookies.

Not that Vertie ever wore white gloves. Her grandmother-in-law was more likely to be found in jeans, cowboy boots and a Stetson driving that Jeep of hers down the side of a mountain. Irene and Vertie were as different as could be, but somehow mother-in-law and daughter-in-law managed to scrape along in relative harmony in that big old Newsome mansion. Probably because Vertie spent most of her time traveling the world.

Tala had no intention of becoming the third-generation Newsome widow in that house. Not if she had to clerk at the Food Farm until she died.

Or spend the next twenty years shoveling elephant dung.

CHAPTER THREE

"IT'LL TAKE ME a couple of hours to pick up the stuff for the lion cage at the co-op and drive back out here," Tala said an hour later as she was about to get into her truck. "And I need to stop by my in-laws'. Maybe I can see my kids after school. Is that all right? I can hardly wait to tell everybody about Baby."

"You can't mention Baby to anyone, Tala." Pete's voice was gruff.

"But—"

"The minute you tell even one person, the story'll be all over town. Next thing you know, we'll have the sheriff and the Wildlife people banging on the front gate with a search warrant."

"I'll swear them to secrecy," she said, but her voice had dropped. She sighed as he simply stood and looked at her. After a moment, she said, "Of course you're right. But what am I going to tell everybody about why I spent the night here?"

"Tell them your car got stuck. Tell them you had a flat tire. But whatever you do, and I can't emphasize this enough, do not tell them about Baby. Promise?"

She nodded. "Promise."

"Besides, if we're actually going to do this crazy thing, build a lion cage, I need to come with you to make sure you get everything on the list. You got no business picking all that stuff up."

"Oh, they'll load it for me. And they won't question what I need it for. When Ad…when my husband was alive, we were always doing things to fix up the farm. They'll just assume I've gotten up enough gumption to start another project. If you come along, it'll be all over town in thirty minutes."

"Why?"

Tala grinned at him. "Because you people are considered deeply weird, Dr. Jacobi. Elephants in the middle of Hollendale County? Haven't you ever lived in a small town?"

"Yes, but it was a small college town. You call my father Mace. How come you keep calling me Dr. Jacobi?"

Tala wanted to say because he made her uncomfortable, but she didn't. She merely ducked her head, whispered, "Okay—Pete," and climbed into her truck.

"Hey, wait a minute." He laid a large hand on the open windowsill. "You taking the job or not?"

"I don't know."

"The Food Farm isn't likely to go out of business or fire you in the near future. That's a mark in their favor." He heaved a sigh. "But we're not going anywhere either. I guess we could use somebody like you around here."

She stared at him, then without a word put her truck in gear and drove off.

Talk about grudging! she thought. Mace must have told him what to say. And he was right. The Food Farm wasn't a piece of cake, but at least it was steady and secure. And indoors. She had to admit, she really couldn't handle working at the sanctuary and at the Food Farm. She'd have to choose one or the other. And this paid more.

If she could work from seven in the morning until three in the afternoon, she could actually pick the kids up from school, attend their practices, be a real mother for a change.

And maybe she could explain to them in a way they'd understand that she still owed Adam a debt.

PETE THRUST HIS HANDS into his pockets hard enough to burst the seams and stared after her truck. He heard a stamp and turned to find Sweetiepie staring at him from about twenty feet away. The other two elephants had apparently departed for the woods at the back of their fifty-acre pasture. They were already invisible in the underbrush and might not surface again until it was time for their evening hay.

"So, what are you waiting for?" he asked.

Sweetiepie swished her trunk, lifted it and opened her mouth.

"Man, are you spoiled." He sauntered over, reached up and began to scratch her tongue. She sighed in ecstasy. "How come I can do this all day and you don't pat *me* on the head?"

She ignored him, merely closed her eyes and shifted her feet.

"What's she got that I haven't? Other than enough

hair to stuff a mattress and a pair of legs that belong in a Vegas chorus line?'' He stopped scratching for a moment. Sweetiepie nudged him gently. ''Okay, okay. It's cold out here, you know, and your tongue is not exactly velvet. As if you cared.''

Sweetiepie closed her mouth and swung away. ''Thank you very much, Pete,'' he called after her. She ignored him.

He never ceased to enjoy watching them move. From the back, Sweetiepie looked as though she were wearing baggy gray underwear. Without any evidence of speed, she covered an enormous amount of ground. He'd be willing to bet Tala would laugh that great laugh of hers the first time she saw them take off for the boonies. The thought gave him a glow that surprised him.

At that moment Baby roared. So now he had a wounded big cat to look after as well as a woman that couldn't even look after her own children, but had the strength and guts to drag wild animals into her truck in the middle of the night. What kind of woman was she?

A woman with big dark eyes who stirred his blood.

He found Baby sitting up in her cage with her bad leg held off the ground. As he watched, she roared again, then began to pant in obvious discomfort. He expected her to be in some pain, even with the drugs, but she could have developed an infection in the wound. That would be extremely bad news.

He'd become a vet partly to gain his father's approval, but mostly because he hated watching animals suffer. He knelt beside the lion's pen, and pressed his hand against the steel mesh, ready to pull it away if she snapped at him.

Thank God her shoulder felt cool. She reached around and licked the wound with a tongue that he knew was rough enough to rip the skin off his hand. "It's okay, Baby," he whispered. "I'll make it better."

He found a syringe, filled it, jammed it into the muscle of her rump and thrust the plunger home before she realized what was happening. When she did, she tore the syringe from his grasp and shook it free on the floor of the cage.

Great. Now he'd have to wait until the drug took effect, then get it out safely. If there was one thing he'd learned, it was that hurt animals didn't often appreciate or cooperate with his efforts.

"GO FOR IT, I say." Vertie Newsome raised her glass of iced tea and took a deep swig.

"I swear, you'd tell her to go for it if she were planning to bungee-jump off the Grand Canyon," Irene Newsome said. "She can't seriously consider taking a job working out there alone with those men and a herd of wild elephants."

"Sure she can," Vertie said. "If I was twenty years younger, I'd go for that Mace myself. Do you good to get mixed up with a man again, Tala. It's been over a year."

"Vertilene Newsome, I swear!" Irene said.

Tala leaned back against the down cushions on the white wicker love seat and sipped her hot spiced tea from one of Irene's antique Belleek cups. Normally she enjoyed watching the sparring matches between her in-laws, but today she was just too tired. Besides, she needed to drive the fencing and cement sacks in the back of her truck to the sanctuary soon, so she'd have time to go home to bathe and change before her shift at the Food Farm.

She'd given the women a truncated version of her adventure in the sleet, but had changed her encounter with Baby to windshield wipers that had ceased to function outside the gates to the sanctuary.

"Of course, if I were you, Tala, I'd go for the younger one. Man, is he a major stud muffin." Vertie smacked her lips. "I always like a real big man." She wiggled her eyebrows suggestively.

One look at Irene's scandalized face sent Tala into gales of laughter.

"Tala, you cannot take that job," Irene said. "Think what people would say."

"I've never much cared about that in the past."

"That was because you had Adam behind you," her mother-in-law told her. "Now you are a single mother with two children, honey. And whether you care about your reputation or not, *they* certainly do. Rachel especially. She's right at that age where she wants to fit in. I really don't understand why you won't move in here with us. It's not like you couldn't have your own suite of rooms. You could come and go whenever you wanted." She paused for a moment, then added, "With Lucinda in the kitchen, I know you'd put on a few pounds, and you'd see so much more of the children. You deserve the money Adam's daddy took away from him when he decided to become a warden instead of a banker. I wish you'd let me give you at least a little money, make things a little easier for you."

"We've been over all that before, Irene," Tala said. She tried to keep her voice level, but she was so tired, she heard the edge of exasperation creep in. "Mr. Newsome left that money in trust for his grand-children for when they went to college or wanted to start their own families. He didn't want you to give Adam or me a penny. Adam refused to take anything from you, and I have to abide by his wishes. The children aren't suffering, Lord knows, and I'm doing just fine. I promise you."

"But it's so unfair," Irene said. "I know Hollis would have come around in time, when he saw how happy you made Adam. If he just hadn't had his stroke so soon… I could make you an allowance and never even notice the money was gone."

Tala covered Irene's small hand with hers. "You're spending a ton on the kids as it is, and I am more grateful than you'll ever know. They need so much I can't give them."

"But with an allowance, you could quit your job, go back to school. It would be so easy…" Irene's voice trailed off helplessly.

Tala leaned back. "I know it must seem crazy to you, Irene. It would be easy to let you spoil me rotten and make all the decisions the way Adam used to, but if I'm ever going to stand on my own feet, I have to start somewhere and just keep going until I get there—wherever *there* is."

Vertie patted her knee. "Hush, Irene. She's right.

We are here to do what we can when we can, and for as long as we can. But it's Tala's life, and she's got a darned sight more of it left to live. So if she wants to bungee-jump off the Grand Canyon, then I do say go for it.''

"And the first warm day you'll fly off to Nepal or Bali and leave me to handle the town gossip," Irene snapped, then looked contrite. "I'm sorry, Vertie, that was uncalled-for.''

"But true. All right, I promise. I will stick around at least until June when the kids are out of school. Then I'll drag both of them off somewhere for the summer. Tala and you, too, if you'll come.''

"Oh, no. I belong here." Irene reached across and laid her fine-boned hand with its sprinkling of liver spots and beautifully manicured pink nails on Tala's knee. "Do what you have to, dear. It would be marvelous for you to have the afternoons free. The children miss you at their practices. Vertie and I are a poor substitute.''

"You'd never know Rachel misses me," Tala said. "She wishes I were the one going off to Nepal.''

"She's just going through a bad time since Adam…died," Irene said.

"Since some fool shot him to death over some out-of-season deer kill," Vertie said. "He didn't die, Irene. He got himself murdered, and the devil that killed him is still walking around looking for more deer to poach.''

"Please, Vertie," Tala said.

"I'm sorry, but it makes me so damned mad. In

my day we'd have caught the sum'bitch and strung him up to the nearest oak tree. The hell with due process.''

Tala stood up quickly, set the fragile cup on the table and bent to kiss Vertie's cheek. It felt like crushed velvet—soft, but with a myriad tiny imperfections and striations. ''I love you, Belle Starr, Queen of the Outlaws, and you, too, Irene.''

''So, you going to take the job?'' Vertie asked in a raspy voice that showed how close she was to tears.

''Maybe. I'll talk to Beanie on my shift tonight. Please don't mention a word to the kids until I'm sure.''

''Of course, dear,'' Irene said, then followed her to the door and touched her cheek. Her eyes were full of concern. ''You've got dark circles the size of dinner plates under your eyes, and I swear you've lost some more weight. You have to remember to eat, Tala. Promise?''

''Yes, ma'am.'' She kissed Irene's cheek, walked to her truck, climbed in and waved to the two women standing at the top of the porch stairs.

They stood arm in arm, united for all their differences. Vertie, tall, angular and hawk-faced, her still-thick gray hair pulled back into a bun at the back of her neck, in her faded jeans, heavy fisherman's sweater and white Nikes. Irene, shorter than Tala, and plump as a partridge, with her immaculately coifed golden hair, her beige wool skirt and baby blue cashmere twin set, wearing high-heeled taupe pumps that showed off the trim ankles that were her greatest vanity. As Tala climbed into her truck, the women turned and went back into the house. A united front as far as the rest of the world was concerned.

If either woman had an inkling how difficult it was for Tala not to be a full-time mother to her children, they would have shipped the pair of them home to her farmhouse in a heartbeat, and volunteered to ferry them home after their practices every afternoon.

But Rachel wouldn't come back to the farm. She swore she'd never set foot there again so long as she lived. She never wanted to see the deer or the possums or raccoons again. So far as she was concerned, if Adam hadn't devoted his life to wild animals, he'd still be alive.

And by extension, if he'd married some safe debutante instead of Tala, he'd never have felt he could follow his dream and become a warden. He'd have been a nice, rich banker living in a big house in town. Rachel was full of anger, and Tala didn't know how to help her.

And the only night Cody had spent on the farm in the last three months he'd cried and had nightmares about his father all night long until Tala slept in the rocking chair beside his bed and held her hand on him. At least at his grandmother's he could sleep.

As she started her vehicle, a bright red Jeep pulled in behind her and honked its horn. She turned off the engine and jumped out of the truck. "Rachel, Cody, Irene said you wouldn't be home for an hour yet." She opened her arms and Cody flew into them. Rachel stood by the Jeep with a scowl on her face.

"Mom!" Cody said, and kissed her cheek. "Mrs.

Johnson was sick, so Rachel's stupid cheerleading practice got canceled and Mrs. Lippincott gave us a ride home so we wouldn't have to walk.''

She looked over Cody's head. ''Sorry about your practice, Rach, but I'm glad I got to see you.''

Rachel shifted her book bag and walked past her mother and up the steps. ''We'll never make it to the State finals at this rate,'' she snapped, then turned around to stare at her mother. ''What's the big deal?'' Her face clouded, and Tala saw a flash of anxiety in her eyes. ''Nobody's sick, are they?''

Tala slid Cody to his feet and walked over to touch Rachel's shoulder. Rachel didn't exactly flinch, she just moved out from under her mother's fingers.

''Everybody's fine so far as I know, Rach.''

''Great. I got homework. Bye.'' She walked up the steps and into the house.

Cody made a face at her retreating back. ''Boy, is she ever a pain. How come I can't be an only child?''

''Little late for that, I'm afraid, Cody bear.''

''She's not mean to anybody but you—well, mostly.''

''Is she mean to you?''

Cody snickered. ''No way. I'm a big martial-arts type, Mom. Yee-hah.'' He proceeded to throw his fists and kick out, just missing his mother's shoulder.

''Very impressive. But don't use it on your sister or anybody else, you got that?''

''Oh, Mom.''

She glanced at her watch. ''Drat. I'm late. I love you, Cody bear. And tell Rachel I love her, too.'' She kissed the top of his head. He waved and scurried up the steps and into the big house. Tala watched him go as she climbed into her truck. She felt her eyes sting with unshed tears. He looked so much like the pictures of his father at that age.

She drove out and turned toward the road to the sanctuary. She barely had time to drop off the supplies and get to the Food Farm on time.

Most people, looking at Cody, would assume he was over his father's death. Tala knew better. Cody kept his feelings all inside, while Rachel bared her teeth at the universe. They both probably needed to talk to a psychologist of some kind, but the closest one was fifty miles away, and he didn't have much of a reputation.

She'd have to muddle through and try to help them. Herself, as well.

As much as she longed to be with her children, Tala could not give up the farmhouse, the house where she and Adam had been married, had loved and given birth to their babies, and where Adam had lain in his coffin before he was buried in the little cemetery behind the Episcopal mission with the other Newsomes.

The day they were married she'd sworn to him she'd preserve the place as long as she lived, so that no matter how much development, how many vacation homes went up around her, the farm she'd inherited at Bryson's Hollow would always stay a refuge for the wild creatures he loved so much. In the end he'd given his life for them. The least she could do was keep her word.

No untenanted farm survived long these days without squatters and thieves and even arsonists destroying what they could not appreciate. She simply could not abandon the place, even if she'd been able to afford something halfway decent in town.

But with a day job, she could bring Cody home for at least part of the summer, and perhaps even convince Rachel to give the farm another try. Tala had always found the woods healed her wounds. They might heal Rachel's, too. A few days' fishing on the banks of the stream where she'd fished with her daddy might possibly smooth out her daughter's soul.

One step at a time. First the new job, then work on getting the kids home.

"TOOK YOU LONG ENOUGH." Pete loomed huge and grumpy outside her truck door. "You get everything?"

"Yes, Doctor. Including premixed cement that sets up in any temperature. Regular cement would stay wet for a month in this cold air."

"Oh. Yeah. Guess you're right."

He sounded surprised—maybe he didn't think women knew things like that. She brushed past him, and her shoulder touched his chest. She caught her breath and kept walking, although her heart thumped.

He, on the other hand, shied away as though she'd attacked him.

"Where are you planning to build Baby's cage?" Tala asked, ignoring both his reaction and hers. She glanced back at him, and was startled to see that the tips of his ears were red. And he was suddenly breathing as though he'd been running a marathon.

He cleared his throat. "Mace and I talked it over. Round back under the overhang and behind the hay storage. Be protected from the wind, and the hay offers good insulation. Plus nobody'll see her if they drive in." He refused to meet her eyes.

"If you could teach her to keep her mouth shut we'd be in business," she said.

"Move over. I'll drive the truck around back. It's still pretty slippery where the elephants have trampled the ground."

Tala opened her mouth to protest that she was capable of driving in mud, but then she shut it. She barely had enough room in the passenger seat by the time he'd fitted his bulk behind the driver's seat. He'd had to move the seat all the way back to get in. She wouldn't be able to reach the pedals until she moved it to its former position.

A few moments later they were at the site for the cage. The location was perfect. The overhang offered protection, and the steel outside wall closed off one side, so they only had three sides to construct.

Mace was already digging postholes in the dirt. Tala climbed out and looked at the perimeter. "Doesn't look very big," she said.

"Not nearly big enough if she were healthy and we were going to keep her forever," Mace said, resting on his digger.

"She can't stay where she is," Pete said. "She's already getting antsy. This way, at least she'll be able to pace, and we can add a ladder or two so she can climb, although lions don't actually do much climbing in the wild.''

"Have you tried to find a home for her yet?"

"You've only been gone a few hours."

Tala dropped her head. "I meant to get back sooner. I'm sorry. About the job…"

"Say yes, m'dear," Mace said.

"I have to speak to the manager at the Food Farm tonight. Give him a chance to meet your offer. I can't just leave him in the lurch. But if he says no, and if you'll really let me work from early until school lets out, and let me have the weekends off, I promise I'll work very hard for you."

"Wonderful!" Mace said, and clapped his hands. Pete merely turned his back and mumbled something unintelligible.

"I hate to leave you with this now, but I've really got to go home and get ready for work," she said. "And I think I left my gloves inside last night. May I go get them?"

"Of course. Pete and I will unload so you can take your truck. Call after you've spoken to your manager. If he does offer you more money, we'll meet his offer. If you have to give him two weeks' notice, so be it. We want you, m'dear."

Tala smiled and walked around the edge of the building, leaving the men hauling posts and wire out of the truck. Maybe Dr. Mace wanted her. She wasn't sure about Dr. Pete.

She opened the small door to the side of the overhead and walked inside the workroom. The light was dim, and the room felt even colder than outside. The faint aroma of raw meat met her nostrils. She looked over at Baby's cage to see whether she was still sleeping.

Empty!

She felt her blood chill as she peered into the dark corners. She hoped Baby couldn't fit between the bars on the elephants' enclosure, but if she could, the lion could be anywhere in Hollendale County by now.

Tala opened her mouth to yell for Pete and felt something heavy bump her leg. Without moving her head, she looked down. Baby stood beside her, butting her big golden head into the side of Tala's knee like a house cat. But hard enough so that Tala had to brace her other hand on the medicine cabinet beside her to keep from falling over.

Baby butted her again, then rubbed her body along Tala's legs, crossed over in front of her and collapsed into a big yellow heap on the concrete. She lay there rumbling contentedly.

"Okay, you're not hungry—at least I hope you aren't," Tala said with more conviction than she felt. "And you've been around people, although God knows what they did to you before they shot you. I doubt seriously you know I rescued you last night, but maybe you're just cold and lonesome."

Baby rolled her eyes and yawned. Even without all her incisors, her mouth looked capable of biting Tala's head off in one gulp.

Tala was trapped. The cat lay across her boots. Her body wound around so that in order to move, Tala would have to dislodge her feet and step over the mound of lion. Assuming Baby would let her. How much time would it take before Pete realized she'd been inside too long?

She couldn't wait. She'd better try to get herself out of this.

"Sweet Baby," she crooned. "Is your shoulder better?" Slowly, carefully, Tala bent her knees until she could touch Baby's head. She began to scratch behind the cat's ears. "My cats always loved this, let's hope you're cat enough to do the same."

The rumbling increased. My word, Baby was purring! Or as close to a purr as she could get. Tala began to stroke the animal's head. "Aren't you a sweet ole baby girl?"

A moment later she nearly toppled head first on top of the lion as the door behind her opened and hit her in the rear.

"Hey, can't you find your gloves?"

"Pete, stay out," she hissed.

He poked his head around the door. "Holy hell. You okay?"

"I'm fine." Tala tried to stand up, but couldn't with Pete halfway in the door. Baby looked over Tala's shoulder and lashed her tail, annoyed at the interruption.

"Stand up very slowly," Pete told her. "Then when I open the door, I'll grab you and drag you out."

"I don't think that's a good idea," Tala said. "Or necessary. I think she just got lonely. I've been scratching her ears."

"Do what I tell you, woman. We'll worry about

what *she* wants when we've put a steel door between the two of you.''

''All right.'' In spite of her bravado, Tala felt a rush at his peremptory tone. He was worried.

Or maybe he just didn't want to have to deal with the consequences of having to explain her carcass to the authorities.

She stood slowly. Baby rumbled again, but she seemed more disturbed at the loss of physical contact than angry. Tala felt the breeze from the slightly open door, and reached back. Pete's big rough hand engulfed hers. ''Hang on.''

He shoved the door open, yanked her around the edge, and almost dislocated her shoulder. He slammed the door and dragged her into a fierce bear hug, lifted her off her feet and swung her away from the door. ''Dammit, don't ever do that again.''

She forced her mouth away from his breast pocket and said indignantly, ''Me? What did *I* do?''

He held her at arm's length with her feet dangling as though she were a rag doll. ''Didn't you see she was out of her cage?''

''Put me down! By the time I spotted the empty cage, I had a lion on my feet wanting her ears scratched.''

On her feet again, she stood toe-to-toe with him. ''I think I behaved pretty darn well, all things considered. For that matter, so did she. She's a sweet pussycat who just needs a little affection!''

''Oh, my sainted aunt!'' Pete struck his forehead with the flat of his hand.

"What's the matter?" Mace came running around the corner of the building.

"She's out is what. And little Miss Cat Lady here has been scratching her ears. I told you she was trouble."

"Me or the cat?"

"Both, dammit!" Pete stalked off to meet his father. "How the hell are we going to handle the lion now? Even if we finish setting the posts today, the concrete won't be solid until morning, and then we still have to stretch the fence and cover it over."

"We could shoot her," Mace said solemnly. Tala caught his wink, but Pete obviously didn't.

"Are you crazy?" He stopped. "Okay. You got me. But we can't leave her loose in the workroom either." He turned to Tala. "Could you tell if she knocked down the enclosure?"

"Didn't look like it, but I must admit I didn't check closely."

"Then she probably came out over the top. We can wire down some steel fence on top of her enclosure in about an hour and get her back into it with the capture gun if we have to, although I suspect another hunk of meat will do it."

"Promise you won't hurt her?"

"We will *not* hurt her. Not unless it's her or us. In the meantime, I can sucker her into the guest bathroom with another hunk of deer meat. She'll be okay." He touched Tala's shoulder with surprisingly gentle fingers. "And you. You okay? Did I hurt you?"

"Not a bit." She smiled at him. "I'll give her the meat if you like."

"Sure you're up to it? She must've scared you pretty good just now." He smiled, his hand still kneading her shoulder. For a moment she wanted to relax against him, feel those hands on other parts of her body. Enough, she admonished herself.

"I'm fine," she said and moved away.

Suddenly he sobered. "The instant you forget you're dealing with a wild animal, you're dead. Trust me on that. She may act like a pussycat, but she weighs two hundred pounds, and she's used to raw meat. At the moment she's well fed and still not feeling in hunting trim."

"But won't she smell fear?"

"Sure. So fake out your pheromones. Don't be scared, be aware. And don't take chances."

Mace came down the steps of his trailer unwrapping a piece of meat. "That beast is eating all my venison, drat it!" He handed it to Tala.

"Go in through the front," Pete said. "Open the door to the guest bathroom, then open the door to the exam room, show her the food, toss it on the bathroom floor, and once she's in, shut the door on her. I'll be right behind you. Think we need the rifle for safety, Dad?"

"No!" Tala wailed.

"Your safety is more important than she is," Mace said. "Take the gun, Pete. Better safe than sorry."

"All right," she said. "But you won't need it. I promise I'll make this work."

Tala wished she felt as confident as she tried to sound. She knew the scary bit would come from the time the cat saw the food until Tala could shut the bathroom door on her and walk away. Suddenly, Pete's huge presence—even holding the rifle—was no longer threatening. He was comforting.

He stood in the hall doorway with his hand on the knob behind him as she inched open the door to the examining room. "Here, kitty, kitty, kitty," Tala called. She heard Pete's snort behind her.

The cat still lay by the door, but on her back with all four feet in the air. She rolled her eyes, saw Tala, and struggled to her feet quicker than Tala would have imagined possible. She put no weight on her left leg, but she still managed to move quickly toward the meat. Tala stood behind the hall door, held out the meat, threw it into the bathroom and shrank back.

The cat ignored her, limped into the bathroom and sank onto the bath mat. Tala shut the bathroom door quickly on the sounds of crunching, then shut the door to the examining room and practically ran into Pete's arms through the other door. This time she buried her face gratefully against his chest.

He held her awkwardly and patted her back. "You did great. We'll take it from here."

Her heart beat so hard she heard it in her ears.

"Hate to say this, m'dear, but didn't you say you had to drive all the way home and get back to town before four?" Mace said from the doorway.

"Lord, yes!" Tala ran past the two men and to

her truck. As she drove by, she called out the window, "I'll call you about the job!"

"Now sit, stay," Mace Jacobi pointed his finger at the lioness, who once more reclined on her blanket in her newly covered cage. She regarded him with wide yellow eyes as innocent as a week-old kitten's.

"Even house cats don't sit and stay," Pete said, slipping the fencing tool back into the leather pouch strapped around his waist. "Have you taken a look at what she did to the bathroom? Shredded shower curtain, shredded bath mat, and deer blood from the inside of the bathtub halfway up the walls. It's going to take me half the night to get the smell out."

"Better than having her roaming around here while we worked." Mace clicked his tongue. "That's a gutsy little girl we've hired."

"You've hired, you mean. Assuming she agrees to take the job. I had nothing to do with it."

"The girl made the final decision, son. Besides, I think she needs help."

"Right. She's not even raising her own kids."

Mace glanced at him. "That bothers you, doesn't it? And we're not just talking about Tala Newsome."

Pete sighed. "Forget it, Dad, we have things to do."

"They'll wait. It's time we didn't forget it," Mace said, easing one hip onto the examining table. "After your mother died, the only way I could find solace was by working. You were so young…"

Pete walked to the corner and unbuckled his tool

belt. "Not too young to feel locked out of your life. That's probably the way her kids feel."

"I—we—thought you were too young to under-stand what was happening to her. She couldn't bear for you to see the way she'd deteriorated."

"I thought she didn't want me."

"She longed for you. I talked about you endlessly. At first she'd cry, but then she sort of disconnected, from me, from life. I tried to call her back, but I felt so helpless. She wanted you to remember her the way she was before she got sick. Maybe it was the wrong decision, but it was the one we made. Isn't it time we got past it?"

"I'm long past it. I know you did what you thought was right at the time. But after she died, we never talked about her. I felt as though you'd shut me out all over again. I guess that's most of why I became a vet—to become part of your world, make you proud of me."

"Son, I've always been proud of you. I knew you could be an extraordinary vet. That's why I was so hard on you. I couldn't let you slide by."

Pete stared at his father. "You thought I'd try to slide by? Because you were my father? That proves how little you know me."

Mace sighed and dropped his gaze. After a mo-ment, he said softly, "Son, when you and Val—"

Pete interrupted him. "What happened between Val and me is nobody's business but ours. We've got steel poles to set and not much daylight left to set them in." With that, he walked out the door.

CHAPTER FOUR

TALA SLID behind the customer service counter at the Food Farm. Beanie believed managers shouldn't put in overtime. He never stayed a minute past five. After that she was on her own.

She'd hated telling Beanie about the new job offer. After all, he'd been willing to hire her after Adam died and had promoted her to assistant manager. She wasn't surprised he'd tried to make her feel guilty for leaving, even for a better job. What did surprise her was that he'd hit on her.

She'd known Beanie Waldrop all her life. He'd already been divorced twice. He'd never given her an inkling that he might consider her as...what? A date? A convenient lay?

And then tonight, out of the blue, stroking her hand and telling her that he was sure going to call her.

How come she could empathize with a lion and a bunch of elephants, but didn't have a clue about men?

Did Beanie think she ought to be grateful to have a man—*any* man—meet her needs?

Lord knows she had them. She missed warmth,

companionship, the kind of gentle, tender loving she'd had with Adam.

She felt disloyal that sometimes she longed for somebody wild and dangerous.

Pete's face rose up behind her eyes.

Nope. *Too* wild and *too* dangerous. And without the least bit of tenderness. Except this afternoon, holding her, kneading her shoulder, rescuing her...

"Mom!" a soprano voice called from the doorway. Her heart did a flip as she saw Cody running toward her. Rachel sauntered along behind him with her hands in the pockets of her jacket, ignoring her mother and acting as though she were merely here to pick up some fresh caviar and truffles.

Vertie brought up the rear, glanced from Rachel's studiously bland expression to Tala and sighed.

"Cody, Rachel!" Tala held out her arms. "Twice in one day. It's a record!" She couldn't leave the customer service desk without locking everything up, but she could stand at the end of it with her arms open wide. Cody bounced into them.

"Oof! You don't have to tackle me," Tala said. She kept one arm around him as she reached for Rachel, who avoided her, but finally leaned forward to kiss the air in the vicinity of her mother's cheek. Then she looked around furtively as though she'd been shoplifting.

"Needed a couple of things for supper," Vertie said. "So I decided to bring these two with me."

"Thank you, Vertie. I feel like I haven't seen them since last Christmas."

"Aw, Mom, you saw us this afternoon. And it's

almost this Christmas already," Cody said, then sobered suddenly. "It's the second year without Dad."

"Your daddy used to say nothing can hurt Christmas," Vertie said. "We'll try to have fun for his sake."

"Yes, we will," Tala said to Cody, still curled under her arm. "And guess what? I've got a new job."

Rachel who had wandered off feigning an interest in the tomato plants, stopped in midpoke, but didn't turn. Tala heard Vertie's quick intake of breath.

"Tonight's my last night at the Food Farm," Tala said to Cody, but she kept her eyes on Rachel. "No more nights. I'll be working only days, and no weekends. Isn't that great?"

"No weekends?" Cody pulled away from her and wriggled like a pup. "You'll be able to see me play. Coach says I'm the fastest running back he's ever had."

"Wonderful. I can hardly wait. I can pick you up after school most afternoons."

"I don't go home after school most afternoons," Rachel said. "Neither does Cody." She sounded as though she were explaining quantum physics to an orangutan.

"I meant after your cheerleading practices," Tala said. "Won't that be great?"

Rachel shrugged and moved on to the instant pudding. She plucked a packet of diet butterscotch from the shelf and wandered back to drop it into Vertie's basket.

"Diet?" Tala asked.

"I can't afford to gain one more ounce," Rachel said, running her hands down the sides of her jacket. "Coach says I could stand to lose a few pounds for when they toss me in the air, you know?"

Vertie harrumphed. "You're too skinny already. You take after your mama. Don't you let some fool coach talk you into something stupid like sticking a finger down your throat or living on half a cup of lentils a day."

"Oh, Great Gram, don't be silly," Rachel said. She ignored Tala. "At least I remember to eat three times a day." She stalked off toward the fish counter at the back of the store.

"She's a pain in the butt," Cody whispered. "Somebody ought to deck her."

"Well, not you," Tala said. "Just remember when you get to be thirteen and you turn into a pain in the butt yourself."

"Aw, Mom," Cody said. "Hey, can you pick me up Saturday morning? We've got a game at eleven."

"Unless something weird happens with this new job."

"Great." He bounced off after his sister.

"You notice neither one of them asked what the new job is," Vertie said. "Selfish little monkeys. You could be robbing banks for all they care."

"No—if I got caught I'd go to jail. Rachel would be embarrassed. Vertie…" She hesitated. "I think Beanie hit on me tonight."

Vertie made an annoyed sound in her throat. "Took his time doing it, didn't he? He's been after you since you came to work here."

"Really?"

"Sometimes you can be blind as a bat. Cody could probably do with a man in his life, but not Beanie Waldrop."

"Cody is not a wimp," Tala said, squaring her shoulders. "He plays killer right field and take-no-prisoners football."

"He worries all the time."

"He doesn't trust life any longer. Vertie, I don't know whether to push him or coddle him."

"At least Rachel doesn't worry."

Tala laughed. "No, she gets mad. At me, mostly."

Vertie touched her shoulder. "Encroaching teen-age insanity."

"I know, but it does get tiresome always to be the bad guy. If there was a mile-wide asteroid falling out of the sky on her, Rachel's last words would be, 'Mother, this is all your fault.'"

"All you can do is hang in there. She really doesn't mean it, you know." Vertie pointed to a lady standing in front of the counter. "You have a customer. We'll stop by after we check out."

Tala turned back to the counter to field a question from the customer who absolutely had to have mango chutney. Which they didn't have.

Twenty minutes later Cody ran a grocery basket, now half-full of bags, up to the counter. Again, Rachel sauntered behind him. "Hey, Mom," he said, "Gr'Gram says to ask you what your new job is."

Vertie gave an exasperated snort.

"I'm going to be working at the elephant sanctuary."

Cody's eyes lit. "Cool. Can I ride the elephants?"

"No way," Rachel wailed. "You can't."

Tala looked at her daughter. "Why not?"

Rachel looked up as though she could see the gods above the ceiling. "It's bad enough my mother is a checker in a grocery store. Now, I'm supposed to tell everybody you're shoveling elephant—"

"Rachel!" Tala snapped. "Don't finish that sentence. I'll be spending most of my time working on the computer, but if I have to shovel elephant dung, I will. And if you and your friends don't like it, I'm sorry. You can thank the elephants for your next pair of Adidas."

"I'll thank Gram. She'll be the one paying for them." Rachel turned on her heel and stalked out.

Tala was torn between abandoning her post, chasing her child outside into the parking lot, removing the girl's head, shaking out whatever substitute she was using for brains all over the asphalt, and bursting into tears.

"Told ya she was a pain in the butt," Cody said. "Don't pay any attention, Mom. I think it's great, don't you, Gr'Gram?"

"Totally rad. Now take these groceries out, and you and your loopy sister put them carefully—I said carefully—into the car while I say goodbye to your mother."

"Okay. See ya Saturday morning, Mom. Love ya."

"Well, that certainly went well," Tala said. "Maybe I should tell the Jacobis I can't take the job."

"You do and I will slap you silly," Vertie said. "That's the happiest I've seen Cody in a couple of weeks. And Rachel would say the same thing if you'd just been chosen to be CEO of General Motors."

"Nothing I do is right."

"She's scared to care about anything and anyone right now. And she's got to blame somebody, because if Adam was shot over something random and stupid, then something equally stupid could happen to you—or to her."

"I know you're right. But I worry she's developing the wrong values."

"That's because you're her mother," Vertie turned and walked to the door. As the electric eye swung it open, she laughed and said over her shoulder, "Don't worry. This phase will pass."

Tala's replacement came in at a quarter to one in the morning, full of apologies and excuses. Wearily, Tala handed over the duties to her, and had walked halfway to her truck in the parking lot before she recalled that, barring unforeseen events, tonight was her last night in the place.

"Hoooray!" she shouted. Then she looked around guiltily. No one had seen her. She felt incredibly buoyant despite her weariness. She climbed into the truck and turned the key.

Nothing. Not a click, nor a whir.

"Damn! Not tonight of all nights." She tried to crank the truck several more times, then gave up and popped the hood. Before she could get out of the truck, however, a dark figure loomed outside her window.

"Trouble?" a baritone voice asked.

She recognized that voice and relaxed. "Stupid thing won't start, Billy Joe," she said. "I was just about to try to find out why."

"Let me. Cold out here."

Trooper Billy Joe Nutworth was another of her friends from high school. A couple of years younger, maybe. He'd married Eunice Milman a few years back. They had a nice house and a couple of kids now. She saw them regularly at church, but in the last year, she hadn't had much energy for socializing.

"Well, shoot, Tala, here's your problem." Billy Joe raised his hand, but not high enough so that Tala could see what he was holding. "Cable's come off the battery. Let me get a wrench from the squad car, I'll have it back on for you in a minute."

"Thanks, Billy Joe," Tala said.

Five minutes later he slammed the hood. This time when Tala turned on the ignition, it caught perfectly. She leaned out the window. "You're a genius. How on earth could something like that happen?"

"Jarred loose over some of them roads you drive is my guess," Billy Joe said. "You got time for a cup of coffee before you go home? I'm flat freezing here, and I got a thermos in the car."

Sitting in a patrol car at one in the morning drinking bad coffee out of plastic cups with Billy Joe was not Tala's idea of fun, but he sounded kind of plaintive and lonesome. Besides, she could use a shot of caffeine to keep her from falling asleep and driving off the side of the Hollow road on her way home. "Sure," she said, and climbed out to join him. He handed her a cup of steaming black brew, which, when she tasted it, was pretty good.

"Fooled you," he said. "Eunice makes the coffee. That woman can flat make coffee."

"It's great. Just what I needed."

"Anything interesting happening down your way?" Billy Joe asked.

"Like what?"

"Like maybe something new on Adam's shooting, for instance."

She felt a stab of pain. To Billy Joe, Adam's death was the most interesting story that had happened in Hollendale County for some years. Of course he'd want to keep up. She shook her head. "You'd know before I would. The Tennessee Bureau of Investigation told Sheriff Craig that if they ever find the rifle, they can probably match the bullet that killed him."

"Shoot. Sheriff doesn't tell us anything. How can the TBI be so sure? Ballistics don't usually do too good on a rifle."

"It's an odd size. Maybe from an antique rifle."

"Huh. That so?" He stared at his coffee. After a moment he raised his head. "Just trying to think if I knew anybody around here's got antique guns. Can't think of anybody offhand, but I'll keep an eye out."

"Thanks, Billy Joe." She reached for the door handle. "And thanks for the coffee."

"Sure. I'll get Eunice to call you for dinner some night when I'm not working. Oh, heck, probably when I'm not on nights, you are. Isn't that always the way."

She opened her mouth to tell him about her new job, but after Rachel's reaction, suddenly she felt very reticent. So she just smiled and climbed out of the patrol car.

"You let me know if anything funny happens down your way, you hear?" Billy Joe said, leaning over to call out her window. "Prowlers or anything. Mighty lonesome in the Hollow at night, you being all alone down there the way you are. I can swing by there anytime. Always glad for a little company, 'specially with a woman pretty as you are.'' He grinned at her, and gunned the engine.

She stood staring after him. Had he just hit on her? Twice in one night? And this one a married man? She must suddenly be giving out signals that every rutting male in three counties could read. What on earth was different?

Pete Jacobi. That's what was different. Whatever he'd stirred up inside her must have percolated straight out of every pore in her body and started floating off into the atmosphere, screaming a sexual availability that she certainly didn't consciously aspire to.

Or did she?

CHAPTER FIVE

TALA TURNED DOWN the gravel driveway to her farm and heaved a sigh of relief when the headlights that had been tailgating her all the way from town swept on.

They were probably lost and hoping Tala's truck would lead them to a crossroads they could identify. They'd have to drive another twenty miles before they reached the next town. With the Brysons in Florida, and Mrs. Halliwell, the only other person who'd lived in the Hollow in recent years, in a nursing home, few people used the Hollow road any longer unless they were visiting Tala.

If the people in the car behind her were lost, sooner or later they'd turn around and go back to Hollendale for directions.

She walked through the front room of the old farmhouse, into the kitchen and out onto the screened back porch. She filled a large bucket from a metal garbage can of crimped oats that sat beside the washing machine, opened the back door and banged on the iron bell that hung beside it. She walked down the stairs into the backyard, setting off the motion-detector light, cast the oats onto the grass verge and walked back inside.

She heard the rustle at once. The deer had been waiting for her. When she and Adam had first installed the motion-detector lights, the deer had been wary, but each generation seemed to have taught the next not to worry. Now even spotted fawns came up to eat at night.

She stood in the darkness of the porch and watched them. Cody badly wanted a dog, but Adam had been afraid even a small dog would spook the deer. As he always said, the deer were there first.

Suddenly a gray doe with a notched ear froze. She raised her head. The others followed suit, listening to sounds that Tala could not hear. Then, as one animal, their white flagged tails went up and they bounded into the trees.

What on earth had spooked them?

Even the coyotes didn't hunt silently. Poachers out jacklighting at two in the morning?

The outside light went out and left the backyard in silent darkness.

The deer didn't spook over possums and raccoons.

Suddenly, she was spooked, too. Had she locked the front door? She ran through the house and slammed the bolt home, then ducked down to get the shotgun from under the couch beside the fireplace.

If the people in the car that had followed her wanted to ask directions, why didn't they simply drive down her driveway with their headlights on? In these parts, sneaking around at two o'clock in the morning was a good way to get yourself shot.

She heard a twig snap and the crunch of dead leaves. Her grandfather had taught her to track when she was small. She recognized the steps of a creature that walked on two legs.

Whoever or whatever was out there knew how far out to stay to avoid triggering the motion detectors.

Her heart hammered, and her mouth was suddenly so dry she couldn't even cough. She crouched on the floor, shotgun at her feet, and slid the box of extra shells into the pocket of her jacket.

She remembered Billy Joe's remark that he'd be glad to keep an eye on things, but it couldn't be him out there, she decided. He'd pull in and park.

The telephone stood on the kitchen cabinet twenty feet away. If she stood, she'd be silhouetted against the single lamp that burned on the side table. Besides, who would she call? All at once she felt as though she and whoever was outside were alone in the universe.

She had no idea how long she hunkered over, straining to hear the sound of a closer footfall.

Just when she decided she'd imagined the whole thing, she heard another twig snap. And then the footsteps moved away. This time, whoever was out there made no attempt to conceal the sound. She snapped off the light and peered over the windowsill. Her eyes adjusted quickly to the darkness.

She hadn't imagined it. Under the trees a tall, bulky shadow moved up the hill and disappeared.

Could it have been a coon hunter? He had no hounds. A deer poacher after her deer?

No one could be after *her*.

She was badly rattled. She pulled her grandmother Sakari's old drunkard's–path quilt and a couple of throw pillows off the couch, made herself a make-shift pallet on the floor and lay down with the shot-gun cradled in her arms like a lover. If whoever was out there came back, she'd be ready.

She'd grown up in this house, raised by the grand-parents who'd been stuck with her when her mother deserted her the day after she was born.

When Sakari died and left Tala the farm, she and Adam had moved into the old house to raise their children. With Adam in bed beside her, she'd never felt isolated or afraid.

She nearly reached for the phone to call Pete, but stopped. What did she want him to do? Come run-ning to protect her? No, she had to learn to protect herself.

Did some burglar plan to rob the place? Or did a squatter plan to move in without realizing someone still lived here?

TALA WOKE with a start at dawn. For a moment she couldn't remember why she still wore her jacket and lay on the hearth rug. She shivered under the quilt.

Somewhere between sleep and waking, she'd heard another sound.

She must have been sleeping much harder than she'd thought, having one of those dreams that seem so real at the time and so silly later. She could swear she'd heard the roar of a big cat carried on the wind.

But Baby was a good ten miles away.

She stood in the shower for a long time, and washed her long hair, which probably was still laden with the perfume of lion.

Times like this she longed to cut it. But Adam had been adamant that she keep it long. He liked it that way. She toweled it as dry as she could, then let it hang down her back while she fixed herself hot oatmeal and toast for breakfast.

She straightened up the house quickly. It never seemed to need much cleaning lately, with no children and no husband. Then she took a bag of cat food down to the old barn to fill her cats' big bowl. It would last them several days. The stream at the foot of the pasture ran cool and clear, so water was never a problem.

She reached for the hasp on the barn door and stopped with her hand in midair. Surely she hadn't left the door ajar that way. The old tractor and all Adam's tools were inside. The tractor was old, but still serviceable. The tools, however, were top-of-the-line and extremely expensive.

She slid the door open eighteen inches. Immediately four cats began calling to her and wrapping themselves around her ankles.

At first glance everything seemed normal. The aged yellow tractor sat in the center under the hayloft with its front-loader turned down toward the floor.

At the back, Adam's electric saw, router table, lathe and workbench seemed undisturbed. She walked over to his tool cabinet and opened it. A little dusty, but neat. She probably ought to sell the tools to somebody who enjoyed woodworking and cabinetmaking as much as Adam had, but so far she hadn't been able to part with them.

The light from the doorway illuminated the dusty clay floor and the footprints of her shoes.

She stooped to look more closely and felt the same instant thrill of fear she'd felt last night when she'd heard those careful footfalls. There was another set of tracks—size 12 to 14 boots—coming from the open door, circling the tractor, and returning to the door.

She filled the cats' bowls, set the bag on the work-table and looked more carefully. Nothing seemed out of place.

Maybe last night he'd cased the place, and planned to come back with a truck this morning when she wasn't here.

Except that ordinarily she *would* be here until she left for the Food Farm at three-fifteen this afternoon.

She swallowed, picked up the nearly empty bag of cat food, pulled a heavy padlock and key from Adam's tool chest and locked the barn behind her.

The minute she reached the kitchen, she dialed the sheriff's office in town and asked for Sheriff Craig personally.

"Hey, Miss Tala," he said when he came on the line. "How's my favorite girl?"

"Probably scareder than I have any reason to be," she said. When she told him what had happened, it sounded pretty weak. But he took her seriously.

"Sometimes we get drifters looking for a warm bed. Could be nothing more than that. Tell you what. I'll have Billie Joe and the other boys on call tonight check on you regularly, starting about three or so this afternoon when you leave for work."

She was about to tell him about her new job, then changed her mind. One way to find out whether or not they did check was to be here to meet them this evening when and if they came by. "Thanks, Sheriff," she said. They talked small talk for a few minutes, and when she hung up, she felt considerably better. Pretty silly, really.

She wound her braid around her head and pinned it down tight. The weather had begun to warm up, but it was still cold enough so that she'd need her fuzzy hat with the earflaps while she shoveled elephant dung. She set the timer for the lights, and climbed into her truck, which started at first crank.

"IF YOU STILL WANT ME, I definitely want the job," Tala said to Pete as she climbed out of her truck.

Pete blinked.

"I mean, we didn't set a definite time yesterday."

"Eight's fine."

The three girls came around the corner of their enclosure chirping like birds and swinging their trunks in greeting. In an instant Tala was surrounded.

Pete watched her eyes widen. "Just stand still," he said.

To her credit, Tala didn't move. While the three huge animals swayed and dipped their trunks to touch her shoulders. It was the way they always greeted one another after they'd been grazing in separate areas of their paddock for even a couple of hours.

Pete saw the glint of fear in her eyes, saw her breath on the cold air.

Then her glittery laugh rang out, and again, Pete's heart turned over at the sound.

After a moment, Tala reached out and carefully caressed each trunk gingerly. The girls chirped and swayed a moment longer, then turned away and moved off into the back pasture in tandem.

Tala didn't move. Her eyes were enormous. "You okay?" Pete said, laying one large hand on her shoulder. "You did fine."

"I've never seen any living thing quite that big and quite that close," Tala whispered. She looked up at him and smiled. "Except you, of course."

He felt his face flush. "Not exactly in the same category."

"Near enough. How's Baby?"

"Restless. We're expecting a shipment of zoo food this afternoon. Mace is getting pretty annoyed at sharing this winter's stock of deer meat with her."

"I'm so sorry. I should have brought some stuff from home."

"Deer?"

"Adam didn't hunt, but he did accept the occasional roast from one of his buddies. Some of the packages are pretty old, but the meat should still be edible. I'll bring it tomorrow." She looked stricken. "But you won't need it then, will you?"

"Sure. Always good to supplement with real meat. Wait and see the giant salamis she'll be getting when the frozen stuff arrives."

"Can I put it on my Visa?" she asked.

"What?"

"I mean, I can't really spare that much cash.

Maybe I should have kept my job at the grocery store and worked this one, too, at least for a couple of weeks. By the time I'm through paying you for Baby, there won't be much left over, will there?''

"You're serious, aren't you?" Pete asked. "Get inside. I'm cold." He practically shoved her in the front door of his little apartment. "Sit down." He realized when he saw those big dark eyes staring up at him how peremptory he sounded. "Please," he finished.

She sat, still swathed in coat, wearing gloves and a funny Sherlock Holmes hat that made her look as though she had hound ears. Adorable.

He yanked off his own gloves and jacket and sat across from her with his arms resting on his knees. "We didn't make this deal to get slave labor out of you."

"But you said…"

"Dammit, forget what I said. This is a sanctuary, after all."

"For elephants," she said in a small voice.

"Elephants, lions—it's all the same, whatever I said. I'll find Baby a home, but until I do, she's my problem, or my foundation's, which is the same thing. I intend to work your can off, but I also intend to pay you for it."

"Oh," she whispered.

He stood and walked to the exam-room door. "So let's get started." He flung over his shoulder, "Pour us a cup of coffee first. Black. One sugar."

"Yes, Pete," she said softly.

He turned around and glared at her. He could

swear he'd caught a smile in her voice, but by the time he saw her, she'd wiped it off her face. So maybe she wasn't as scared of him as she'd seemed.

Well, he'd have to see about that.

Baby stood up when Tala walked in and began to chuff at her expectantly.

"Hey, sweetie," Tala said, hunkering down by the cage. "Feeling better today?"

Baby butted her head against the enclosure so hard the fence wobbled. Tala poked her fingers through and scratched the lion's ears.

"We're going to have to dart her to change the dressing and check for infection," Pete said. "While she's out we'll move her to her new enclosure."

"Do you have to? Knock her out, I mean."

"Just because she didn't take your arm off yesterday does not mean she'll leave mine attached when I start probing that wound."

"Oh. I guess you're right."

"Damn straight I'm right. Now, it's about time you learned how to shovel elephant dung."

"Where's Mace?" Tala asked as she followed Pete's instructions. The piles were odorous and steaming, but Tala pitched in as though she'd been doing it all her life.

"Sleeping in. Had a long day yesterday. He works hard, but it takes him a little longer to recover than it used to."

"He's still a relatively young man."

Pete sighed. "I think he burned out dealing with all the fund-raising and bureaucratic hoops he had to jump through at the vet school. He maxed out his retirement several years ago, so he up and retired. He's still a good teacher. And a good vet.''

"Did you ever think maybe he came because he thought you needed him to deal with all *your* bureaucratic hoops?''

Pete stopped with his pitchfork in midair. "Maybe. Sooner or later he'll find something else to do that turns him on.''

"You don't think working with you does?''

Pete shrugged. "Never did before.''

By the time the elephant enclosure was ready for the girls to return, Mace still hadn't surfaced. The day had warmed up considerably, and the sun shone in a cloudless winter sky that was clearer than summer could ever be.

"Come on," Pete said as he closed the gate. "I need to show you over the paddock. We'll go check out the girls.''

She trotted along behind him to the enclosed shed behind Mace's trailer. Pete opened the door to reveal a four-wheel, off-road vehicle with its wheels covered in mud. He pulled it out and straddled it. "Climb on behind.''

"I've never ridden one of those things," she said. "They're dangerous.''

"They're necessary when you've got this much land to cover. Hop on, and put your arms around my waist.''

He felt gloved hands clasp his waist and her body against his back. Her face didn't even come to his shoulder. Even through the layers of cloth and down, he was aware of her warmth against him. He found himself hungering for her.

The thought of looking down into her eyes as she lay beneath him distracted him so totally he darn near turned over the four-wheeler on a root.

They were airborne for a moment. Tala screamed and buried her face even deeper in his shoulder.

He slowed. "Sorry."

He drove along wooded trails and through open pastures surrounded by old-growth trees. Evidence of elephants was everywhere, from the leaves and bark stripped from the small trees, to the muddy paths, to the long grass that had systematically been torn up in great swaths.

He stopped by the side of a shallow pond that measured about eight by fifteen feet. "A year ago this started as one footprint that filled with water. Now it's one of the girls' favorite bathing spots in the summer."

"What do you do in the winter? I know elephants love water."

"We have to make do with hot water from the hose in the shelter. When and if I get the money, I want to put in a heated pool for them. There's Sweetiepie." He pointed. Tala raised her head from his shoulder.

"Where? I can't see anything."

"You have to learn to see them." He pointed. "See? That gray thing that's starting to move. Sweetiepie is kind of a loner. Sophie and Belle are probably together somewhere." He accelerated and Tala clung once more.

Nice. Worth riding all day for. He drove down a forested path, turned a corner and slammed on his brakes. Belle and Sophie stood no more than five feet away, happily stripping leaves and stuffing them into their mouths. They barely looked up.

"Okay, girls, see you for dinner," Pete said, turned the four-wheeler and began to drive sedately back. "We've got the property sectioned off into fifty-acre areas. We monitor the destruction of plants in one section so we can move the elephants to another paddock and let the land recover before they do any real damage. Next month they move next door. We pull a wire fence across the opening to this pasture until they're used to going to the other. Works fine."

"One little wire?"

"Sure. Elephants don't mess with electric fences. Of course, we still keep the high-perimeter fences and the front gate. That's as much to keep the public out as to keep the girls in."

On their way back Sweetiepie swung in behind them, overtook and passed them as though they were standing still.

"Wow!" Tala said in awe, as the baggy gray rear end reached the end of the elephant house and disappeared through the plastic door.

"Thinks she's going to cadge some extra food when we get back."

"Will she?" Tala asked.

"Probably. She's more demanding than the others. And older. She had an infected tooth that didn't respond until a week ago. She dropped a few hundred pounds while I was treating her.''

When they walked into the enclosure, Mace had just forked a half bale of hay inside. Sweetiepie stood placidly ripping out flakes with her trunk and placing them gently into her mouth.

''Morning, all,'' Mace said cheerfully. ''Sorry I overslept.''

He still looked tired, Pete noted, and the hands that held the pitchfork shook slightly.

As usual, Baby stood and began to rumble the moment she saw Tala, who went to her immediately.

''Her cage needs cleaning badly,'' Tala said. ''Can we put her in the bathroom again while I scrub it down?''

''No way,'' Pete said. ''She tore it up completely yesterday. Dad, have you checked her new cage?''

''Concrete's set. Won't be completely dry for a couple of days, but I don't think she can rip out the posts. I spread a couple of bales of hay on the floor, put a water trough in there for her and a pan full of meat.''

''Then let's do it,'' Pete said. He was aware of Tala's eyes on his back as he loaded the pistol with the sedative dart and walked over to Baby. When he aimed the gun through the fencing at her rear she snarled at him, and took a swat at the fence the instant the dart embedded itself in her rump.

''Get out of here, Tala,'' Pete said quickly. ''Go turn on the computer or something.''

''I want to watch.''

''I'll call you when she's down. Go.''

He kept his eyes on the cat until she settled on her haunches, and five minutes later keeled over on her side and began to snore. "Okay, Dad, let's work on her in there. That way if she comes out of it we can still slam the door on her."

A few moments later, Pete was kneeling inside the cage, examining Baby's wound. It was healing faster than Pete had expected and showed no sign of infection. To be safe he gave her another shot of antibiotic.

"You were supposed to call me," Tala said from behind him.

"I was busy. Dad, you wait here, I'll get the hay cart. We can move her on that."

"Can I help?" Tala said.

"Stay out of the way. If she wakes up I don't want to have to worry about where you are."

But she didn't wake. Pete locked the door on her new cage securely. When he went back in, Tala was already filling a bucket with steaming water and disinfectant.

"Those blankets will need to be washed at least twice," she said. "Do we add lion poop to the pile of elephant poop, or do we start a new one?"

"Add, m'dear, by all means," Mace said. "In the meantime, however, it is after noon, and I have had no breakfast. You, I suspect, could use some lunch."

"I don't usually eat lunch," Tala said.

"You should. I shall fix us all sandwiches."

"Dr. Jacobi, Mace, you can't keep feeding me…"

"Indeed I can," Mace said. "And I intend to. Consider it my pleasure and a perk of the job. I have to feed myself and Pete anyway. Why not you?'' He ducked out the door and shut it behind him.

Tala had already scooped up the lion droppings into the manure bucket and had begun scrubbing the concrete floor with a heavy long-handled brush and hot soapy water.

''I'll do that,'' Pete said. ''You still haven't looked at that computer.''

''Oh, no. This is what you hired me for. I'm used to it.'' A stray lock of dark hair had come loose from her braid and fallen across her forehead.

Pete reached over and tucked it behind her ear, then his fingers slid down her cheek.

She was probably as startled as he was by the gesture.

For a moment their eyes met and held. He could feel his pulse thrumming in his ears and see hers throbbing at the side of her throat. Lovely throat, fine and slim and pale.

He took a deep breath. The spell shattered. She turned away to scrub fiercely, and said in a carefully conversational tone, ''Why elephants?''

''They grow on you. And I found out how desperately they need the help.'' He looked away. ''There are a great many abused and starved elephants in this country. Let's just say I'm trying to pay off an old debt.''

AFTER LUNCH Tala finished scrubbing the lioness's old cage, and while Mace and Pete disassembled it, she cranked up the computer and began to find her way around it.

Before Adam's death, she'd taken several computer courses at the junior college in hopes of eventually getting a degree in education so she could teach, but her other duties kept getting in the way. And Rachel had taken the family computer to her grandmother's house to do homework, so Tala had no computer at home any longer.

She didn't have the sanctuary password to connect to the Internet, so she couldn't check out their Web page. Maybe Pete would trust her with it tomorrow.

"If you're going to pick up your children, m'dear," Mace said from the doorway, "better close that thing down and get going."

Tala glanced at her watch. The day had gone like the wind. "Lord, yes," she said as she scrambled for her things. "I meant to check Baby. Is she awake?"

"And anxious for dinner. Let me walk you to the gate, then you won't have to get out to open it." He handed her a plain metal key ring. "Here you go, m'dear. The big key is the gate padlock, the others are labeled, including the one for Baby's cage. I wouldn't advise you to open it, however."

Tala felt a wave of gratitude. "You're sure? About the keys, I mean."

"Of course. Pete got the set together while you were working in here. You might arrive before we're up, or need to get in at some other time. You work here, after all."

As he stood at the gate and waved her through, he called, "See you tomorrow." Pete was nowhere in sight. She felt a surprising letdown. How could she have thought he was hateful? Angry, obviously. But she might be angry too, if she'd seen half the things he'd seen.

And he was trying to do something about it in a small way.

Just the way Adam had tried to do something about the small world he lived in.

And it had killed him.

CHAPTER SIX

"I'VE INVITED the doctors Jacobi to dinner tonight," Irene said to Tala as she watched her children climb the stairs to their bedrooms. "If you are going to work for them, then we must get to know them."

Tala's heart sank. She'd spent all day with Pete and Mace. The last thing they would want is to be hog-tied into one of Irene's semiformal dinners at the last minute. And Tala was exhausted. Last night's pallet had been pretty uncomfortable.

"I'm sure they're sick of the sight of me."

"They're bachelors—well, Mace Jacobi is a widower, but I don't think his son has ever been married. Not that I can find, at any rate. And bachelors are always delighted to be invited out for a decent meal."

"Dr. Mace is a good cook."

"Ah, but it's not the same as Lucinda's cooking."

"Besides, it's a school night. Cody and Rachel have homework."

Irene waved the problem away. "They probably got their homework done in study hall." She called up the stairs after them. "Rachel, Cody, did you do your homework?"

Two affirmative sounds came from upstairs. Irene

beamed. "See. No problem. Now, you go home, get cleaned up—put on a dress, darling, for a change."

Tala sighed. "Okay, but I may fall asleep in the shrimp bisque."

"As long as you eat some of it first." As Tala walked to her car, Irene called after her, "What's it like being able to pick up your own children after school again?"

"Wonderful. I actually got to watch five minutes of Rachel's cheerleading practice. Those girls are really good. I had no idea Rachel had gotten that limber. I never could do the splits, even at thirteen."

Irene laughed. "Three days and you'll be praying for the good ole days of car pool."

Tala came close to tears on her drive home. What was she nervous about?

Too much rode on this dinner. What if everybody hated everybody else? Pete Jacobi could be a royal pain when he chose, and he didn't look like the crystal-wineglasses-and-lace-tablecloth type. She wanted her family to like him, despite his temperament.

What if Rachel did one of her numbers? Cody wouldn't be a problem. He'd be delighted to hear elephant tales, but Rachel? My Lady of Perpetual Disdain?

Adam had always demanded obedience from the children, and miraculously, they had never given him any trouble. She didn't know his secret.

If she had time, she'd try to stop by the library tomorrow afternoon before she picked up the kids and get some parenting guides.

The Land Rover was already parked in front of the

Newsome house by the time Tala got back. She hadn't bought any clothes since Adam died—except for the black dress she wore to his funeral. Probably an appropriate choice for tonight's party, but she'd been afraid Rachel and Cody would recognize it. So instead she wore a dark green sweater, a long black skirt, ankle boots and a black blazer. She'd styled her hair into a long French braid with a green cloisonné clasp holding it together.

She heard Mace's cheerful laugh the moment she opened the front door. In the living room, he stood at ease with one elbow resting on the mantelpiece, a glass of sherry in one hand, the other in his pocket. He looked every inch a college professor, beautifully tailored tweed jacket and all.

Pete sat in obvious discomfort on the peach damask sofa. The sofa tended to devour anybody that sank into its heavy down cushions, and Pete was no exception. He was so tall that his knees stuck up above his waist. He wore a dark blue shirt, a slightly askew knitted tie, a tweed jacket similar to his father's, jeans and clean brown suede desert boots.

Pete's jacket seemed two sizes too small, stretched so tight across biceps and shoulders that it wrinkled, and as rumpled as though he'd plucked it from his wastepaper basket on the way out the door. The sherry glass in his fingers looked as though it might crack from sheer terror. If voices could break glass, then perhaps a scowl that registered that high could do the same thing. When he saw Tala, he tried to get his feet under him to stand up. She waved him down.

"Tala, honey, you look lovely," Vertie said from

the staircase behind her. Vertie wore a heavily embroidered hot-pink and turquoise Mexican shirt with fringe on the sleeves, a pair of hot-pink Wranglers, turquoise cowboy boots and enough turquoise and coral jewelry to pay off the national debt of a small nation.

Irene turned and saw her mother-in-law and blinked. "And you, Vertie dear, look downright astounding. Shall I pour you a sherry?"

"Good God, Irene, it's darned near seven o'clock. I want a real drink." She grinned at Pete, who manfully struggled out of the sofa. "I'll bet you played offensive lineman, didn't you, honey?" She held out her hand, and when Pete nodded sheepishly, she laughed as she turned to Mace. "Dr. Jacobi. Nice to see you again." The moment he took her hand, she withdrew it, walked over to the drinks cart in the corner of the room, poured herself two fingers of bourbon, sipped and caught her breath. "Sherry, my foot. Any of y'all want to switch to bourbon?"

Pete looked as though he'd be grateful, but he kept his mouth shut when he caught his father's eye. Best behavior must not include bourbon.

Irene turned back to her guests.

"By the way, Irene," Vertie said, "I asked Lucinda to set an extra place. Since we were having a dinner party, I didn't think you'd mind an extra man."

Irene looked at her quickly. Tala could tell she was almost afraid to ask.

"Don't worry. He's presentable. Vincent Oxley.

You've met him at council meetings. He's developing those new condos out by the country club.''

Irene relaxed. "How nice, Vertie. How do you know him?''

"His daddy was on one of my tours a few years back. Vincent looked me up when he came to town last year, and today when I ran into him on Main Street, seemed like I ought to ask him over.''

Lovely, Tala thought. Now not only would the Jacobis have to deal with her family and children, but a perfectly strange real-estate developer, to boot. What a delightful evening this was shaping up to be.

The doorbell rang, and a moment later Vertie ushered Vincent Oxley into the room. This time Pete made no attempt to stand, or even offer his hand, although Mace came across to be introduced.

Oxley was tall, slim, graying, probably in his mid-forties, and showed a little too much collar and cuff for Tala's taste. But she supposed real-estate types had to be well-groomed. She'd never much cared for French cuffs, either, even with gold studs in them. When she shook hands with him, he held on a millisecond too long, and smiled a bit too warmly.

Or maybe not. He was just as charming to Irene. "Miss Irene, I have been meaning to call. I believe that with my construction background and your land, we might do some business.''

Irene actually blushed. "Vertie's the land baron in the family, not me.''

At that point Lucinda stuck her head in the living-room door and said, "Y'all better come on to dinner or that tenderloin's gonna be too done.'' Then she turned to the staircase and yelled, "Rachel, Cody, get yourselves down here."

The shrimp bisque was delicious, although Cody said there was no way he was eating pink soup.

The wilted-spinach salad was good as well, but Rachel carefully picked every sliver of bacon out of hers and placed it disdainfully on the side of her plate. "Yuck. All that fat," she whispered.

The beef tenderloin was sheer perfection, although the addition of another person made the portions a little skimpy. There were plenty of vegetables, however, and even Pete ate with gusto. And good table manners.

Vertie had angled a seat beside him, and kept leaning over and whispering to him as though she were flirting. Knowing Vertie, she probably was, all seventy-eight years of her. Tala had to admit, he handled Vertie beautifully, with just the right amount of amusement and deference.

Tala was seated next to Vincent Oxley, who was probably charming as well, but she kept losing the thread of their conversation while she watched her children across the table. Rachel, on the other side of Pete, tossed her head and leaned over to whisper to him as well.

Mace Jacobi, as she had been certain he would, entranced Cody and Irene with funny stories about elephants and vet students.

"Can I come ride the elephants?" Cody asked. Tala reached across and just missed landing a toe in his ankle.

Pete's head whipped around. "They don't ride people anymore. They're retired."

"Oh." Cody sounded deflated. His shoulders pulled in. Now Tala wished she could reach Pete's ankle.

"But you can certainly come out and see them, pet them," Mace said. Cody's shoulders straightened. "Your mother is getting to be quite an elephant girl, aren't you, m'dear?"

"Yuck," Rachel whispered. Then said something Tala didn't catch.

"What was that?" Tala asked.

Rachel raised her chin, "I said, Sheena, Queen of the Jungle, right out of those old comic books in the attic."

Irene tittered.

Mace leaned forward and said seriously, "I recall Sheena rode a zebra. Never seen one myself that wouldn't buck off a rodeo rider, but I suppose it's possible. Besides, these are Indian elephants. Less comic book, more Rudyard Kipling." He smiled at her. "Ever read his story about Moti Guj?"

"I *love* that story," Rachel trilled. It was the most animation Tala had seen her show in months. Mace had made a conquest.

"So come and play with our girls," Mace said. "They're every bit as interesting as Moti, though probably not so large."

"Could I? When?"

Mace shrugged. "How about Sunday afternoon? The weather is supposed to warm up."

"Will my mother be there?" Rachel looked over at Tala.

"She's got to catch up with her own work on weekends, I'm sure. But I'll be delighted to come get you and Cody after church if she says it's all right."

"I suppose..." Tala hesitated, sounding unsure.

"Please, Mom, please, please, please!" Cody begged.

Tala sighed. "If you're sure it wouldn't be too much trouble."

"Yes!" Cody said.

Tala glanced at Pete and saw that he was looking at Cody and Rachel in horror. Well, the heck with him. They were good kids, for all their attitudes. Time Dr. Peter Jacobi dealt with the real world.

"Do you mind if I tag along?" Oxley said. "I've never seen an elephant outside of a zoo."

"We don't let the public in," Pete said. He glared at his father. "As a rule."

"Wouldn't be a bit of trouble," Oxley continued.

Damn! Tala didn't want Oxley horning in on the children's afternoon. She said quickly, "I was hoping you'd show me around the new development Sunday, Vincent. One of these days I might decide to move into town."

The glint of a possible sale lit in his eyes. Condo sale, and maybe another kind as well. In his dreams. "Of course, Tala," Oxley said, and covered her hand with his momentarily. "I've got the perfect place for the three of you."

"Oh, Mama, could we?" Rachel asked.

Lord, this was getting out of hand. "I said, Rachel,

I might think about it at some point in the future. Period." She saw that for some reason Pete was downright furious. With her? His father? Her children? Oxley? The world, the galaxy and the universe? Instead, she quickly asked—more to change the conversation than anything else—"Where did the girls come from originally?"

Pete took a deep breath, then said, "I don't think you want to hear about that right now."

"Oh, please, please," Cody begged.

"Okay, but you won't like it," he said. "Sweetie-pie was in a small circus. Her owner died, and if one of the other performers hadn't seen our site on the Internet and notified us, she would have died, too. She was skin and bones when we got her."

"Oh, dear," Irene said. "Perhaps you're right, Dr. Jacobi." She glanced at the children.

"No, Grandmama," Rachel said. "Let him tell us."

Pete turned to Rachel. "Sophie was sold to a roadside park in Florida when she was a baby. When her owner went bankrupt, he simply walked away and left the animals. The neighbors called us. She was so dehydrated we thought we'd lose her."

"Oh, poor thing," Rachel whispered.

"Belle was a circus elephant for twenty years," Pete continued. "Then one day she got fed up with standing on her head three shows a day and went after the man who owned her. From all I hear, he deserved it."

"She hurt somebody?" Irene said. "You brought

an elephant that hurt somebody into Hollendale County, Dr. Jacobi?''

Mace turned to her quickly. ''She's extremely even-tempered when she's well treated. And at the sanctuary, she is.''

''Nonetheless, Tala…and the children. Oh, dear, if I'd known…''

''Don't worry, Mrs. Newsome,'' Pete said.

''She's a dear, sweet girl,'' Tala said. But she hadn't known Belle had hurt someone. Maybe worse than hurt.

''I think I'll come along on Sunday, if you don't mind,'' Irene said with a hint of steel in her voice. ''I haven't actually been out there, you know, not since you brought in the elephants.''

''Fine, glad to have you,'' Mace said cheerfully. Pete didn't look cheerful at all. Tala wished she'd never asked in the first place. And if her mother-in-law ever got even a hint that she was looking after a lion as well as the elephants, well—Irene's reaction simply didn't bear thinking about.

TWENTY MINUTES LATER, as she drove out after the Land Rover and turned toward home, she realized she couldn't be angry at Pete. First, the stories must be true. He'd probably cleaned them up a good deal as it was. Second, she'd been the one to open that particular can of worms. She should have known better.

The same stupid car that had followed her from the Food Farm the other night—or one very similar—followed her with its brights on from the city limits up onto the Hollow road.

She held her hand up to try to shield her eyes from the lights in her rearview mirror. The idiot was going to try to pass on a blind curve! As the car closed on her rear bumper, she felt a jolt.

He'd hit her!

She fought the wheel, suddenly terrified by visions of the steep hillside on her left.

She recovered just as he hit her again. Harder, this time. The guy was nuts!

As she saw the lights close in on her for the third time, she realized she was heading for a curve that she couldn't take at the speed she was going. At the last minute, she wrenched the wheel of the little truck to the right.

The car behind her flew by with no more than an inch to spare, fought its way around the curve ahead and accelerated into the darkness. She glimpsed two males in the front seat, but couldn't see much more.

She had her own hands full. She braked and skidded off the road onto the gravel shoulder, then felt the pickup lurch sickeningly into the shallow ditch on the far side of the shoulder.

The truck rocked and stopped at a forty-degree angle in the ditch. Tala used all her strength to open the driver's-side door, and almost fell onto the road.

The night air was cold, but she felt so blessed to be alive she welcomed it.

Would those crazy people come back when they realized she hadn't gone over the cliff? Maybe not.

They were probably laughing their fool heads off and heading for the nearest roadhouse twenty miles away.

She really needed a cell phone for her car. Irene kept telling her she'd pay for it. Maybe this was one time Tala could let her.

She grabbed her purse, pulled the hood of her car coat over her head, turned off the ignition and the lights on the truck, and slipped and slid her way up the small embankment to the road.

As she let her eyes adjust to the darkness, she remembered the flashlight in the glove compartment. She hadn't changed the batteries since Adam died. He always took care of things like that. She scrambled back into the car, located the flashlight, flicked it, and was grateful when it lit.

Then she reached under the front seat for the Rossi .38 pistol, checked to see that it was loaded and dropped the extra box of shells into her pocket. This was getting to be a habit.

She shone the light on the rear end of the truck.

Very little damage. Mostly scraped paint. Certainly drivable. Except that she'd need something to tie her winch rope to before she could pull the truck out of the ditch. And there was nothing appropriate on the shoulder.

Bother. That meant walking home.

She walked back fifty yards to the place where a deer trail started down the Hollow slope, and began to slide her way down the brow of the hill. She was probably not more than a mile and a half from her house through the woods, but the trail would be steep and muddy. She mustn't slip.

She heard a car coming, and switched off the flashlight. Whoever drove by slowed, but didn't stop. Maybe those idiots had come back after all. They might be feeling remorseful and want to help.

On the other hand, they might be afraid to leave her in one piece. Best not to take the chance.

By the time she reached the trees at the back of her yard, she'd spooked half a dozen deer. This was one night she didn't want to run into a big cat.

She was also cold, thirsty, and dragging what seemed like a hundred pounds of sodden wool skirt.

She stood at the edge of the clearing and looked at the house. Nothing seemed different. The proper set of lights were on inside. No cars outside.

For the first time, she cursed the motion detectors as she ran across the yard lit as though she were on a stage.

Once inside the house, she collapsed into Adam's leather chair.

She looked at the clock and was amazed to see that she'd left Irene's a little over an hour ago. It wasn't even eleven o'clock yet.

Realizing she had no way to get to work in the morning, Tala dragged her wet skirt into the kitchen and dialed the number of the sanctuary.

"Yeah?" Pete Jacobi answered on the fourth ring.

"Pete?" Her voice sounded as though she hadn't used it for the past century. She cleared her throat.

"Tala? What's wrong?"

"Do I sound that bad?"

"You sound like hell."

"Somebody tried to run me off the Holler road on the way home."

"What?" he shouted. "You okay?"

"Okay, home, and very lucky. Thing is, the truck's sitting in a ditch about five miles from here. I didn't see anything to tie the winch to. I don't think it's much hurt, but I'll have to wait for a tow truck tomorrow morning. I hate to do this my second day, but I'm afraid I'll be late coming in tomorrow."

She was babbling and knew it, but didn't seem to be able to stop.

"I'll be there in twenty minutes."

"Pete…"

But he'd already hung up.

SHE HEARD the car door slam as she pulled one of Adam's heavy old sweaters over her head. Pete must have driven at warp speed. She'd barely had time to change into jeans. She cantered down the stairs as he began to attack the doorbell.

"Okay! Just a minute," she called. She undid the chain and clicked upon the dead bolt. The door swung open as she realized she had no idea whether the person on the other side was Pete or a serial killer.

From the wild way his hair stood up on his head, she'd have picked serial killer.

He barreled in, nearly knocked her down, grabbed her around the waist, lifted her off her feet and kissed her hard.

For a moment she hung stiff, and then her arms climbed around his neck of their own volition, her body arched against him through no fault of hers, and her bruised lips parted to meet his questing tongue without any instruction from her brain whatsoever.

He kept one arm around her waist, while his other hand slid up the back of her neck and into the fine hair at her nape. His fingers felt gentle, caressing, but they were about the only gentle thing about him.

Nobody had ever kissed her that hard or that— *thoroughly* was the only word she could think of. He tasted of toothpaste and some wonderful spice that she couldn't identify, but was rich enough to put ten pounds on her if his kiss lasted much longer.

Suddenly he released her and stepped back. "Dammit! Are you all right?"

"I think my front teeth are loose."

"You hit the steering wheel?" He bent down and reached for her upper lip. "Did the airbag deploy?"

She shoved his hand away. "No, I did not hit the steering wheel and the airbag did not deploy."

He got it then, and said sheepishly, "Oh, sorry. Sometimes I don't know my own strength."

"I'll say."

"Look, I'm sorry…"

She took two steps until she was standing close to him again. "Next time, take it easy."

"Huh?"

He really was the stupidest man! She stood on tiptoe, wound her hands in his hair and pulled his head down. As her lips touched his, his eyes closed, he sighed and slipped his arms around her, but this time softly, tenderly, moving down from her waist to her hips. Their tongues met, tasted, roved, touched and caressed one another's mouths slowly at first, then with more urgency.

He cupped her bottom and lifted her. This time her knees refused to obey as they had before. She wrapped them around him, felt him hard and urgent against her belly, and the leap of answering flames in her groin.

She was held by some giant brown bear with huge gentle paws that warmed her body everywhere they touched. Nothing could get through, around, or over him to hurt her. Now that she felt truly safe, she recognized for the first time how frightened she'd been.

She broke the kiss, tucked her head under his chin and let him hold her, let his warmth seep into her.

"I passed your truck up on the road," he whispered into her hair. "If anything had happened to you…"

"It didn't. And it won't, not now."

"I've wanted you since the instant you pulled that hood off and I saw your eyes." He kissed her eyelids gently.

She slid her legs down and pulled away from him to look up into his face.

He ran his thumb along her cheekbone. "Doesn't matter what I'm supposed to be doing. All of a sudden I see your face, your eyes, and I discover I'm standing like an idiot with a shovelful of manure halfway to the pile."

Tala laughed up at him. "You romantic devil."

He flushed. "I'm serious. Wanting you is screwing

up my life, confusing the heck out of me, and causing me problems I don't know how to handle, but I can't deny my feelings.''

She sobered and pressed her face against his shoulder. ''I feel as though I've been hit by a truck.''

He grinned. ''Under the circumstances, that's one hell of a lousy metaphor.'' He slipped his hand under her chin, bent and kissed the tip of her nose. ''You're really all right?''

''I've got scratches on my scratches from stumbling through the woods, and I don't think I'll ever be able to wear those boots again, but that's a small price to pay.''

''For being alive? This isn't a joke, Tala. Let me take a look at your scratches.''

''Please, Pete, I don't dare think about how close I came or I'll start to shake. I'm fine. Don't fuss.''

''I'll fuss if I want to.'' He reached down and swept her into his arms, walked over to the sofa and laid her on it, then dropped to his knees beside her and took her in his arms. ''It's okay to shake. I shook all the way over here worrying about you,'' he whispered against her hair. ''Now show me your scratches.''

She sat up and gave him her best attempt at a grin. ''Forget it, buster. I'm not taking off these jeans so you can play doctor.''

''I *am* a doctor.'' He reached for her ankle. She yipped and kicked at him. In a minute they were rolling together on the couch, laughing like children.

Then, almost as one, they caught their breath. He lay above her, his big chest pinning her under him.

Her dark eyes stared up into his face, and her breath came in quick little gasps.

"God help us both," he whispered as he lowered his face to kiss her.

And jerked away as a siren screamed outside the house. "What the hell?" he said. She turned her head to see the spinning blue, white and red lights outside.

"Oh, Lord," she said. "It's the cops."

A moment later booted feet thudded up onto the porch and rang the doorbell. "Tala?" a voice called. "Tala Newsome? You in there?"

Tala called over her shoulder, "I'm coming, Billie Joe." She sat up, patted her hair and pushed off on Pete's shoulder to stand up. She walked to the door as Pete surged to his feet behind her.

"You all right?" Billie Joe said when she opened the door. He came in without waiting for an answer, saw Pete standing by the sofa, blinked, frowned a moment at Tala, and cleared his throat. "Saw the truck in the ditch. What happened?"

She told him.

"I'll find those little…jerks," Billie Joe said. *Jerk* was obviously not the word he had been planning to use. "And when I do, I will mess with their civil rights real good."

"You think it was high-school kids?" Tala asked.

"'Course it was kids. Out drinking beer they shouldn't 'a' had in the first place and hoo-rawing a lone woman on a lonely road. Didn't think what might 'a' happened if you'd gone off the road. Hell, you could have been killed."

"But I wasn't. You know, Billie Joe, I think the same car followed me home from the Food Farm the other night."

He narrowed his eyes. "You sure? Didn't get the make or license plate or anything, did you?"

"I didn't pay much attention at the time." She shivered. "But I think it was the same car."

"What you doing home this time of night anyway?"

"I meant to tell you, Billie Joe. I took a new job today with Dr. Jacobi and his father working days at the elephant sanctuary."

"Doing what?"

"Whatever needs doing," Pete said.

"Well. I keep saying I need to come by that place sometime, see them elephants of yours, Doc."

Tala saw Pete open his mouth and stepped in with, "I'm sure they'd love to see you, Billie Joe, but we're all pretty busy, and the sanctuary's not really set up for the public."

"Uh-huh. Had any more kids trying to climb the fences lately, Doc?"

"Not since the weather got lousy."

"Maybe before next spring they'll find something else stupid to do." He looked from one to the other. "Y'all want me to call a tow truck?"

"I think I can winch her out of the ditch with the Land Rover," Pete said. "Thanks, anyway."

"Yeah. Well, sure. I'll be by here a couple more times tonight, Tala, and then the late shift takes over. You be careful now, you hear?" He raised an index finger in what might have been a form of salute, turned on his heel and tromped down the stairs. A moment later he drove out of the yard.

"What's that about a car following you home?"

"Nothing. Just paranoid. I've only started realizing how alone I am out here."

"You don't have to be." He moved toward her. "I could stay."

"No, you couldn't. Not in this town. Come on, we have to get my truck out of the ditch so that I can get to work tomorrow morning."

He looked at her closely for a moment, then sighed. "Yeah. Right."

PETE'S LAND ROVER made quick work of pulling Tala's pickup out of the ditch. The right side of the truck was caked with mud, but otherwise the vehicle seemed undamaged.

"A few scrapes of black paint on the left bumper," Pete said, squatting to run his fingers over the place where the other car had hit her. "I think I can get them out with rubbing compound."

"Thank God. I really can't afford to have any bodywork done right now."

He started to climb into the Land Rover, and she put her hand on his arm. "Thanks, Pete. I'll be fine now. I have a shotgun. And I'm about to drop from exhaustion."

He started to protest, then nodded. "I'll follow you and see you safely inside. Don't argue."

He sat outside in his car until he saw her throw the bolt on the front door, then he spun and drove up the hill to the road much too fast.

She watched his taillights go out of sight before she dragged herself wearily to feed the deer, then up the stairs, stripped and climbed into the bed she'd shared with Adam for so many years.

Until tonight, she'd clung to the left side of the bed, as though Adam still slept on the right. Tonight, however, she rolled over on her stomach and moved her body catty-corner until her head lay on Adam's pillow.

There was no longer even a hint of Adam's scent. Now all she felt tingle in her nostrils was that spicy scent of Pete. Why did she feel so disloyal?

Her body ached. Pete's kiss, so unlike Adam's gentle kisses, had broken down barriers she'd kept closed through sheer force of will.

She could no longer tell herself that she was only a mother. Pete had forced her to remember she was a woman as well.

CHAPTER SEVEN

"PETE TOOK OFF for Knoxville before dawn," Mace told Tala when she wondered where he was the next morning. "Said he was going to see an old friend about finding Baby a home. Wanted to check out the facilities himself."

Running away, no doubt, so he wouldn't have to deal with her after that kiss last night. And getting Baby out of his hair as soon as possible in hopes that she'd leave soon after. Then he could go back to being a happy hermit.

Except that she had no intention of begging Beanie for her former job back. She could pick up her kids after school now, make a little more money, and she loved the elephants.

Even if Pete made her uncomfortable, awakened feelings she didn't want to deal with, she'd find a way to handle them. No more frantic midnight kisses. No more erotic dreams that kept her tossing and turning all night. Pete was right. There would be too many problems if they "got involved."

"How's your truck?" Mace asked, breaking in on her reverie.

"It's fine," Tala answered. "Some mud and a

couple of scratches, but nothing worse than I got walking home through the woods.''

''The sheriff have any idea who might have done it?''

''Billie Joe said he'd call me if anything turned up. Probably joyriding kids who had too much to drink.''

''Maybe not. Could have been somebody trying to force you off the road to take you hostage or worse. I think you should move in with your family in town temporarily.''

''Major overreaction,'' Tala said with a good deal of heat. ''Lord knows I love them, but once they get me into that house, I'm afraid I'll never get out. I'm not ready for that.''

''So sell your place and move closer to town.''

''I can't.'' Tala hoped the finality of her answer would keep Mace from asking any more questions. But as he opened his mouth to do just that, Tala felt a whiffle of air on the back of her neck and turned to see Sophie peering down at her. Tala hadn't even heard the elephant approach. Sophie gingerly wrapped her trunk around Tala's heavy braid and pulled.

''Hey!'' Tala grabbed at her scalp as she tried to keep her balance.

''Sophie! No!'' Mace shouted.

Sophie dropped the braid and stared at the pair of them in puzzlement. Then she sighed deeply and swung away.

''What was that about?'' Tala asked in a shaky voice. She massaged her scalp. No harm done, but

Sophie could have scalped her easily, or picked her up and swung her around by her hair like a circus performer. For a moment she was truly frightened.

Mace dropped his arm around her shoulders. "It's all right, m'dear."

She shivered. "What did she want?"

Mace shrugged and dropped his arm. "We'll have to ask Pete, he's the elephant man, but I think she regards your braid as a sort of trunk. She can't understand why it's on the back of your head instead of the front, and why it doesn't work the same way hers does. I think she was greeting you elephant style and expected you to greet her back the same way."

"Oh, poor Sophie! Have I offended her?"

"I doubt it. She's endlessly patient with us human beings, but she does get confused."

"Would she come back if I called her?" She pushed the fear to the back of her mind. Sophie was only being neighborly. Not her fault if she weighed several tons.

"Always speak firmly. Don't shout, but also don't sound wishy-washy. It's fine for them to like you, but they must respect you as well."

Tala took a deep breath, cupped her hands around her mouth and called, "Sophie, come here."

A moment later a large gray head peeked around the edge of the enclosure, and then the whole elephant emerged. She walked hesitantly over to them.

"What should I do now?" Tala whispered when Sophie raised her trunk and opened her mouth.

"Scratch her tongue."

"What?"

"They love it."

Tala reached as high as she could and began to scratch the rough surface of Sophie's tongue. It felt like sandpaper dipped in glue. Unappetizing, but Sophie seemed to accept her apology. After a minute or so, Tala asked Mace, "Can I quit now?"

"I think so. Sophie, go find your sisters."

Sophie sighed again and swung off toward the back pasture.

"Whew! Every time I think I know what I'm doing, I find out I don't."

"Always remember they have their own code of etiquette. The problems arise because we humans don't always realize when we've transgressed it. Now, would you like to take Baby for a walk?"

"Pete would have a fit."

"Pete's not here. She's extremely docile, and she needs to stretch that sore shoulder."

"I'm scared."

"I should hope so." He moved his jacket back to reveal a holster on his hip.

"Tranquilizer?"

"Bullets," Mace said soberly. "If she goes for either of us, there's no time for a tranquilizer to take effect. But I don't think she will."

Baby rumbled her greeting to Tala the moment she saw her.

"Have you sacrificed any more of your venison?" Tala asked as she bent down to scratch behind Baby's ears through the mesh of the cage. "I've got several roasts in an ice chest in the back of my truck, you're off the hook for the moment."

"The zoo food arrived after you left last night, so this morning she's already had a nice big fat frozen sausage. That's probably why she's licking her paws—to get the last bit off."

"So she shouldn't need another snack for a while?"

"Not until late this afternoon. More often than she'd feed in the wild, but she needs the extra weight to get her immune system back to normal. We'll feed her another sausage and some of your meat late this afternoon."

Tala heard a clatter and saw that Mace had dropped a length of heavy steel chain beside her with what looked like a dog's choke collar on the end. She gulped.

"Don't worry," Mace reassured her. "I'll put it on her. I don't think it will be the first time she's worn one of these. Stand back."

Baby limped to the door of the enclosure as though well aware of what was expected of her. When Mace opened the door, she accepted the collar and chain casually, and limped slowly out to stand beside him. Mace wore a heavy welder's glove on his left hand. He handed Tala its mate. "Here. This chain can tear the skin off you if she starts to pull."

Baby, however, still wasn't secure enough on her lame shoulder to do much pulling. She limped along beside Tala chuffing happily and without much obvious pain. She wasn't too much taller than a full-grown mastiff, but Tala felt none of the ease she would have felt with a dog. Mastiffs didn't have six-inch fangs.

"How do the girls feel about her?" Tala asked, never taking her eyes off the cat.

"They ignore her. They wouldn't like her to be higher than they are, but so long as she's caged and stays on the ground, she's nothing to them. They could squash her like a bug if she got cheeky. Even tigers generally leave elephants alone. They have only one natural enemy. As Pogo said, we have met the enemy and he is us."

"How did you and Pete ever get into this?" Tala asked, stroking the top of Baby's head.

"I got in after he'd already bought the land. I was at loose ends after I retired, and Pete seemed to need help with the paperwork to get the elephants approved. This is Pete's penance, not mine."

"Penance?"

"That's his story to tell. Suffice it to say, he feels guilty because he made a professional decision that turned out badly for someone he cared about. He's never forgiven himself. The elephants sense that. Haven't you seen how they respond to him?"

"I thought I was imagining things."

"No. They accept him, but they don't warm up to him. He's never really learned to open up. Most of that is my fault. I was an absentee father after my wife died. Pete was only six, just starting school. I buried myself in my work and shuffled him off on housekeepers. I foolishly thought he'd forget his mother, that my own grief was all that mattered. He grew up believing that the only safety from pain lay in not allowing himself to care about anyone or anything too much. Then, when he did finally let himself care…''

''Please tell me.'' It came out as a plea. If Pete was incapable of caring about anyone, then she'd better know it now before it was too late. Except she feared it was already too late.

''She was a colleague in Ohio. Lovely girl. Val. They lived together. I assumed they were headed for marriage.''

''He dumped her?''

''She died. An accident, but Pete feels it was his fault. I don't know all the details. You'll have to ask Pete. I only know that she died.''

Tala caught her breath. ''How awful for everyone.''

''Pete dropped everything, walked away from his practice and disappeared into Malaysia. I didn't hear from him for three years. Then one day he showed up on my doorstep, told me about the sanctuary and asked if I could help him get all the paperwork organized and deal with the county council for him. He's never been good with people.''

''I've noticed.''

''But until Val died he'd always been fine with animals. Something shut down in him then, some residual guilt or bitterness he can't get rid of. The animals sense it.''

''So he's as much in a cage as Baby.''

''And like any other animal, he hates the bars, but he doesn't know how to break them.'' Mace glanced sideways at her. ''I don't think he can do it alone.''

Well, don't look at me, Tala thought. *I can't handle my own life, much less help someone else.*

PETE COULDN'T DECIDE whether he wanted to leave Mary Ann and Jim Hildebrand's big-cat sanctuary early and get home while Tala was still there, or dawdle so that she'd be gone. One part of him longed to see her, but the other part kept telling him they were both better off in different hemispheres.

In a way, he envied the Hildebrands. They had each other. But, he wondered, would they be able to run a sanctuary for some thirty big cats if they had children? The sanctuary seemed to take all their time and most of their money, although Jim, like Pete, did his own veterinary work.

Until he'd met Tala, Pete had never considered what it might be like to have a family—wife, children, catcher's mitts, school tuition, prom dresses, new sneakers, a regular house, a mortgage.

When he and Val had been together he'd never thought further than his career. And he'd believed Val felt the same way.

Was there any way to balance the needs of a family with the needs of the elephants?

Could the Newsomes ever accept him and his way of life if he were to court Tala openly?

Irene Newsome might not blatantly pressure Tala, but the gentle suggestion to conform was there, all right. No doubt in her mind, being assistant manager in a grocery store was a whole lot more respectable than running around with an eccentric who kept elephants.

And in some ways, Pete was a rival to her dead son. No matter how hard she tried, Irene Newsome was bound to see Tala's interest in any new man as disloyalty to her children's father. Tala's children would view him the same way.

He turned the corner, saw the start of the elephant fence and glanced at his watch. His heart leaped like a schoolboy's. She should still be there. How would she greet him? Would she ignore that kiss?

How was she going to take the news about Baby?

She'd grown attached to Baby; heck, he was attached to the big cat as well.

As he turned into the entrance to the sanctuary, Tala came around the corner of the shed trundling a wheelbarrow overloaded with two teetering bales of alfalfa. She saw him before he had a chance to get out of the truck, dropped the handles of the wheelbarrow and ran over to open the gates for him.

In spite of himself he smiled. She definitely moved like a female. Despite her thin body, she bounced in all the right places. Her braid swung over her shoulder, and she flipped it back with a practiced hand.

When she smiled at him, he forgot all his doubts.

He pulled through and parked by the shed. She swung the gates closed and followed with her hands in her pockets, suddenly hesitant.

So was he. He felt embarrassed about last night. What the heck, it was just a kiss. Still, his voice sounded brusque even to his ears. "So, that's settled."

"Huh?"

"Baby. I found her a home."

Tala's face fell; her eyes widened. "Oh." Then after a long pause. "When does she leave?"

He couldn't bear the loss he heard in her voice. He reached for her hand, pulled it out of her pocket and enveloped it in his. "You knew we couldn't keep her."

Tala took a deep breath and stood very tall, which brought her up to about Pete's chin. "I know. How long before she leaves?"

"Come on," he said gently, and led her to the front door of the office and into his living room. "Sit," he said.

She sat. She refused to look at him.

"It's a sanctuary devoted strictly to big cats."

"Big cages?"

"More like fenced enclosures. Trees, grass, ladders for them to climb on, buildings on stilts constructed like dens. Plenty of fresh running water, food and excellent care. Jim Hildebrand's a vet specializing in big cats."

She nodded.

He took both her hands. "You can visit her. She'll be less than a hundred miles from here. Maybe, in time, she'll even be able to join a pride, if they'll accept her without her front claws. She'll be with her own kind."

"I wish we could take her back to Africa."

"She's never been to Africa, Tala. She was born and bred right here, and she's lived with people all her life. She couldn't function on her own."

"I know that. I really do. It's just that…I'll miss her."

"She won't be going anywhere for a few days, until we're sure that shoulder is healing properly."

Tala smiled quickly. "Oh, I'm so glad."

Her hands closed on his convulsively. They felt soft, warm, small. There must be some way he could make this easier for her. "The hardest thing I had to learn," he said softly, "was that letting go is part of the contract we humans sign when we take over the care of any animal."

"Not just animals," Tala said in a small voice. "Sometimes we have to let go of people, too." She looked down at his fingers caressing the backs of her hands and withdrew them with a quick intake of breath.

"We took her walking," she said to break the tension.

"You what?"

"It's okay. She was a real lamb, Pete. Just like a big dog on a leash. And Mace was right there with his pistol."

"I'll kill him," Pete said, and surged to his feet. "You don't have the experience, but he's supposed to know better."

"Don't you dare." She stood up and grabbed his arm. "I should never have told you. Mace said you'd act stupid."

"Stupid? *I'm* stupid?" He turned toward the door.

"She needed the exercise. Isn't that part of the contract, too? Do what's best for the animal?"

"Not when it puts *you* in jeopardy." He strode toward the door. That heavy jaw of his was set like an iron bar.

Tala ran after him, grabbed his arm. "Stop it. Listen to me. I wasn't in jeopardy. Neither was Mace. He had a pistol with him, but he didn't need it. She walked on the chain like a large yellow dog. She's certainly done it before. Besides, she'd been fed one of those salami things early this morning. She wasn't at all interested in munching down on us."

"Cats don't have to be hungry…"

"Mace says they do. Or angry or threatened. And she wasn't. She may not warm up to *you,* but—" She stopped, eyes wide, her mouth in a silent O. "I didn't mean…"

He shook her off. "Sure you did." He sighed and ran his hand through his hair. "Isn't it time you picked up your kids?"

She glanced at the clock over the computer. "I've still got an hour."

"You might as well go on. You're sure not getting anything accomplished here."

She stared at him hard for a moment. "I was before you showed up and stopped me." She pushed past him and ran to her truck.

He strode after her. "And fix your hair. It's full of alfalfa. Wouldn't want the kiddies to be embarrassed by the little hayseed, would we?" He stomped off to find Mace and left her to open and close the gate herself.

Why in hell had he said something as nasty as that? Why did he vacillate between wanting to rip her clothes off and make love to her until she screamed, and wanting to dip that stupid pigtail in an inkwell and make her cry? He was a big boy now.

He should be above hitting back when he was hit—
particularly when his opponent didn't even know
they were in the ring together. On top of that, she
was way below his weight class and didn't understand the first thing about cruelty. Next he'd probably
take to pulling the wings off butterflies.

He longed to chase her down the road, take her in
his arms and tell her he was a total jerk who didn't
deserve to be on the same planet with her. Instead,
he stomped over to the wheelbarrow she'd left beside
the gate and kicked one of the tires as hard as he
could.

For a moment he thought he'd broken his toe. He
relished the pain. It was not nearly as much as he
deserved.

He trundled the wheelbarrow around the corner
toward the elephant enclosure. A moment later he
heard the gate slam. What a louse he was. What a
lovesick nincompoop.

He ought to fire her and get her out of his hair
before he did real damage.

TALA STOMPED on the accelerator and did a two-
wheel drift around the curve that led away from the
sanctuary. What an almighty bullying jackass that
man was! How she could have kissed him last night,
allowed him to comfort her, she simply could not
conceive.

Obviously he hated people. Probably children people most of all. Her children, at any rate. She looked
at her watch. She'd left a good hour early, but he

had certainly suggested it, so if he tried to dock her pay she'd dock him, see if she didn't!

She pulled her braid over her shoulder and looked at it in the rearview mirror. Okay, so there were a couple of strands of hay caught in her hair and a couple of tendrils had come loose. Did that make her a hayseed? Would her children give a darn?

Actually, she thought, Rachel probably would. Cody wouldn't even notice. She yanked on the blasted thing. She hated it! It had darned near gotten her scalped this morning, it weighed so much it gave her headaches, and it kept getting in the way of every job she tried to do. Adam had loved her long hair, said it made her look like an Indian maiden. She'd kept it because it gave him such pleasure.

On Main Street, she pulled across two lanes of traffic, ignored the raised fingers and honking horns, braked into an angled parking space, climbed out and locked the truck behind her. Still fueled by her anger, she stalked into Estelle Marie's House of Style and slammed her purse on the counter.

"Hey, Tala," Estelle called from the first chair. "Need some shampoo?"

Suddenly Tala's knees began to shake. She gulped, picked up her purse and started to walk, no—run, from the shop. She stopped with one hand on the door, closed her eyes a moment and turned back to Estelle. "Can I get my hair cut without an appointment? I have to pick up the kids in an hour."

Estelle put down the bodybuilding magazine she'd been reading and pulled herself out of her chair.

"Sure. Nobody due until five-thirty, after work. You could stand to have those split ends cut off."

Tala took a deep breath. "I want you to cut it three inches long all over my head."

Estelle gasped. "What? No way, Tala. You've worn your hair long forever."

"That's my point."

"I won't do it."

"Then I'll find someone who will."

"Nobody in this town'll do it, Tala. What's got into you?"

"Then I'll go home and whack it off myself." Tala shoved the door open.

"No!" Estelle shouted. "Don't you dare. Tala Newsome, you come back in here this minute and tell me what on earth has got into you."

"We're wasting time, Estelle." Tala picked up a new copy of the latest hairstyles magazine and began to flip through it. "There," she said, and held the magazine out to Estelle. "That's what I want right there."

Estelle took the magazine as though it were a pit viper. She stared at the picture a moment, then looked up at Tala.

"Can I wear my hair that way?"

"Well, sure, honey. You got that perfect oval face and those high cheekbones. And *good* hair. It's straight, but it's thick and heavy. You'd look precious like that. But are you sure you know what you're doing?"

"Tell me, Estelle, how long would it take to grow my hair this long again?"

Estelle shook her head and shrugged. "Lord only knows. Years."

"But it would grow back eventually."

"Well, sure, I guess."

"And how long have I worn it this way?"

"Ever since I've known you. Since elementary school, I guess."

"That's long enough to wear one style. Do it."

"Miss Irene'll kill me."

"It's my hair."

Estelle frowned at her a moment, then nodded. "Okay, but only if you'll let me cut off the braid and redo it for you so you can pin it on if you want to."

"I can't afford that."

"Won't cost much. We got a deal? I'm protecting myself from Miss Irene here."

"Fine. Now, before I lose my nerve. I can't be late picking up the kids."

"I TOLD YOU, you little creep, don't hang around me and Ashley when we're waiting for Mama," Rachel said as she climbed into Tala's truck.

"You're the creep," Cody retaliated. His voice went high and soupy, "Oh, Kevin, you are just too amusing." He made a gagging sound. "Rachel's got a boyfriend, Rachel's got a boyfriend."

"You shut up!"

"Knock it off, both of you," Tala snapped. After a moment's annoyed silence, she added, "So, how did school go today?" Soupy and stupid. No wonder they sniped at each other with a mother as boring as that.

"Fine," they said in deflated unison. A moment later, Rachel screamed.

Tala nearly drove into a tree.

"Your hair! What have you done?" Rachel howled. She began bouncing up and down on the seat.

Cody leaned forward. "Mama?" he said hesitantly. "You cut your hair?" he whispered. A moment later he began to wail.

"Hush, both of you," Tala said. "It's hair, people, it's not brain surgery."

"But why?" Rachel said. "Your beautiful hair? Daddy loved your hair."

"Daddy's not here, and frankly, it had gotten to be a real pain. I needed a change." Why should she have to justify a haircut?

"Oh, Mama!" Cody sobbed.

Rachel had gone still. Tala could feel her daughter's eyes on her, but she said nothing.

They pulled into the Newsome driveway. Without a word, Cody dived out of the car and dashed for the front steps. Rachel slid out behind him. Tala longed to drive off and face Irene and Vertie when she felt stronger about her decision, but by then Rachel would have them believing she'd shaved her head and her eyebrows, too. She sighed, turned off the engine and opened the car door. As Rachel reached the front steps, she turned and looked at her mother with such fury that Tala stopped dead in her tracks.

"It's him, isn't it? You cut it for him!" She flung

herself into the house and a moment later Tala heard her footsteps pounding up the staircase.

"What on earth?" Irene's voice came from the front hall. "Tala, what is wrong with those children? Oh, my God!"

CHAPTER EIGHT

THE NEXT MORNING Tala climbed out of her truck prepared to do battle with both Jacobis if they said one word about her hair. She walked into the office and found Pete hunched over a cup of coffee reading the newspaper. He looked as though he hadn't slept for a week.

"Good morning," she said, tossed her head and waited.

"Morning," he grumbled. He squinted at her. "You look different." He waved a hand. "You've done something with your hair."

She hung her coat on the hook beside the door.

"I like it," he said. "Makes you look—I don't know—sexy."

She turned to him. "You like it? Really?"

"Yeah."

Mace walked in from the back room, saw her and stopped dead. "Well, m'dear, when you make a life-style change, you go at it with a vengeance, don't you."

"Don't you start."

He put up his hands and laughed. "None of my affair." He chortled. "But you're really going to confuse Sophie."

She started to laugh, choked, grabbed her jacket and flew out the door with her shoulders shaking.

"What the hell?" Pete said.

"Go after her, you young dolt. She's crying."

"Huh?"

"Go! Or I will disown you."

Pete took one look at his father and followed at a run, not even bothering to pick up his jacket, although the temperature hovered around thirty-one. He caught sight of her running around the end of the elephants' enclosure.

Heading for Baby's cage.

He found her hunkered down on a stack of alfalfa bales beside the cage. She looked much like a wood elf with her short cap of hair. He reached for her, yanked her to her feet and held her at arm's length. "What the hell did I do now?"

She wrenched away and dropped back onto the bales. "I'm not crying because you did anything. Well, you did, but not the way you think." She sighed. "I spent half the night trying to convince my children and my in-laws that I hadn't lost my mind, and that cutting my hair was not a sign that I intended to run away to New Orleans and take up naked barroom dancing. And then this morning you're so *nice*."

"Tala, it's only hair. *H-A-I-R*."

"To my family and this entire town my stupid hair had all the symbolic value of a Russian icon."

He sat on the bale beside her. "So, why'd you cut it?"

"I was sick and tired of getting headaches from

the weight on my neck and having to walk around with wet hair streaming down my back and wasting half my life on it. I wanted to feel *new*."

He leaned back. "So they're right. It was a symbol."

"A symbol? Of what?"

He turned her to face him, leaned forward and took her chin in his other hand. "You're changing. It's scaring the heck out of them." He kissed her gently. For a moment she held herself stiffly, then with a sigh she came into his arms.

The gentleness of his kiss turned fierce. Her lips opened to him, and her tongue answered his. Her hands went around him so that he could feel her fingers pressing into the muscles of his back through the thin shirt he wore.

He sank onto the alfalfa still holding her, slid her across his lap, then opened the snaps of her coat one-handed so that he could feel her body against him.

Cold as he was, he was as hard as a rock. His jeans were pure agony. He brought his free hand up the nape of her neck and ruffled the short hair under his fingers.

He'd never been kissed like that, not once. She gave as good as she got. She didn't back off, but melted against him, her hot tongue meeting his...

Baby gave a full-throated roar six inches from their knees. It sounded like an explosion. They both jumped. A moment later she sprang off his lap and took off toward the office.

Panting despite the cold, Pete leaned back against the hay. "Thank you very much," he snapped at

Baby, who regarded him with the malevolence of a football coach who caught his quarterback in the sack with a girl the night before a big game.

Baby roared again.

"Oh, shut up. You accomplished your mission. Next time I'll throw a blanket over your cage, missy, you see if I don't."

Baby followed his steps with a roar for every two. Jealous. The darned cat was jealous of Tala. Didn't want to share her—well, definitely not with Pete.

Neither would anyone else. He was right. Her kids and her in-laws were scared.

Damnation. So was he.

TALA WORKED like a demon throughout the day and refused Mace's offer to join him and Pete for lunch. Instead, she sat beside Baby's cage and shared her tuna sandwich with the lion.

Pete apparently wanted to avoid Tala as much as she wanted to avoid him. He took off on his four-wheeler toward the back pasture right after their encounter. She took refuge with a lion, he took refuge with elephants. Which one of them was crazier?

After lunch, she hunted through Pete's desk until she found the shoebox full of slips of paper, business cards, letters and notes from which the Jacobis wanted her to assemble a list of possible supporters for the sanctuary. She set up a new data file and began entering the information. It was slow going. Both Pete and Mace had the stereotypical doctor's handwriting—practically illegible. After an hour or so, she began to figure out the quirks they both used.

Their handwriting was very much alike. Awful in the same way.

At about two, Mace walked into the office, handed her a can of soda and plunked himself down in the chair beside her desk.

"Take a break, you deserve one."

"I can't. This is going to take longer than I thought, and I won't be here tomorrow or Sunday. I'm really going to have to push to get it finished if you're going to mail your letters next week."

"They can wait. We don't even have the letter written yet." He pointed at the computer. "If you can do all that, how come you were working at the Food Farm instead of in an office?"

Tala flushed. "I took typing in high school, then a couple of evening computer classes at the college a couple of years back, but there wasn't time or money to go for even an associate degree. There aren't that many office jobs in town. I took the best I could get."

"Sorry. Didn't mean to intrude. Having said that, here's another intrusion. Why is your family so bent out of shape over your hair? I don't think I've known a dozen women in my life who didn't change color, cut or style every six months."

Tala leaned back and rubbed the back of her neck. The short hair tickled her fingers. "I let it grow in the first place because we didn't have money when I was growing up for such frills as haircuts. My grandmother, Sakari, which means sweet, by the way—not that she was—butchered it herself until I started kindergarten and saw other kids. After that I had a fit every time she reached for the shears. When it got long, she told me my hair was probably the only thing attractive about me and said I'd better hang on to it."

"Charming."

"It turned out she was right. Adam, my husband, loved it, and so did Irene and Vertie, probably because he did. Yesterday when Irene and the kids saw what I'd done, it was like I'd made this big announcement." She sat erect and said in a deep voice, "As of now, your son and the father of my children is dead, gone and forgotten." She slumped. "Bang, just like that."

"And what were you thinking?" Mace asked gently.

"That I was sick to death of all that hair."

"So there was no declaration of independence involved?"

Tala dropped her head for a moment, then leaned her elbows on the desk in front of the computer keyboard. "Maybe a little. I'll never forget Adam, and I'll be part of the Newsomes forever, but I've got to find out who I am, learn how to live my life without Adam looking over my shoulder making all the decisions."

"Your family understand that, surely, if they love you. But you're too young to spend the rest of your life alone."

"It's too soon to think about that," Tala said, although lately she'd been thinking about it quite a lot. She leaned back and drove her fingers through her hair. She couldn't stop relishing the feel of it. "I think Irene and Vertie want me to find some clone of Adam who won't disturb the equilibrium of the clan—someone they can absorb. They tend to do that in the nicest possible way. And it's simply easier to let them.''

"Did you convince your children you're not forgetting their father?"

"Who knows? Rachel is still miffed, but Cody didn't make a big deal over it once he got over the initial shock. He keeps everything inside, so I'm not certain how he feels deep down. Kids hate change. Adam's death affected them in ways I'm only beginning to see. This is something else that's different for them. And God forbid I should actually start to see someone..." The sentence trailed off. She dropped her eyes.

"God forbid," Mace said cheerfully. He lobbed his empty soda can across the room and hit the open wastebasket dead center.

Tala banged hers down on the desk so hard it splattered on her mouse pad. She wiped the liquid away quickly with her sleeve and said, "This is the only life I've got. I've got to learn to do it better."

"I think you do it admirably already."

"No, I don't. I don't have a clue about being a mom, and this is hardly a great career path... Oh, Mace, I'm sorry. That was a stupid thing to say."

"But accurate. However, one step at a time. You may be surprised. Now, cut along to pick up your children."

"I left early yesterday."

"I am the boss. Or one of them."

"Yes, sir." She shut down the computer, slid the keyboard back on its drawer and stood up to ease her back. As she passed by him on her way to the coatrack, she dropped a kiss on his head. "Thanks for bucking me up."

LATE THAT AFTERNOON, Pete came back, found Tala gone and stalked around grumbling over his chores until Sweetiepie gave him a solid thump on the head with her trunk, not hard enough to raise a lump, but definitely enough to get his attention.

"Ow, dammit!" he snapped.

She harrumphed and moved away to join her sisters over dinner. Catching the looks the three gave one another, he wondered if they'd decided that he needed a wake-up call, and selected Sweetiepie for the job. Actually, he suspected she'd volunteered.

"Serves you right," Mace said. He knelt in front of Baby's cage and tossed her second feed of the day through the narrow opening. Baby chomped down on her dinner with evident delight. "You have been a pain in the butt. What's with you and that girl anyway?"

"She's not a girl, Dad, she's a mother."

"And?"

"She has other priorities that come way before this job or anyone here."

"I see. And you're jealous?"

"No, I'm not jealous. Because I have other priorities as well. Besides, I don't do children."

"They're very little different from puppies and kittens."

"Rabid puppies and spitting kittens, maybe."

"Oh, come now."

"I never learned the first thing about parenting, Dad. And I'm a damned sight too old to start off with a ready-made family. Beside that, even if I were a recombinant DNA of Judge Hardy, Mr. Cleaver and Sheriff Andy, I couldn't make any headway against a dead hero. Whatever Adam Newsome was in life, now that he's dead, he's perfect. I, as you may have noticed, am not."

"Neither was he."

"Yeah, but he's not around to show his warts. And I'm glad of it, because I don't mess with married women. Am I evil to feel this way about him?"

"You didn't know him. His absence has no reality for you. Tala may well feel the same about Val."

"How does she know about Val?" Pete laid his pitchfork down and stared at his father.

"I told her. Not much. I don't know much myself, after all. Just that you lived together, she died, and you can't forgive yourself for it for some reason."

"Drop it."

"Sooner or later you're going to have to lance that particular boil, son."

"That's my problem. I'm going for a drive."

"What about dinner?" Mace called after him.

"I'll pick up a burger in town." He slammed the door after him.

Mace raised his eyebrows at Baby. "He might have offered to bring us one, don't you think?"

A moment later the door opened again and Pete

stuck his head in. "You want me to bring you something?"

Mace grinned. "No thanks. But it is nice to be asked."

The door slammed again, and a moment later Mace heard the gates slide open and Pete's Land Rover drive through.

"Ah, a quiet evening," Mace said. "Just one lion, three elephants, a TV dinner and TV to accompany it. Life is good."

As he walked by the girls, he said, "Let us hope that the poor wretch manages to wind up in Tala's bed and doesn't make it home before morning."

The girls swung their trunks at him.

HALF AN HOUR LATER, Pete ate his burger with one hand on the wheel. He casually drove by the Newsome house, and just as casually checked to see whether Tala's truck was in the circular driveway. It wasn't, and his heart lifted. Maybe she was home alone.

He told himself that he might as well drive through Bryson's Hollow as anyplace else. The road was pretty, although he wouldn't be able to see much of it in the dark. He slowed beside the precipitous driveway that led down to Tala's house. He could see lights inside, but couldn't tell whether her truck was parked outside or not. He couldn't simply show up at her front door uninvited, could he?

He drove another five miles without seeing another driveway to turn around in. She truly was isolated out here. Now that the other farmers were gone, scrub trees and underbrush were reclaiming the hill-sides fast.

He didn't see how anybody could ever have made a living out here anyway. Subsistence farming must have turned into starvation farming years ago. No wonder the Newsome kids didn't want to live out here. Why had Adam Newsome forced it on his family? And why did Tala remain?

He finally found a flat, graveled shoulder, and managed to turn his car around. What the heck, that cop said he'd be checking on her. What was wrong with her employer checking on her as well? He turned into her driveway and bumped down until the outside lights came on. Her truck was there. No squad cars this time. Unless her kids had come home with her, she was probably alone.

She opened the front door before he got his feet out of the truck. He wished he'd brought a sack of burgers—at least that would give him some excuse for showing up unannounced. He suddenly felt as shy as a sixteen year old.

She waited at the top of the stairs without speaking.

"I was out this way anyway, and I thought I'd check to see whether you got home all right."

"I'm fine."

No invitation to come in. He jammed his hands into his pockets. "Fine." He stood there unable to think of another word to say.

"Pete…"

"Tala…"

They spoke at once, stopped, and grinned at each

other. She stepped back. "Come in. I've got cham-omile tea brewing. You like tea?"

"Sure." He would have liked battery acid if she'd offered him a cup of that. He followed her to the big country kitchen with bright yellow painted cabinets that looked as though they'd been there since the house was built. Probably had a dozen coats of paint on them. The yellow-checked curtains at the windows were obviously homemade. The round oak table in the center of the room looked old, but hadn't been fine when it was new, nor had the oak ladder-back chairs around it.

But everything was clean, bright and cheerful. The room smelled of warm cinnamon.

"Please sit down," she said, and reached for a plain white cup and saucer out of one of the tall glass-fronted cabinets. She set a large covered tin on the table and popped the lid. The aroma of warm spice cookies filled the room. "Cody just casually mentioned on his way home from football practice this afternoon that he needed to take cookies to practice tomorrow. He's known about it for weeks, probably. Lucinda would have baked them, but she does more than enough. Baking cookies is one thing I'm good at. The last batch is cooling." She blew her new bangs off her forehead.

Her face was pink and damp from opening the oven. She looked luscious. Her shirt showed the curves of her body, and he noticed that he could see the outline of her nipples through the cloth. He felt his own skin begin to heat, his breathing speed up.

"I can't eat Cody's cookies." He couldn't take his eyes off her.

"Go ahead. There's at least twice as many as he needs. When I get uptight, I bake." She caught her breath.

"Are we still on the hair thing?"

She poured his tea, topped up a heavy china mug for herself and leaned against the counter. "No. They've stopped talking about it. Now Irene just looks at me and sighs."

He sighed as well. The way her jeans stretched across her flat stomach, leaving hollows beside her hipbones... He wondered what she wore under those jeans.

He realized he'd been silent a moment too long and tried to remember what they'd been talking about. Oh, yes. "She'll get over it."

She closed her eyes and whispered, "You know why I'm uptight. You and I are practically strangers. We don't know a thing about each other, and half the time we're sniping away like a pair of shrikes, and then out of nowhere..."

He started to get up, but she raised her hands. "No. You stay right there with the table between us, please."

"We know plenty about each other."

"No, we don't. You're practically the weirdest man I've ever known, maybe *the* weirdest. Instead of baby-sitting a bunch of elephants in the back of beyond, you could be running a clinic or being vet to a big zoo."

"I've done that."

"Did you hate it? Screw it up? Mace said you disappeared for three years before you showed up at his door with your land already bought."

"That's about it."

"No, it isn't. I refuse to get involved with a total stranger just because he knows all the right buttons to push."

"Who's involved?" He set his cup down and pushed away from the table. "Thanks for the cookies."

"Don't you dare get huffy!"

He stopped, closed his eyes and turned back to look at her. Their eyes met, and held much too long.

Without a word, he wrapped his arms around her, felt her open her soft lips to his questing tongue and gave himself up to the sheer joy of feeling her against his body, tasting the chamomile on her tongue, smelling the cinnamon and sweat on her skin.

After a moment she began to push away, but he said, "No," against her mouth. He couldn't bear the weight of his jacket. The heat was like being back in the jungle again where every breath was an effort.

She shoved him away and looked up into his face. "Don't get involved my foot." She stroked his jaw.

He buried his face against her neck. "Mace should never have hired you. I ought to have made you drive on to Dr. Wiskowski's vet clinic in town when you showed up with Baby."

"She'd have died if you hadn't taken her in." She stroked his hair. "Lord, I must be every bit as needy as Billie Joe thinks I am."

"Huh?" He pulled away and looked down at her.

She rolled her eyes, turned away from him and evaded his hands. "Seems like lately every male I meet acts like they'd be doing the poor little widder lady a big favor if they took me to bed and eased all that tension I'm bound to be building up not having a man around."

"I knew that Billie Joe was up to more than police business."

"He's got a perfectly good wife and children. Honestly, I'll never understand men if I live to be a million years old."

"Heck, Tala, you're a beautiful woman living out here all alone."

"I'm not beautiful and I'm not helpless, and I can take care of my own needs, thank you."

He raised his eyebrows. She blushed. "You know what I mean."

"Well, I don't have a wife and I'm not the one with kids waiting at home." The moment he said the words he could have cut out his tongue.

Her eyes widened, she caught her breath. "Oh. I see."

"I didn't mean that the way it sounded."

"Listen, buster, in these parts, unless you plan to find yourself some sixteen year old, you're likely to come up with somebody who's got some living behind her." She considered. "Around here, even the sixteen year olds probably have at least one baby trailing along behind them. I'm not entirely certain why *you* don't. Most men your age, if they're available, are already paying child support to at least one other family."

"Drop it."

"No. Mace told me the woman you loved died. Is that what it is? I can't possibly compete with a dead woman."

"And I can't compete with a dead man."

"What?"

"Not a dead man whose family name is on the bank, the hardware store, the town square and the library, and whose murder is still the most celebrated unsolved crime in Hollendale County, Tennessee. Not with his mother, his grandmother and his children all snarling at me like junkyard dogs every time I take a step toward you. At least Val's buried in Cleveland."

"But her ghost is right here in this room. Whatever you may think, Adam's is not. He'd be the last person on earth to stand between me and another relationship. You're the one hanging on to Val's ghost. What I want to know is why."

"Because I killed her, dammit! How do I get over that?"

CHAPTER NINE

"I DON'T BELIEVE that for a minute. You couldn't kill anybody," Tala said, but she sat down hard on the kitchen chair and pulled the tin of cookies toward her. Without taking her eyes off Pete, she picked up a cookie and began to chew it voraciously, then while she was still chewing, she reached for another.

"You keeping track of how many Cody needs to take to school?"

She glanced down at her hand. "Oh, Lord." She snapped the lid back on and shoved the tin away from her. "I always do that when I'm upset."

"You must have the metabolism of a gazelle."

"Don't change the subject."

"Val died because she did something I was supposed to do. That's enough."

"It is not enough. I mean it."

"I don't want to talk about it."

She reached for his hands, held them across the table and said gently, "Please, Pete."

His shoulders drooped. "All right. You won't like it."

"Did you love her?"

"I was too busy with my career to think about whether I was in love or not. We liked each other.

We were good together. We were in the same practice—an excellent, big practice. We sort of drifted into a relationship. After a while, it seemed logical to move in together.''

"Logical?"

He leaned back and looked up at the ceiling as though he were traveling back all those years. "I was totally focused on becoming the best and most successful vet I could be.''

"To show your daddy," Tala whispered.

Pete looked up and frowned. "Yeah. That was always part of it. I wanted to be so good he wouldn't be able to ignore me any longer.''

"And Val? Was she that focused?"

"I thought so. We both had our priorities…''

"But she wasn't at the top of your list."

He sighed. "No." He glanced up and spread his hands. "But I didn't think I was at the top of hers either.''

"Where did you suppose you were heading?"

"I never thought about it. I guess I thought we might get married eventually, have kids. Once we could afford our own practice, had built our reputations. We were both saving as much money as we could. Setting up a practice and buying equipment takes cash.''

"Is that what Val thought too?"

"She started telling people we were engaged. That was okay with me. Then after two years together she said we should take our relationship to the next level. I didn't know what she meant.''

"She meant marriage."

"She never actually said the word. Half the time we were on opposite shifts and only saw each other going and coming. Half the time we were so tired we fell into bed without even a good-night kiss. What kind of a marriage would that have been? There was plenty of time for marriage. That's what I tried to tell her, and I thought she was okay with it."

"She wasn't?"

"One morning after she left for work I found a letter lying on the kitchen table. It offered Val the partnership she'd been discussing with the owners of a small-animal practice in Beverly Hills. She'd written me a note on it. 'Unless you have a better offer, I'm going.'"

"Oh dear."

"She'd apparently been talking to these people for months without even mentioning it to me, and now she was going to walk out just like that." He snapped his fingers.

"I realized then how much she meant to me, how much I depended on her. But she was pressuring me to do something I wasn't sure I was ready for. I was scared, and when I get scared I lose my temper. I drove to the clinic, dragged her away from a poodle with ear mites—I'll never forget that—and we had the mother of all fights."

"What happened?"

"She yelled, I yelled, she cried, and finally we agreed to talk sensibly that night when we'd both calmed down. To give us both some breathing space, I swapped duties with another doctor who was supposed to do tuberculin testing on a herd of Guernseys seventy miles north of town. Seemed like a good idea.'' He sounded bitter.

''Anyway, twenty miles outside of town I decided to go back to the clinic and make up with Val, but when I got back she'd already left on an emergency call. A big old African bull elephant at the zoo. Ordinarily that would have been my call. I always took the elephants when I was available. I went after her to give her a hand if she needed one. Then I was going to apologize, and ask her to marry me. What I should have done in the first place.''

He looked down at his hands. ''I didn't get the chance.''

''Why not? What happened?''

''The bull had torn a ten-inch gash in his trunk. And he was in musth.''

''What's musth?''

''Males get these major testosterone surges from time to time.''

''They want to mate?''

''They want dominance, not sex. Some elephants stay even-tempered. Others go crazy. That particular old guy had never shown any symptoms before, but everybody takes extra care around them. Val understood that.''

''Maybe she didn't know he was in musth.''

''She knew.'' He pointed to his eyes. ''They've got these glands on their cheeks below their eyes. They secrete fluid when the bulls come into musth. She discussed it with the keepers. When a bull's in musth, it's a good idea to put off treatment, but this bull couldn't wait. Elephants can't eat without their trunks. They die. And their trunks get infected very easily. He had to have stitches and antibiotics immediately.''

He closed his eyes. ''Everybody followed procedure, that's the sad part. Four keepers with elephant hooks, and extra leg chains to keep him from moving. Val shot him full of tranquilizer. By the time I walked into the cage he was on his knees. I'd have sworn he was past caring what anybody did to him. I'd have done the same thing Val did.''

''What *did* she do?''

''She'd already sprayed anesthetic on the wound, but she had to give him a couple of shots of local anesthetic around the wound site before she started stitching. I called to her, told her I'd take over. She looked up at me the moment before she stuck the needle in.''

He dropped his head into his hands. ''I'll never know whether she hit a nerve or what. He came off the ground in an instant. I heard the chains snap and yelled at her to get back. He caught her chest high with his brow bones. Her head hit the concrete wall.'' He closed his eyes. ''Massive skull fracture. I'll hear that sound until the day I die. She died on the way to the hospital.''

''It was an accident. A terrible accident, but it wasn't your fault. The same thing would have happened to you.''

''It didn't happen to me. It happened to Val. If I hadn't called out, would she have seen the danger and gotten out of the way in time? Could I have moved faster than she did? Would I have used more tranquilizer? More chains? I don't know. I'll never know. You want to know the funny thing?'' He didn't sound amused. ''While she was in the ambulance dying, I was back in the cage stitching up that elephant.''

''Oh, Pete.''

''It was the least I could do. I killed them both.''

''Them? They killed the poor elephant?''

He shook his head. ''They wanted to, but I fought them, got everybody I knew to fight them. Even her parents didn't want the elephant killed.''

''Then who?''

''They did an autopsy. Thank God her parents had gone back to their hotel when the doctor told me how sorry he was about both of them—Val and the baby.''

Tala simply sat and stared at him with her mouth open. Then she jumped up, came around the table, knelt beside him and put her arms around him. For a moment he resisted, then he put his head on her shoulder and wrapped his arms around her. She could feel his shoulders shake and knew that he was crying.

She'd have been willing to bet this was the first time he'd ever cried. He'd been bottling all this up inside for almost four years. Was this what the elephant sensed? This pain inside him?

Without a word, he wrenched away, stood and strode to the living room. He couldn't leave. Not like this. She held out a hand to him, ''Pete, wait. Please don't go.'' She heard the front door slam, stood and ran after him. ''Pete!''

He stood outside on the front porch, facing the

dark front yard. She stood quietly beside him, not quite touching, but close enough so that she knew he could feel that she was there.

After what seemed an eternity, he said, "That wasn't for Val, that was for me."

"Grief is grief."

"You don't understand. I lost *myself* when Val died. The thing that made me a good doctor, that gave me empathy with the animals. I don't have it any longer. They know it. They don't trust me. You've seen the way Baby and the elephants act around me." He turned to look at her, but in the shadows, she couldn't see his eyes. "That's why I'm so damned jealous of you. You have the gift I lost when I lost Val—when I threw her away."

"So that's why you went to Malaysia—to try to get it back?"

"At the time, I didn't realize that's why I went, but yeah, I guess so."

"It didn't work?"

"Nothing is ever going to work. You asked me why I'm not running my own clinic. That's why. Oh, my hands are still good. I'm still a pretty fair diagnostician, but the feeling, the connection that I had, not only with the animals but with people, is gone. They don't warm up to me."

"I warmed up to you."

"Not at first."

"I caught on pretty quickly when I saw you with the girls. And you cared enough to start the sanctuary after you left Malaysia. Why *did* you come home?"

"Malaysia was so damned frustrating. Never

enough resources or enough government support. I couldn't make a dent. Too many people, not enough habitat. Here, at least, I can help a few elephants live out their lives in peace and relative freedom.''

''That's empathy, isn't it?''

''Not enough. At least the girls don't think so. There's still a barrier between us. They want more from me than food and baths and a decent place to live. They always seem to be reproaching me for my failures.''

''But you're putting your money where your mouth is, Pete. Maybe that doesn't count with the girls, but it ought to make you feel better.'' She waved a hand in the direction of the sanctuary. ''Land isn't that cheap even around here, and then there's the barn and the fences—it all must have cost a great deal of money.''

''That's the final irony. When we started telling people we were engaged, Val and I made each other beneficiaries of our estates and our insurance policies so that if something happened to one of us, the other one could still start a practice. Hers was double indemnity. And she had a trust fund from her grandmother. I'm not rich, Tala, but I can afford to spend the rest of my life looking after old, sick elephants.''

''Mace said it was your penance. He was right, wasn't he?''

''In a sense, it's Val's memorial.''

''Not memorial. Shrine.'' She felt her temper rising. ''No wonder the girls get exasperated. They're not a bit happier watching you whip yourself than they would be if you whipped them.''

"What?"

"Stop beating yourself up."

"You're a fine one to talk, withering away out here in the boonies while somebody else raises your kids."

She shoved him around so that she looked up into his face. She tried to keep the anger out of her voice when she said, "I stay here because I promised Adam I would. Eventually he wanted to turn this place into a sanctuary, too—but for the deer and the birds and all the other animals whose habitat is being eaten away every day. He was trying to buy the Bryson place when he died."

"Then why not rent it out? Get someplace in town?"

"I could never rent it for enough to cover a house payment in town. I'm trying to earn enough to pay our way because Adam's father disinherited him when he married a trashy little Bryson's Hollow girl and went to work for the Wildlife people instead of joining his father at the bank."

"Adam died on the job. He must have left *some* money."

"Not enough for three people to live on comfortably. That's why I live here." She turned away.

"That's the only reason?"

"No." She dropped her head into her hands. "Rachel won't come near this place. She says she hates it and the animals. And Cody has nightmares when he's here."

She raised tearful eyes. "My family has owned this land forever. I *will* turn it into a nature preserve somehow, someday, the way Adam wanted. I don't have any other way to give *him* a memorial."

Her voice had risen dangerously. "I'm trying to do what's right for everybody, and making a really lousy job of it. I'm doing the best I can with what I've got, Dr. Jacobi, and I don't give a damn whether you agree with my choices or not."

"Wait a minute," Pete said. "That wasn't an attack. Okay, maybe it was, but I warned you that I get mean when I get scared."

"What do you have to be scared of, may I ask, Dr. I-have-enough-money-to-play-with-elephants-the-rest-of-my-life?"

"You!"

"Me?"

"You and your family. In case you haven't noticed, I'm not good with families."

"There's no reason you should bother with mine."

"Fine. Then I'll say good-night." He started for the door.

"Good night," Tala said coolly. She felt her face flush. Thank goodness he'd mentioned how he felt about her children and brought her back to reality. The way she'd been going—practically throwing herself into Pete's arms—she'd never become a person in her own right, never become emotionally self-sufficient.

She had no more business getting attached to the Jacobis and becoming trapped in their orbit than she did getting trapped in that mansion with Irene and Vertie.

From the porch steps she watched him climb into

the Land Rover and take off. At the top of the rise, he suddenly slammed on his brakes. A moment later he backed down the hill. The instant the car stopped, he jumped out of the car and walked to the porch. To apologize? To hold her? Oh, Lord, she did want him, but she only said, "So why'd you come back?"

"Because your damn barn's on fire!"

CHAPTER TEN

"ADAM'S TOOLS are in there!" Tala shouted as she raced toward the barn. "And the tractor!" Smoke eddied through the closed barn doors and a thin lick of orange flame showed through the high window. He could see the barn cats silhouetted in the smoke. They were already streaking for the safety of the woods.

"Tala, come back here!" Pete yelled, and raced after her.

She already had the doors open and was forcing her way through the smoke toward a yellow tractor when he grabbed her arm.

"Get out of here! Call 911."

"But..." she choked.

"I'll get the tractor out." He began to cough. "Go!"

"Adam's tools!"

"Forget the tools! Go!"

He climbed on the tractor, prayed it worked the way his own did and turned the key in the ignition. The smoke was damn near impenetrable now. His eyes closed of their own volition. He forced them open as he dragged a corner of his shirt across his nose and mouth and floored the tractor.

It lurched forward and chugged toward the open doors. That's when he spotted the source of the flame—a couple of bales of ancient, moldy straw in the corner by the door. In another couple of seconds the whole place might go up.

He turned the tractor on its axis, lowered the front-loader, slipped it under the bales and surged forward toward the wall they stood against. For a second, the wall held, and he was afraid he'd have to back up and try again. He wasn't certain he'd have the time before the barn was engulfed—and him with it.

The boards fractured with an explosion like a howitzer's.

He pushed the entire flaming mess into the yard in the bucket of the front-loader. He kept driving forward, afraid that the whole structure of the barn would collapse on him before he could get out.

Miraculously, the roof trusses held. The minute he was free of the barn, he lifted the steel bucket of the front-loader like Lady Liberty holding her torch.

"Pete!" Tala screamed from the back porch.

He jumped off the tractor and ran to where she stood. "Where's your garden hose? We need to wet down the barn."

"But the flames..." She pointed to the bucket high above their heads.

"Leave 'em." He glanced over his shoulder. "Wet down the barn first to make sure nothing else is catching. That bucket's steel. They'll burn themselves out. Did you call the fire department?"

She was running toward the hose attached to an all-weather spigot beside the back steps. "Yes, but it may take them fifteen or twenty minutes to get here.''

"Give me that.'' He wrenched the hose from her hands none too gently. "I'll do this. You watch that thing up there and make sure it doesn't catch the trees.''

"It's been too wet.''

"Probably,'' he said as he pulled the hose toward the barn. Thank God the weather had been above freezing most of the day and the hose was drained properly. If it had been full of ice, they'd have been sunk.

He stood outside the barn and played water over the area where the bales had been burning. He heard a few sizzles from the old wooden pallets they'd sat on, and there was enough steam to cook a million lobsters, but no flames, at least from what he could see.

The yard lights had come on and stayed on, but the inside of the barn was lit only by the flaming torch fifteen feet up in the front-loader.

He heard the sirens miles away, and the answering yips of coyotes in the woods. He didn't look up until he was shoved out of the way by a big man completely enclosed in an orange fire suit. "Here, buddy, I'll take over.''

"You guys got here fast,'' he said. "I think it's pretty well out.''

"Yeah? Look over your shoulder.''

Pete looked. The flames from the front-loader still burned cheerily, fed, no doubt, by the barn boards he'd picked up when he broke through the wall.

"No problem. It's steel."

"Good thinking."

He realized suddenly as the last of his adrenaline drained that he was exhausted. His lungs burned. His eyes were painfully dry. He leaned over his knees and began to cough. The man on the garden hose shoved him toward the small truck behind the pumper, where half a dozen men were unrolling a firehose.

"Go back there and get some oxygen. You need to be checked for smoke inhalation."

"I'm fine," he said, coughing.

"Yeah, right. Do it."

Two of the men from the pumper aimed their fire hose at the front-loader. Sparks exploded like fireworks as the water hit the flames. After only a minute, they moved to dump their remaining water onto the barn.

Wearily, Pete walked by them, past the pumper, the chief's red car, and toward the EMT van that was last in the parade. He realized he had no idea where Tala was just as she hit him full force, wrapped her arms around his waist and began dragging him faster toward the EMT van. He hooked an arm around her and asked, "You okay?"

"Of course I'm okay."

"You ought to see your face," he said, and reached up to run his index finger down her nose. Her face was covered in smut.

"Me? You could've been killed." She sounded teary for a moment. But only a moment. She finished with, "You idiot!" And shoved him down on the step of the van, then stood over him with her hands on her hips, her face furious.

"You're welcome," he said. Then he grinned and bent double in another fit of coughing.

AN HOUR LATER, Pete, Tala and the fire chief sat on the back porch steps as the volunteer firemen finishing coiling their hoses.

"Don't normally find cases of spontaneous combustion in straw that old," the fire chief said, shaking his head. "Only in fresh wet hay."

"It wasn't spontaneous combustion," Pete said. "Somebody set that fire."

"I'd be inclined to agree with you, but we're not likely to get evidence." He pointed at the tractor, still sitting in the center of the yard with its smoking remains lifted on high. "Not much chance to find signs of accelerant on those charred little bits of wood from the barn."

"I realize that."

"'Course, if you hadn't broken the wall that way, whole barn would 'a' gone up and you with it. As it is, the place is one muddy mess, but a lot of scrubbing and a few boards to repair the wall is all it's gonna take to put everything back in order."

"So who did it?" Pete asked.

The fire chief shook his head. "Kids, most likely."

"I'd padlocked the door," Tala said. "How could anyone get in?"

"Most likely busted out that window, set some kind of simple timer inside—lit candle would do it, give 'em enough time to hightail it outta here. If the doctor here hadn't seen the smoke and shoved those bales out through the wall, whole place would 'a' burned over before we arrived. Lucky, Mrs. Newsome. Real lucky.''

''You must have set some kind of record to get here so fast,'' Tala said. ''Thank you so much.''

''Our pleasure.''

More than anything, Tala longed to lean over and rest her head against Pete's shoulder. She didn't think she'd ever been so tired. But if she did, it would be all over town before morning that Tala Newsome was lollygagging with that elephant guy. That sort of problem she didn't need. Tough enough to explain his presence in the first place.

The entire yard, front and back, was ablaze with light now. She'd set the lights to burn continuously, although the constant to-ing and fro-ing would have kept them on in any case. ''The deer won't like this,'' she whispered.

''Huh?'' The fire chief asked.

She shook her head. ''Never mind.''

''Well, I'll be going then,'' he continued. ''I'll send somebody out to check out what we've got tomorrow when it gets light.'' He heaved himself up from the steps and eased his back. ''If we got us a bunch of kids going around setting barns on fire in the country, we could have us a major problem. I want it solved quick before they move on to houses and maybe folks who can't get out in time.''

''I don't think it was kids,'' Pete said softly as the chief made his way down the steps.

''Who else could it be?'' Tala asked.

"Think about it. Somebody tries to run you off the road, you notice somebody walking around in the yard the other night, opening the barn—could have been scouting out the place to set the fire."

"But why?"

"Damned if I know. You don't have any enemies, do you?"

She sat up. "Certainly not."

"Your husband did."

"Adam ticked off a few hunters and fishermen who didn't have licenses, but then so did all the other wardens."

"They weren't killed. Your husband was."

"Whoever did it probably shot by pure reflex and ran clear across the country once he saw what he'd done."

"Unless he lives here, has a good job here, a family."

"Local people who poach deer out of season usually do it to feed those families," Tala said in annoyance. "And they fully understand that if they get caught they'll be fined, lose their licenses and probably do some jail time. They don't like it, but they'd never kill over it. Besides, nobody around here hunts with fancy rifles that shoot special shells. Adam's killer was somebody from outside. Lord, Pete, it's been well over a year since he died. This can't have anything to do with him." She turned away. "I don't want to talk about it anymore."

"I'm sorry," he said, and picked up her hand.

She caught one of the firemen watching, started to remove her hand from Pete's, then squared her shoul-

ders and held on. Everybody knew she worked for
Pete. No reason he couldn't offer her a little comfort.

The trucks started their engines and began to back
up the driveway. Tala heard the squeal of air brakes,
and a moment later a car door slammed in front of
the house. This time she did lean over against Pete's
shoulder. It felt like leaning against a nice warm
boulder. He lifted his arm to slide it around her and
cradle her against him.

"What on earth happened here, Tala?"

Tala jumped guiltily. Pete dropped his arm as
Irene and Vertie trotted around the corner of the
house.

"My Lord, look at that!" Irene said, staring at the
gaping hole in the side of the barn, the muddy run-
nels that surrounded it. "Are you all right?"

She gave Pete a cool glance, and sat on the step
below Tala, putting her hands on Tala's knees.
"Your face! You didn't get burned, did you?"

Pete stood and moved away with his hands in his
pockets. Vertie walked over and stuck out her hand
to him. "Pete, Sheriff Craig said when he called to
tell us about this that you're a hero. Saved the barn
and probably the house too."

"No, ma'am. I just saw the smoke is all."

She thumped his shoulder. "Not what I heard. My
word, what a mess!" She walked through the mud
in her cowboy boots and peered into the hole in the
barn. "Usually these old barns get too damn dry to
burn. No resin left in the wood."

"This had help," Pete said, then wished he'd kept
his mouth shut.

Irene was on his words instantly. "What do you mean? Tala?"

"Pete thinks somebody set some old bales of straw on fire. Probably kids."

"I swear! What is the world coming to?" Irene stood and pulled Tala to her feet. "Come on, you're getting into my car and coming home with us."

"No, I'm not. I don't have anything packed—"

"We'll wait."

"Come on in the kitchen. It's freezing out here," Tala said. "I'll fix us all a cup of tea." She turned. "Pete?"

"I ought to be getting home."

"Not on your life, Pete," Vertie said, hooking her arm through his. "We want to hear all about it, start to finish."

Ten minutes later the four of them sat around the kitchen table with mugs of Earl Grey tea in front of them. Tala knew Pete felt ill-at-ease, but she wasn't certain she could stand up to Irene's need to cosset her without him. She wanted her own bed tonight, and she wanted it badly.

"Now. From the beginning," Irene said, setting down her mug.

"Who's watching the kids?" Tala asked.

"Lucinda ran over to sit after the sheriff called," Irene said. "Didn't wake them up." She waved a hand. "I wish they didn't have to know at all."

"Me, too, but it'll be all over town by morning."

"Enough!" Vertie said. "I want to hear all the details."

Between them, Pete and Tala told the story. Neither of them mentioned why Pete was here in the first place. Neither Vertie nor Irene asked, but Irene kept darting glances between the two of them. Tala could tell she was concerned, but there was no way to reassure her mother-in-law without making matters even more complicated.

"Well," Vertie said after the story was complete, "we're all lucky it's been so wet, otherwise the trees might have gone up, and I'm not real anxious to lose all the timber on my land any more than you are to lose yours," she said.

"Your land?" Pete asked.

"One of the pieces of land I own is over there someplace," Vertie said, pointing toward the creek and the back of the property. "I'm letting it go a couple of more years before we do some selective logging on some of the hardwoods. My daddy bought it years ago to hunt on."

"You're not considering clean-cutting it, are you?" Pete asked.

"Lord, no! I don't believe in that. Ruins the looks of the place, causes erosion, and whatever they say, planting all those neat little pine trees in even rows looks awful. Not a bit the way nature intended. Adam got his hankering for the woods from my side of the family. I ran wild on that mountain when I was growing up, and then so did he when he was old enough."

"And then you went off to boarding school and Bryn Mawr and married a banker," Irene said dryly. "Why do you always try to convince people you're some sort of hillbilly?"

"I don't have to be fixey like you if people think I'm just a good ole country girl."

"Well, you're not." She turned to Tala. "You coming with us or not?"

"Not." Tala smiled at her. "I'm going to sleep late, but I'll be over to have breakfast with Cody and Rachel if you'll have me. Then I can run Cody to football practice and Rachel to cheerleading. I can talk to them about the fire then."

"But Tala…"

"I'm fine."

"If anything happened to you, too…"

"It won't. I promise."

After more protestations, Irene finally gave in, kissed Tala, hugged her hard and walked out the front door with Vertie sidling along after her.

Pete followed. Tala looked at him helplessly.

"You are coming, aren't you, Doctor?" Irene said.

"Yes, ma'am." He touched Tala's hand, and whispered, "This time I think Mrs. Newsome's right. You ought to go with her. I don't want you staying here alone."

"I'll be fine. I'll call you in the morning."

She stood on the steps until both cars had driven away. Then she turned wearily back into the house, locked all the doors and pulled the shotgun out from under the couch. She stopped with one foot on the stairs. Adam's tools. She had to protect them from the elements.

She spent half an hour dusting off the worst of the smut, covering the tools with tarpaulins and weighting the edges with concrete blocks. By the time she was finished, she considered sleeping on the sofa again to keep from having to walk upstairs, but decided against it. No sense in getting the sofa filthy, because she certainly was.

Upstairs, the face she saw in the bathroom mirror startled her. "No wonder Irene was upset," she said.

She stripped off her smoky clothes, dropped them in a pile on the bathroom floor, laid the shotgun on the floor beside the bed and climbed under the covers.

Pete couldn't be right, she thought as she drifted off. She didn't have any enemies.

Despite her exhaustion, or maybe because of it, she tossed and turned with terrible dreams all night long. Twice she sat up in bed, certain that she heard Baby roaring for her. She dreamed that the big cat was sitting on the end of her bed watching her sleep.

At last she drifted off as one final cry from Baby seemed to be carried on the wind.

THE TELEPHONE DRAGGED her from the first real sleep she'd had all night. She rolled over, coughed and answered it.

"Mom?"

She came instantly awake and sat up. "Cody? You okay, baby?"

"I'm not a baby, Mom. Gram says the barn almost burned down last night."

"Just a couple of bales of that old straw. No big deal."

"Wow! Cool! I wish I'd been there to see it."

"I'm glad you weren't." She cleared her throat.

"Good grief, Cody, it's only seven in the morning. I thought your football practice wasn't until eleven."

"We're not having practice. That's what I called about. Look outside."

Tala looked through the curtains at her bedroom window. Rain sluiced down the windowpanes. "Is cheerleading practice canceled, too?"

"Uh-huh. Rachel and Ashley are going to the movies. Me'n Mike want to go too."

"What do you want to see?"

She heard the hesitation. "See, there's this cool cartoon thing with monsters and aliens."

"You'll have nightmares."

"Will not!" Cody said hotly. "I'm not a baby." Then softer, "It's rated G."

"Well, let me talk to your grandmother."

A moment later she heard Irene's voice. "It is rated G."

"How about the one Ashley and Rachel want to see?"

"PG, but the reviews say it's very tame. Some new version of one of the old fairy tales. It stars some hunk they're crazy about who looks like a beardless child of twelve." She lowered her voice. "Frankly, dear, an hour or two of Ashley is about all I can stand. Put her and Rachel together, and it's instant migraine."

"I'll take them off your hands. Maybe take them shopping and lunch before the movie."

"At the moment they're up in Rachel's room being remarkably quiet. Let sleeping dogs lie, and I mean that literally. They probably won't straggle out until nearly time to leave for the movie. I'll take them on my way to the garden-club luncheon. You can just turn over and go back to sleep, then take a hot soak. Give yourself a manicure and a herbal mask. Pamper yourself. After last night, you could use a little pampering.''

"That sounds wonderful. Shall I pick them up after the show?''

"No need. Vertie's already said she'll stop for them on her way home from the stable.''

"Stable?'' Tala asked

Irene sighed cavernously. "Vertie's latest madness. She's decided to learn to ride reining horses. At her age. I swear, the two of you will send me to an early grave. In return, you come for dinner tonight, stay over, and go to church with us tomorrow morning. Deal?''

"If you're sure it's no bother.''

"You should know Ashley's spending the night again, so you'll have to listen to her at dinner.'' Irene laughed. "That'll show you how lucky you are to have Rachel. She may be snippy, but at least she shuts up occasionally.''

"I need to figure out what to do about the barn.''

"Not in this weather. I swear, Tala, if you *don't* agree to pamper yourself, I *will* make you come into town and chauffeur the kids!''

Tala looked out at the deluge. Not much to do today except assess the damage. She certainly couldn't clean up the mess in the rain. "You win,'' she said.

"Good. See you at six. And you will spend the night tonight. Promise?"

"Absolutely."

"I'M GOING INTO TOWN, Dad," Pete said, shrugging into his heavy jacket. "We could use a few things from the grocery store."

"In this weather?" Mace looked up from the paperback techno-thriller he was reading. He was stretched out on Pete's couch, his pipe sending curls of smoke over his head.

"The girls are fed and indoors. Baby's dry and gnawing on her breakfast. Not much else to do."

"You going over to Tala's?"

Pete stopped with his hand on the door. "Maybe drive by just to check, see she's okay. Heck, Dad, I'd do the same thing for any employee."

"Of course, son," Mace said and went back to his book. "Any employee, indeed."

Pete thought he saw the edges of Mace's lips curl into a smile, but with his gray beard, it was hard to tell. Pete pulled up his hood and stepped out into the icy rain that sluiced down from the eaves of the building and landed in a waterfall on his head. Damn, he must be crazy to go out on a morning like this.

He stopped by the store, and received a remarkably nasty glare from the manager. Must know who he was, Pete decided. And resent him for stealing his night manager. He ignored the dirty look, picked up milk, cookies, coffee, Mace's tea, some Granny Smith apples, eggs and a supply of man-size frozen dinners for the microwave.

He stuffed the bags into the rear of the Land Rover. In this weather nothing would spoil. The dinners wouldn't even start to defrost.

He had a few other stops to make before he went home.

First, he went to the fire station. He found the volunteer fire chief playing gin with the only other fireman on duty.

"Chief, mind if I speak to you?"

The chief looked over his glasses, laid down his hand and stood. "You look a good deal better than you did last night," the chief said, offering his hand. "How's the cough?"

"Gone. The eyes'll take longer to stop burning, I think."

"Probably right. What can I do for you?"

Pete steered him outside the dormitory into the firehouse proper where the pumper stood, already shining after its midnight run, water still beading on its red paint from an early-morning wash.

"Hope you don't mind my coming by like this. I wondered if you'd had any thoughts about the fire last night."

The chief leaned his big body against the wall of the station, and braced one foot against the wall. "Why?"

"Because Mrs. Newsome's had some other—I guess you'd call them incidents—lately. She's had prowlers, and somebody tried to run her off the road the other night. I don't believe much in coincidences."

"Wish I could help you, son, but I got nothing to

go on. Hell, Mrs. Newsome's a fine woman. Her husband, Adam, was a credit to the community. Damn shame what happened to him.''

''Can you think of any reason for somebody to try to scare her?''

''Nope. Folks like her. Lived here all her life. And she's had a hard row to hoe, what with Adam being killed and all.''

''Maybe someone trying to drive her off her land?''

The chief laughed. ''Lord, there's half a dozen farms for sale around here bigger and better than hers, even a couple in the Hollow. Most people can't make a living farming this up-and-down country. No reason anyone'd want that land especially.''

Pete had to be content with that. His next stop was the sheriff's office in the Hollendale County courthouse. He didn't really expect to find the sheriff working on a rainy Saturday morning, but he had to try.

Billie Joe lounged behind the counter with his shiny brown boots crossed on a scarred wooden desk and his nose deep in the *Hollendale County Register*.

''Excuse me,'' Pete said.

Billie Joe nearly toppled over backward. He put down the paper, thumped both feet onto the floor, peered at Pete, then stood and came around the desk with his hand extended and a big grin on his face. ''Got us a real hero, Doc,'' he said. ''Want to shake your hand.''

Pete shook his hand and asked if Sheriff Craig was available.

"He's in, but whether he's available..." Billie Joe looked over his shoulder.

"Could you check?"

"Sure." Billie Joe knocked on a partly open door at the back of the squad room, slipped in and came out a minute or so later. "He says to come on in."

Pete had seen the sheriff a few times, but didn't know him. He was a big man. Not as tall as Pete, but a good deal broader, with a belly that was fighting to stay above his Sam Brown belt, and the broad shoulders and barrel chest of a man who would still be formidable in a fight.

After some small talk, Pete leaned forward. "I know this is one hell of a lot to ask, Sheriff, especially when I don't have anything to offer in return."

"Uh-huh."

"I need to know about Adam Newsome's murder."

The sheriff leaned back and eyed Pete speculatively. "Well, now. You got some reason?"

"Tala Newsome is working for the sanctuary now. Dad and I would like to avoid putting our foot in it with her, if you know what I mean."

"Uh-huh." Craig didn't sound convinced.

"I know it's an ongoing investigation, and I wouldn't want you to reveal anything that's not public knowledge."

"That's mighty big of you." No warmth here. Pete had the feeling Craig saw right through him.

A formidable man.

"I could check out the newspaper files, but I

thought there might be something you could tell me that wasn't in them. Is that possible?''

"Can't remember what was in 'em and what wasn't.'' The sheriff templed his fingers and braced himself with a knee against his desk. "Why don't you ask and I'll answer what I can.''

"Fair enough. Where was Newsome shot? And how many times?''

"One shot through the heart. Rifle slug. Left a hole in him the size of your fist. Miracle the bullet was still in him and not halfway to Chattanooga. Died instantly. Probably never knew what hit him.''

"Where?''

"Well, we don't rightly know.''

"I beg your pardon?''

"See, the body was moved after he was killed.''

"How do you know?''

"Nope. Out of bounds.''

"Okay," Pete continued. "What kind of a rifle was it?''

"Something old. Unusual shell. Haven't been able to match it to anything yet.''

"No suspects?''

"Nope.''

"What do you think happened? Can you tell me that?''

"My guess is as good as anybody else's.''

"His family thinks it was probably a poacher.''

"Yep. Adam Newsome was about as strict as you could get on hunting out of season or going above your limit. Hell, he'd have arrested the governor or the president of the biggest oil company in the world if he'd found either one standing over a dead deer out of season.''

"You think he did?''

"Probably some outsider with a fancy rifle down here for a little out-of-season sport—the kind of rich guy who thinks the rules don't apply to him. He's crowing over this fine deer—''

"Did you ever find a deer carcass?'' Pete interrupted.

"Nope. Either the guy took it with him, or it's so deep in the woods it'll never turn up. About all that would be left now would be some bones—probably minus the head if it was a trophy buck.''

"Sorry. Go on.''

"Anyway, he's crowing over this deer when up pops old Adam Newsome, all five foot ten and a hundred and sixty pounds of him just madder'n hell. Gonna arrest the sum'bitch. Guy panics, ups with the rifle, and maybe it goes off accidentally, or he freezes on the trigger. Suddenly he's looking at a dead warden. He could call somebody, turn himself in. Or he could just walk away.

"He doesn't do either one. He hauls Adam's body off to whatever vehicle he's come in, drives him around a while looking for a place to dump him, and then rolls him out on the side of the road and keeps driving. Probably to New York City or Chicago.''

"And the deer?''

"Took the deer.''

"Unless he was a pretty strong guy, he'd have been pretty worn out dragging a dead hundred-and-sixty-pound man and a deer any distance, even in two trips. Not to mention the possibility of running into a witness.''

''If he had an off-road vehicle, he could drive in, pick 'em both up and drive out again.''

''You find any tracks?''

''We looked, but it was raining pretty hard. Any tracks wouldn't have lasted long.''

''You ever consider there might be more than one of them?'' Pete asked.

For a moment, Craig didn't answer, then he said casually, ''Could be.''

''Maybe one outsider with a fancy gun, and somebody local setting him up on a deer stand while he drove deer for him to shoot.''

''No way to prove it. Now, I got one for you.''

Pete nodded.

''Why are you really asking all these questions?''

Pete hesitated, then he said, ''Too many bad things are happening to Tala Newsome. I want to know whether somebody who had anything to do with her husband's killing could be bothering her.''

''Don't know why, not unless she knows something she's not telling.''

''I'm sure she'd tell you anything that would help find Adam's killer. If she knew she knew it, if you get my drift.''

''Yeah. But why wait this long to go after her?''

''No idea. One final thing. Tell me about him— Newsome, I mean.''

''I told you. Real stickler. Smart. Not a tree hugger, but a real conservationist. Knew it was either hunt or watch deer starve, but didn't hunt himself.''

"Did he carry a gun?"

"Pistol. Found in his holster."

"So he wasn't sufficiently worried to take his gun out? Could he have known the person who shot him?"

"I'd hate to think that. Now, if that's all, I got me a bunch of reports to finish. That's why I come in on Saturday." He grinned. "Usually I don't get bothered."

"Sorry, Sheriff." Pete stood. "One more thing. What kind of a husband and father was he?" This was certainly not a question that had to do with Newsome's killing, but Pete realized he was hanging on the answer. He had to know what he was up against. How big a shadow did Adam Newsome cast?

Craig leaned back, closed his eyes and considered for a moment, then he opened them and stared hard at Pete. "Preoccupied. One of those boys that was raised rich, thought he liked living poor, but actually had Tala smoothing the path for him, making sure he never caught on to how hard it got for her sometimes."

"And as a father?"

"Tough, but fair. Liked his family, but didn't have much time for them. I've heard him get a little testy a couple of times when the kids wanted him to do something or go somewhere with them. But he loved them. Loved Tala, too, although I don't think he knew he'd never be half the man he was without her. But I also don't think he ever regretted his decision to marry her, even though it cost him his inheritance."

"But his family wasn't his first priority?"

The sheriff nodded. "But then you could say the same thing about me. You, too, probably. Men tend to lose sight of the things that really matter." He grinned. "'Course, I married me a wife who makes damn sure I don't forget that she and the kids come before even this job."

"Thanks, Sheriff."

As Pete was walking out of the sheriff's office, Craig said to his back, "I'm one of the few people around here to know what Tala's name means. You interested?"

Pete turned. "Of course."

"Most folks never knew Tala's grandmother had a sense of humor. Sure didn't show it much, but then she never had much to smile about. When old Sakari brought that baby home from the hospital, said she was as hungry as a wolf cub. So that's what she named her—little wolf. Fits."

Little wolf. It did fit. Loyal, loving, family-oriented and willing to fight if she had to. As Pete drove away, he thought what the sheriff had told him about Adam. He and Adam probably had more in common than Pete wanted to believe.

He'd certainly been more than preoccupied when he was living with Val. He'd been oblivious. All that had mattered was the blasted job, building a career, showing his father what a great vet he was.

Maybe it was time for him to change that. Maybe a good place to start was with her family. If all he'd wanted from Tala was a roll in the hay, maybe he could have persuaded himself that what her family and the town thought of him didn't matter.

He wanted her in his bed, all right. Any man would be crazy not to.

But he wanted much more than that. He wanted her in his life. Every day, all the time. And he wanted to be part of hers—a big part.

He had precious little to offer. He wished he'd made some sort of effort to become a part of the town before now, because Tala was part of a community that cared about her. People respected her. Somehow he had to make them accept him.

He drove past the Newsome mansion, looking for Tala's little truck, but it wasn't there. She must still be at the farm—or maybe trying to buy enough wood to close up that gaping hole in the barn wall.

At least he could take care of that for her. Besides, he had an excuse. He wanted to check the damage by daylight.

If she was there, maybe one thing would lead to another.

He slammed on his brakes as a big eighteen-wheeler ran one of the few traffic lights in town as it turned from yellow to red. Damn thing was as big as Sweetiepie.

Suddenly he grinned. Did he say he needed something to offer to make her family like him? Shoot, he had plenty to offer her kids, at least.

He had elephants.

CHAPTER ELEVEN

PETE'S HEART SANK when he drove down Tala's driveway. Her truck was nowhere in sight. After the night she'd had—they'd both had—Tala ought to be tucked up in front of a roaring fire with a glass of wine and a good book.

Then he remembered her children's Saturday schedule. Maybe Cody's football coach thought he could toughen them up by giving them pneumonia. Pete had suffered under a number of coaches like that.

If Rachel's cheerleading squad practiced in a field house, the rain wouldn't bother them.

He could still do what he came for—or ostensibly came for. Check out the damage to the barn. He pulled on heavy work gloves, climbed out of the Land Rover and walked around the house to the backyard. The elderly yellow tractor still held its front-loader aloft, but the hydraulics had slackened overnight, so that now it sagged at shoulder level. The rain and water from the hoses had stirred up the blackened mess inside into a foul stew. It needed to be dumped, but he didn't know where to do it.

The wind blew the rain away from the hole he'd made in the barn wall. Still, the floor was muddy from the fire hoses. He ducked inside and let his eyes adjust to the semidarkness. Rain drummed on the metal roof like birdshot.

He bent to see if any signs of accelerant were visible on the bits of wood he'd left standing when he'd driven through. But there wasn't enough light and anyway he wasn't certain what to look for.

Nothing else in front seemed to have been disturbed. He walked to the back of the barn and found Adam's tools carefully covered by waterproof tarpaulins held down at the corners with hunks of concrete block. Tala must have come back out here last night to protect them after everyone left.

She'd been out here alone. He should have stayed, no matter what Irene and Vertie thought. At least he could have done this small task for her while she stayed safely in the house.

At any rate, the table saw would make cutting the boards to repair the barn a simple task. He measured the length and width of the hole he'd made, and calculated the number of boards he'd need. He'd stop by the hardware store on his way home.

Then one day next week after a couple of days' drying time, he'd spend an afternoon repairing the damage.

In the meantime, at least he could get the tractor back under cover. He pulled off his gloves, stuck them in his pocket and opened the doors of the barn from inside.

He started the tractor, lowered the bucket to a horizontal position that would keep it from dumping the muck it still held and carefully backed into the center of the barn. He'd leave Tala a note so that she wouldn't think it had been stolen.

As he climbed down, he heard a sound behind him.

"Pete?"

His heart lurched at the sound of her voice. He hadn't heard her truck or her footsteps over the din of the rain on the metal barn roof.

He tried to wipe the goofy grin off his face, and turned to look at her.

She'd shoved the hood of her jacket back. The rain glinted like diamonds on her eyelashes. In the semi-twilight under the eaves her eyes were huge and ink black.

"I..." he began, ready to explain what he'd been doing. The words died in his throat. Afterward he didn't remember moving.

She was in his arms, her body pressed against him. A moment ago he'd been miserably cold and wet. Now he felt as though his skin were smoldering.

He was rock-hard, and knew she felt him even through the layers of clothes between them. All his good intentions to remember her reputation, her family, to take things slow, exploded in pure desire.

He crushed her mouth with his, devoured her lips and tongue with his own, held her against him with one arm while he curled his fingers in her short hair.

And she was with him, her mouth as hungry, as fiercely demanding as his. Her hips moved against him slowly, rhythmically. He lost all rational thought.

He only knew he wanted her as he'd never wanted

anyone before. The cold, the rain, the mud, the layers of clothes—there were no barriers strong enough to disarm his passion.

She broke the kiss and stared up at him with glazed eyes. He could feel her heart beating wildly through her jacket.

"Not here," she whispered. "We can't…there's no place…"

He shook his head like a punch-drunk fighter trying to survive a standing eight count. He set her down, still groggy, still in the moment.

She broke from him, turned and ran toward the house.

"Oh, God," he breathed. What the hell had possessed him? At least she had the sense to run before he stripped them both and took her on a bale of wet hay in a forty-degree rain.

He wasn't an animal, dammit! He had to tell her, somehow make her understand he'd never hurt her, never seduce her into doing something she didn't want to. Even if he burned to a cinder.

He raced through the driving rain, up the back stairs and through the open porch door. Light streamed from the open kitchen door beyond, revealing a pair of mud-encrusted loafers beside the threshold.

He used his toes to lever off his own muddy shoes beside hers.

Across the threshold her wet jacket lay in a sodden heap on the tile of the kitchen floor. He tossed his own jacket onto the back of a kitchen chair and walked into the living room in his socks.

She stood across the room facing him, head high, two red patches along her lovely cheekbones. Her left hand gripped the back of a worn plaid chair. Her wet jeans clung to her, and the cold made her nipples stand out through her thin sweater.

Her eyes met his and held. They were a doe's eyes, knowing yet wary. Like a doe, she stood poised between flight and capitulation.

He held out his hands to her. Then he dropped them and simply stood there holding her gaze, not daring to breathe.

For an interminable moment they stood silent. Then she reached out to him.

He closed his eyes and breathed again. Thank God.

She came to him slowly, on bare feet. He ran his fingers over her forehead, down her cheek, across her lips gently, as he might touch a bird.

She closed her eyes and swayed against him. He lifted her chin and brushed her lips with his, then kissed her eyelids, her earlobes and the pulse that throbbed at the base of her throat. Her arms circled his neck. She sighed and melted against him.

He slipped one arm under her back, the other under her knees, and picked her up. Her bones felt fragile, hollow.

He carried her up the stairs, realizing halfway that he had no idea which bedroom was hers. He nudged the first door open, saw the double bed, and carried her through. He set her on her feet, but kept his arm around her waist.

"Tala?"

She smiled softly and touched his cheek. A moment later she pulled her sweater over her head, dropped it on the floor at their feet and slid her hand down his chest to his waist and below. For a moment he was afraid he would explode when she touched him.

"It's all right," she whispered.

He bent to kiss the soft skin of her breast where it swelled above her bra. He kept repeating a litany in his head, "Go slow, take it easy, careful, gentle..."

He felt her fingers lock into his hair. Her back arched, she moaned and shivered in his arms, pressed her hips against him. He lifted his face to kiss her.

She bit him.

Her teeth closed softly on his lower lip and worried it as her fingers dug into the ridges of muscle along his spine. He felt a jolt of electricity along every muscle and all his good intentions exploded into naked passion.

One moment he was running his lips gently over the silky skin of her breast, the next she was on the bed.

Afterward he couldn't remember how they'd gone from half-clothed to fully naked, or when slow and tender erupted into passion that was more like fury.

She was hot and wet and open when he touched her. She pulled him down to her, holding him, arching against him and whispering, "Pete, Pete, Pete," over and over in a voice he'd never heard her use before.

For him the joining was like diving off a cliff or out of a plane without a parachute. He knew vaguely that at some point he'd hit the ground and fracture every molecule in his body, but the ecstasy of the flight was worth it.

She was hungry, moving under and against him, her ankles locked around his waist, her head thrashing from side to side, eyes half-closed, half-blind, meeting him thrust for thrust as she made those sounds over and over in her throat.

Suddenly she threw back her head, her eyes closed, and arched against him, every muscle strained, and he felt her spasm.

He crested as she began to come down the other side, only to have her arch against him again and join him in one final mindless freefall.

He collapsed in her arms, forgetting for a moment to be careful of his weight on her slim body. She held him in her arms as lightly as though he'd been a child.

Then he remembered and rolled away, pulling her on top of him. She dropped her head down on his chest under his chin and sobbed with the effort of breathing again.

"I think I'm having a heart attack," he gasped.

"Me…too." She began to laugh.

What if he'd hurt her? "Tala, I swear, I never…"

"Yes, you did." She snuggled down and began to nibble the mat of sandy hair on his chest.

As completely exhausted as he was, he felt sensations he knew he couldn't possibly be having so soon again.

He closed his eyes and relished the feel of her naked breasts against his chest. His hands slid down to the curve of her hip just below her waist. He wanted to know her body, every inch of her. He'd wanted to explore, to make tender, leisurely love, to know her in every sense.

Instead, there had been this cataclysm. He'd never been so completely out of control.

And why had he ever thought she was shy? Or fragile? He began to chuckle.

"What?" she asked, momentarily raising her head from its place under his chin.

"You, m'dear, as my father would say, are a wild woman."

He knew he shouldn't have said something like that. He tensed for anger, wounded innocence.

What he got was surprise. "You know," she said, "I guess I am. I never knew that."

He sat up against the headboard and held her away from him. "I beg your pardon?"

She rolled off, turned over and sat against the headboard beside him. "I said I never knew I was capable of that…what just happened. It's a funny feeling—like suddenly finding out you've got multiple personalities and there's a whole other person hiding inside that you never realized was there. I don't know whether I like it or not."

"Oh, like it, lady. Please like it, for my sake."

"For your sake?" She smacked him lightly on the shoulder. "Selfish thing."

He wrapped his arm around her and felt her snuggle against him. "Then I don't have to feel guilty."

She sat up and turned to face him. "Why would you feel guilty?"

"I'm damn near six-six and I weigh more than a hundred pounds more than you do. And..." He put an index finger against her lips. "And I had all these fantasies about how gentle and tender I'd be if we ever got this far. That was something out of *Call of the Wild*. You're lucky I didn't break you in two."

She smiled lazily, and ran her tongue over his finger, evoking additional frissons to his awakening lower regions.

"I don't break so easy," she said, and bent to lay her head on his stomach. "It was wonderful, like falling down a well or stepping on a land mine."

"Neither one of those is close to my top ten most wonderful experiences. What are you doing down there?"

"Going to sleep," she said drowsily. "I think I'm probably going to ache all over," she whispered. Her voice trailed off. "Lovely."

He slid back down onto the pillows so that her head was on his chest, and pulled the quilt from the far side of the bed over them both. She made a soft purring sound.

His own eyes felt heavy. He held her against him, his arms across her slim body, and listened to her breathing. As he drifted off, he thought, "Well, hello, mystery of the universe."

HE AWOKE when she began to move. She stretched like a cat waking from a nap, sat up and yawned lazily, then bent and kissed him.

Not too soon now to make love again. Feeling her naked body stretch against him woke him in more ways than one. He cupped her breast, ran his thumb across her nipple and heard that lovely little sound again. This time would be slow, gentle, leisurely— all the things he'd planned for the first time.

Suddenly her eyes opened wide and she sat bolt upright. "Oh, Lord, what time is it?"

His left wrist was out of sight somewhere under her thigh. She glanced at the clock beside the bed, yelped and rolled away to stand up.

"Come back to bed."

Instead, she ran to the bureau in the corner of the room, opened drawers and began dragging out what looked like underwear.

"Tala?"

She threw up her hands. "Oh, Pete, I promised Irene I'd be there for dinner at six. It's almost five-thirty now! I'm going to be so late!" She started toward the bathroom, stooped to kiss him quickly, but eluded his hands when he reached for her.

"Stay where you are, Pete," she said. "I'm sorry, really I am." The bathroom door slammed, and a moment later he heard the shower start.

Damn! His body had already started something that it obviously was not going to be allowed to finish. So much for slow, gentle lovemaking. He sighed, stood and started trying to reassemble his clothes.

He managed to find his shorts, jeans and flannel shirt. Remarkably, his wallet, keys and comb were still in his pants pockets. He located his soggy socks, sat on the bed to pull them on. Like encasing his foot in damp kelp.

He dressed quickly then made up the bed carefully

so that if Irene or one of the children should see it, they wouldn't wonder what their mother had been doing in it.

A moment later the bathroom door opened.

"When will you be home?" he asked, watching as she stood at the bureau holding up a pair of plain gold hoop earrings.

"That's just it. I promised to spend the night at Irene's and go to church with them tomorrow." She reached into her closet, pulled out a pair of black wool slacks and a bright red sweater, then tossed a nylon backpack onto the bed. "I'll have to pack at least a change of clothes for morning." She rummaged around on the floor of her closet, giving him an arousing view of her slim rear end.

"There—" she held up a pair of black leather pumps "—I've got stuff to sleep in and makeup at the house."

She glanced at the clock again. "Irene's going to kill me! She hates it when people are late for dinner."

"You won't be very late." He grumbled, "Not at the rate you're going."

She stopped with one foot in a clean black flat, turned and knelt on the bed. He put his arms around her and kissed her downturned face.

"I wouldn't have agreed if I had any idea we'd..." she whispered. "If I'd even dreamed..."

"Hmm," he said against her throat.

Another instant and she was back at the bureau tossing clothes into the bag. "You have your girls, I have my family. Life is complicated."

"The girls don't fuss if I'm an hour late for dinner."

She looked at him with her eyebrows raised. "The heck they don't."

He grinned. "Okay, so they do."

"The deer are the same way." Her eyes widened again. "Oh, damn and blast! The only reason I went out in this rain today was to pick up a couple of bags of oats for the deer, and they're still sitting in the back of my truck under the tarpaulin."

He stood. "I'll bring 'em in. Where do they go?"

"The big metal garbage can on the back porch. Otherwise we get mice. Oh, and Pete, if you wouldn't mind, could you dump a couple of scoops outside on the back-porch steps? It's so muddy it'll just sink into the ground if I toss it into the yard."

"Your wish is my command."

He found his jacket on the kitchen chair where he'd draped it, and pushed his feet into his shoes. The rain had finally stopped, but everything still dripped. He tossed the two fifty-pound bags of feed over his shoulder, walked into the back porch and emptied them into the garbage can. As he turned to the back steps with a full scoop in his hands, Tala said from the door, "Wow! Impressive."

"Huh?"

"I never saw anybody toss around a hundred pounds quite that easily."

She stood in the glowing light from the ceiling. Her black hair shone in tendrils around her face. She was so beautiful, so desirable he wanted to kick the door out of the way, say the hell with everyone in the world except the two of them and carry her back to bed.

"I've got to leave, Pete, but you stay as long as you like. Just slam the doors behind you."

"No reason to stay without you."

"Are you angry?"

He grinned. "Hell, yes, I'm furious, but at what my father calls 'the general cussedness of things in general,' not at you."

"At least you can kiss me goodbye."

"I'm muddy and wet. I'll mess you up."

"Who cares?" She came to him, stood on tiptoe and wound her arms around his neck. "Goodbye, Pete." She kissed him. "Go home."

"Yeah."

"Pete, darling." She kissed him again.

This time he broke the kiss. "No, you go on. You're going to be late, but only fashionably. Maybe Irene'll forgive you. And be careful. The roads are slick. I'll follow you into town."

"I'll be all right."

"Humor me."

She touched his cheek. "Okay, and thank you."

As he waited for her to pull away in her truck, she lowered her window and asked, "You're still going to introduce the kids to the elephants tomorrow afternoon, aren't you?"

He'd forgotten. He'd dreamed of spending Sunday afternoon drowsing over the Sunday papers with her beside him. "Sure, yes. You coming?"

She made a wry face. "I've got to entertain Oxley." She blew him a kiss and pulled away.

He sat for a moment in the Land Rover, then pulled out after her. He hoped whoever had set the fire wouldn't try any more tricks on her or her house tonight. For a moment he considered mounting a still watch, but Billie Joe would probably shoot him if he found him there alone. Besides, nothing seemed to happen when she wasn't home. At Irene's at least she'd be safe.

Safe from him, too.

CHAPTER TWELVE

"YOU SEE?" Irene said as she kissed Tala's cheek. "I knew you'd glow if you simply spent the day resting and pampering yourself. Doesn't she glow, Vertie?"

Vertie narrowed her eyes. "Uh-huh. Like a lightning bug on a June night. I'd like me some of *that* bubble bath myself."

Tala cleared her throat and hoped the blush she felt wasn't that obvious. "Where are the kids?"

"Upstairs getting washed up for dinner." Irene rolled her eyes. "I'm glad Rachel has a best friend, but occasionally I wish she'd picked someone a little less ebullient."

By the time dinner was over, Tala had a throbbing headache behind her left eye, and her jaw hurt from smiling. Ebullient didn't half define Ashley Rogers. How she managed to put away enough of Lucinda's chicken and rice, broccoli, spinach salad and peach cobbler for three grown men, while managing to talk nonstop—but never with her mouth full—put her up in David Copperfield's ranks so far as Tala was concerned.

And Rachel hung on her words as though they were pearls of wisdom from the ancients.

Several times Tala interrupted to ask Cody about his movie, but one sentence later Rachel and Ashley were back to giving a play by play of the romantic comedy they'd seen, as well as a description of every garment, hairstyle, number of teeth, dimples and muscles their current blond idol displayed in every scene. Between them, they seemed to have total recall and photographic memories.

Then their conversation turned from movie stars to boys at school. "The minute we get into high school we'll both be on the cheerleader squad," Ashley rattled on. "I mean—" she hugged herself "—they'll have to take us. We're better than any of those other dweebs. The dreamiest guys are on the football team. I mean, like, you know, they are just the hunkiest, you know?"

Cody made a "yuck" sound. Tala scowled at him and shook her head. He rolled his eyes.

"I mean, I just love looking up at them." Ashley fluttered her mascaraed eyelashes.

"I mean, even when they get old they're still hunky, you know, like Sean Connery and that Dr. Jacobi."

Tala assumed she meant Dr. Mace. He did look a lot like Connery with his crinkly eyes and gray beard.

"I mean, it's just so cool, like, you know, bringing in the elephants and all."

So Pete was the old one. Wouldn't he love that?

Ashley squealed. "Ooh, Rachel says I can go with you all tomorrow! Isn't that, like, you know, way cool?"

"Rachel," Tala asked, trying to sound as unchallenging as possible, "have you called Dr. Jacobi to ask if Ashley may go with you? You can't simply bring someone else along without checking first, you know."

Rachel refused to meet her mother's eyes. "I talked to Dr. Mace this afternoon. He said fine." She looked up with both a challenge and a slight smile. Score one for Rachel.

"And what did Dr. Peter Jacobi say?" Irene asked. "It is, after all, his sanctuary."

"He was off somewhere. But Dr. Mace said he was sure it would be all right. And he's the father."

And the father sets the rules. No father, no rules. Was that what Rachel thought? If so, she had another think coming.

"Is it okay?" Ashley asked. "I mean, like, you know, I don't want to butt in or anything."

"I'm sure it's fine, Ashley," Tala told her, thinking that poor Pete would be a basket case after two hours of the Newsomes plus Ashley.

"That nice Mr. Oxley will be by to pick you up at two, Tala," Irene said. Nice Oxley to contrast with Weird Jacobi. "He called this afternoon thinking you were here. I didn't want him to call you out at the house in case you were napping."

"Thanks, Irene." She thought she sounded choked and was certain her face was the color of her sweater.

Vertie stared at her so hard she dropped her eyes and took another helping of cobbler, which she didn't really want.

"Here, honey," Vertie said solicitously. "You need a little whipped cream with that." She dumped an enormous glob on top of the cobbler. "Got to keep your strength up for those elephants."

When Tala looked at her, however, Vertie's face was bland.

After dinner, much as Tala longed to hear Pete's voice, she didn't get the opportunity to call him.

Instead, she ended up playing gin rummy with Vertie while Irene played Chopin in the music room. It was almost loud enough to cover the musical noise that came from Rachel's room, but not the bass beat, which thrummed through the house.

At ten o'clock, Tala gave up. She'd call in the morning from the parish hall. She yawned deeply and shook her head. "Sorry, Vertie, I'm about asleep on my feet. Mind if I call it a night?"

"Not surprising." Vertie began to stack the cards. "You planning to tell me about it?"

"What?"

"Nobody's likely to hear us what with Irene in the middle of a polonaise and the newest Beasts from Hell going full blast upstairs. Not to mention the noise Cody's making saving the universe from dragons on the computer."

Tala gulped.

"Irene is blind as a bat not to see it," Vertie said. "I knew the minute you walked—no, floated—in the front door looking like somebody's lit you up inside." Vertie sank back. "Which, come to think of it, is probably about what happened."

For a moment Tala considered brazening it out. Then she nodded. "Okay, but not here. Can I come to your room in a little while? I really could use some advice.''

"You got it. Give me thirty minutes to get my pajamas on." Vertie pulled herself up from her chair and eased her back with one hand. "Can't believe I ache this much from being on a horse for thirty minutes. I used to ride to hounds and follow the dog trials at Ames Plantation for ten, twelve hours a day."

"It's been a while."

"Too darned long. But it's time I started doing something beside tai chi if I plan to ride the roundup in Wyoming this August."

"What?"

"Well, it was either that or a two-week trip down the Snake River in rubber rafts, and I think Cody and Rachel would prefer the roundup, then maybe down to Disneyland for a few days."

"Vertie…"

"I know what I'm doing. Let me be." She straightened her spine and walked up the staircase. "Thirty minutes, young lady."

THIRTY MINUTES LATER, after tucking Cody in and saying good-night to Rachel and Ashley, who turned off the music, but who would probably talk and giggle most of the night, Tala tapped on Vertie's door.

"Come on in."

Tala slipped around the door. She wore plain blue cotton pajamas and a wool robe from L.L. Bean that Adam had given her for Christmas a couple of years back.

Vertie sprawled on a Chinese yellow silk chaise longue. She wore red Tibetan slippers that curled at the toes, and an embroidered mandarin robe that probably belonged in a museum. She pointed to the lady's desk in the corner of the room. "Pour yourself a brandy and come sit down."

"No brandy, thanks."

Vertie patted the leather easy chair beside her. "Come, sit, tell."

Tala sat, primly, her bare feet flat on the floor, her hands folded on her knees. She had no idea how to start.

"There's obviously a problem. What is it?"

Tala took the plunge. "Vertie, what if all you've ever known about making love is one thing and then all of a sudden it turns into this whole other thing you didn't even know existed?"

"Ah." Vertie leaned back and closed her eyes. "Wild, huh?"

"Uh-huh. And so unexpected. I mean, there we were talking about fixing the hole in the barn and then ka-boom."

"In the barn? In that rain?"

Tala blushed. "Not quite, but almost."

"So what's your problem?"

"If, and it's a big if, it happens again, is it going to be ka-boom all over again? I don't see how it can be."

Vertie sat up, leaned over and patted Tala's folded hands. "I take it there was no ka-boom with my grandson?"

Tala started to get up. "Oh, Lord, I can't talk about this with you."

"If not me, then who? I'm an old hen, girl, and I had me one hell of a rooster in my day. Sometimes it was ka-boom, sometimes it was like drifting down the river on a warm day and letting your fingers trail in the water." She sat up. "And sometimes it was wham-bam-thank-ya'-ma'am on the kitchen table when he was supposed to be eating a sandwich before going back to the bank." She grinned. "That was fun, too."

Tala laughed.

"Thing is, it was always different." Vertie leaned back, sipped her drink and closed her eyes with a sigh.

"Before, it was always so tender and sweet, as if he was afraid I'd break or something." Tala couldn't say Adam's name, not to his grandmother.

"Well, I won't say I haven't sampled a few of the barnyard strutters since Edward died, but it's never been ka-boom for me since. It was recreation and a hell of a lot of fun, but not love."

"How can this be love?"

"Oh, honey, it can be hate one minute and love the next. Lord knows how it happens."

"But will we be able to drift down the river sometimes?"

"That's what you need to find out. And the sooner, the better."

"And what about Irene? And Cody, and Rachel?"

"They're going to hate the whole idea until they

get used to it. So don't tell 'em until you're sure and he's sure."

"Of what? He lives in two grubby rooms attached to a veterinary surgery, and an elephant house. His daddy lives in a trailer. He doesn't want to start a veterinary practice here, though Lord knows we could use one what with Dr. Wiskowski getting so forgetful. And he's basically pretty screwed up emotionally. I don't know whether he's capable of dealing with me, much less my family." She threw up her hands. "It's hopeless."

"No, you wait one minute. I'm about to tell you how the cow ate the cabbage, Miss Tala, and you better listen good. I loved my grandson to pieces, but he wasn't a patch on my Edward."

"Vertie…"

"Hush up and listen. All he thought about was that damn job of his. You let him. He never had to deal with any of life's little problems like shopping for sneakers for Cody, or writing the checks for the utilities or buying the groceries, or seeing that he had clean socks and gas in his car. You did all that."

"But he made all the decisions."

"He just thought he did, and apparently, you bought into that because he had an education and picked you up out of the Hollow to marry instead of some debutante from Raleigh. Irene and those children think he hung the moon, but you were the one holding it up while he just pointed at it and told everybody how he'd put it there. I don't know whether this Dr. Jacobi is the man for you or not, but Tala, girl, at your age, *somebody* had better be, because you can't live the rest of your life without passion. This time you make damn sure that you and those children are at the *top* of his priority list, and not dragging up the rear behind a bunch of elephants.''

BY NOON SUNDAY Pete had scrubbed, polished and straightened everything he could. The place would still look ratty in Irene's eyes, but there wasn't much he could do about that now. He'd bathed the girls, too, and scrubbed out Baby's cage.

"You behave yourselves," he said to the girls as they forked hay into their mouths. "I'm counting on you." They watched him as though they understood him perfectly. He was sure they did. Whether they'd do as he asked was a whole other question.

At one o'clock he stuck his head in the door of Mace's trailer. "I'm going to run over and pick up those kids now."

"Oh, son, forgot to tell you," Mace said, lowering the sports section of the Sunday paper. "Irene's driving them over in her car. And they're bringing one of Rachel's little friends along."

"What? Who told them they could do that?"

"Actually, I did. Why? Does it create problems?"

"Hell, no." Pete slammed the door behind him. The world was conspiring against him.

And Tala was spending the afternoon with that smarmy jerk Oxley.

Why didn't she at least call? She knew he couldn't call her, not at the Newsome place. He stomped into the living room of his apartment in time to hear the answering machine start to pick up a call. He dived for the telephone.

"Hello?" His heart sang. Tala at last.

"Pete? Hi, this is Mary Ann Hildebrand."

He leaned on the kitchen counter. "Oh. Hello."

He heard her laughter. "Boy, is that ever a hearty greeting. Who were you expecting? The Prize Patrol?"

"No, I'm sorry. What can I do for you?"

"Well, we were thinking that since the afternoon's going to be warm, we might drive up to your place and pick up that lioness if she's well enough to leave."

"No!"

"She's not? I thought she was doing so well."

"She is, but—oh, hell, Mary Ann, it can't be this afternoon."

"Is there some reason why not?"

"I've got a bunch of people coming. People who don't know about her. I've got her settled down in her cage with enough food to keep her happy, and a blanket over the cage to keep her quiet while they're here."

"Oh. We could come late."

"That's not it. I couldn't send her off without—without letting the lady who found her have a chance to say goodbye."

He expected an argument.

"Of course, Pete. That would be awful. Just to have her suddenly disappear after that woman went to all the trouble of bringing her to you."

"Thanks for understanding."

"But Pete, you know that every minute she's on your place you're technically breaking the law."

"I know. Listen, could you possibly drive down tomorrow? Maybe get here for lunch? Then we could get her settled, and Tala'd have the whole morning with her."

"Let me ask Jim."

Pete held the phone so hard he realized his fingers were starting to go numb. No matter how long Baby stayed, Pete knew it wouldn't be long enough for Tala.

"Pete? Jim says that's fine. Tell Mace we're looking forward to some of his great grilled sandwiches."

"Yeah. I'll tell him."

He'd have to reach Tala tonight to tell her about Baby.

In the meantime, he had an entire afternoon of Newsomes to look forward to, when what he really wanted was to find Tala and take her back to bed.

TALA WAS SO BUSY worrying about the Jacobi-Newsome encounter that she didn't realize at first that Oxley was selling something besides condominiums.

"Call me Vince, hon," he'd said as he guided her to his big Cadillac with a warm hand in the small of her back. "All the ladies do." Then he actually took her hand to help her in, something Tala thought had gone out with the Model T.

She listened with one ear to his sales pitch as she wandered around the three-bedroom town house he showed her in the new development on the edge of town. "A lake and a clubhouse that anyone who lives here can reserve for big parties," he said. "And for the more intimate get-togethers..." He actually leered at her. "There's plenty of room here, sweet thing."

If "intimate" meant Tala and himself he had another think coming. Sweet thing? Really!

She was ready to leave. Three minutes inside the door and Tala already had claustrophobia. More than six people would be cramped in the living room. The stairs were too narrow and too steep, the bedrooms tiny.

The kitchen was shiny and new with wonderful appliances, and the master bathroom was bigger than the second bedroom. What did people do in bathrooms that required all that space?

"I sense that you're not convinced," Vince said, dropping an arm casually across her shoulders. "We have bigger models, and from what I hear about your land, you could well afford one."

"What did you hear?"

"Why, just that you've got a couple of hundred acres."

"Woods, hills, hollows, a creek and a couple of flat pastures. Plus a barn, outbuildings and a house."

"The house and buildings wouldn't be worth much. But people from as far away as Raleigh are starting to look at this area for vacation homes. That hill overlooking the creek would be a perfect place to build a house."

"So my house would be a teardown?"

"Probably. Nobody is going to buy the place to farm."

"Uh-huh." She wanted to get back into that shiny Cadillac and force Vince to drive her to the sanctuary. But she was supposed to keep him away from there. So she made him drag her through more expensive models and endured his hand on her arm, his expensive cologne in her nostrils.

"Want to drive out by your place so I can take a look?" he said. "I've never actually seen it. Maybe you could give me a cup of coffee."

"Sure."

She gave him directions, and twenty minutes later he pulled into her driveway.

"This is really isolated," he said as he opened his door.

She didn't wait for him to open hers, but managed to be out and halfway up the front steps before he reached her side of the car.

"No wonder Mrs. Newsome is worried about you. You really shouldn't stay here alone at night. You'd be safer in town."

"I've always been safe here."

He made pleasant noises about how charming the house was. He followed her into the kitchen, and even went upstairs to the bathroom. She was glad Pete had made the bed before they left.

Finally, she looked at her watch, concealed a sigh of relief and told him she really needed to get back.

She jumped out of the car the moment he stopped in the Newsome driveway. Irene's car wasn't back yet. She waved Oxley off with a promise to call him about the condo, and slammed the front door behind her. She kicked off her pumps, massaged her aching insteps and sank onto the sofa in the living room. She tried to read the Sunday paper, but found she couldn't remember from one paragraph to the next.

Finally, she heard the sound of a car in the driveway. She closed her eyes. Please God it had gone well.

She opened the front door with a broad grin on her face that froze when Cody rushed past her, flew up the steps and slammed the door of his room. She'd had a glimpse of tear-stained cheeks and mussed hair.

Rachel brushed past her as well, calling "Cody, Cody bear!" as she raced upstairs after her brother.

Tala turned to Irene and Vertie, who hung on to one another. Irene's face was gray.

"What happened?" Tala asked.

Irene brushed a hand at her and walked by without speaking. Straight to the liquor cabinet in the living room. She poured herself a wineglass full of sherry and took a hefty swig.

Vertie shook her head. "Don't ask."

CHAPTER THIRTEEN

TALA RACED for the stairs. "Cody, Cody honey! Are you all right?"

His door was locked. Inside she could hear Rachel's voice low and soft and the sound of Cody's sobs. She knocked. "Cody, Rach, open the door."

"Go away!" Rachel called. "I'm handling it."

"Rachel, let me in this minute."

"Please, Mom, go 'way." Cody's voice sounded teary. "I'm okay."

"That's for me to judge. Rachel, I swear I'll break it down."

She heard an expletive from Rachel, but a moment later the latch on the door clicked. Tala opened it slowly to find herself face-to-face with her daughter. "Did he get hurt?" Tala asked.

"No, he didn't get hurt," Rachel said. "He's upset, is all. And he doesn't want to talk to you or anybody else about it."

"He's talking to you."

Rachel drew herself up. "He's my *brother*. It's my job."

"No, Rach, it's mine." Tala walked past her.

Cody was curled on his bed in the fetal position. Tala sat down next to him and put a hand on his body. He drew a ragged breath. "Whatever happened, baby, it's going to be okay. Didn't you enjoy the elephants?"

Wail. Head buried under pillow. Snort of exasperation from Rachel.

"You think?" the girl said. "If you must know, they scared the poo out of him."

"What did they do?"

"They didn't *do* anything." Rachel leaned against the door and a faraway look came into her eyes. "They're really sweet. Cody freaked, is all. He does that sometimes." .

Tala knew that, but had no idea Rachel knew as well.

"Anyway, he'll be fine. He's just embarrassed, and he doesn't need to be." She came over, sat on the bed beside her mother and began to stroke Cody's calf. "Everybody gets scared sometimes, Cody bear," she said gently.

"You don't," Cody answered from under the pillow.

"Sure I do. All the time. I just cover it up better." Without warning, Rachel began to cry. Not sobs like Cody's, just tears that rolled down her cheeks. "I'm scared something else bad is going to happen."

Cody rolled over and buried his face in his mother's lap. "Don't go back to that place, Mom, please, please, please."

She held him and patted his back. "Why, baby?"

"He's scared you're going to die, too," Rachel said.

Tala's breath caught in her throat. "How about you, Rach?"

Rachel dropped her eyes. "Me, too." She looked up at her mother. "I love living here, and I don't ever want to go back to the farm, ever, ever, ever, but all the time I worry about losing you, too."

Tala wrapped her arm around Rachel's shoulders and pulled her into her arms. She rested her cheek on Rachel's head. "It's natural to worry about me," she said. "And more than anything in the world, at this moment I want to say, don't worry. I'll always be here. Everything will always be perfect."

"But you can't, can you?"

"No. Losing your father so suddenly made me realize how uncertain life is. I wish you hadn't had to face that truth yet."

Tala stroked his hair off his forehead. It was wet with sweat, just as it had been when he cried himself to sleep when he was a baby. Even then he'd worried. "But," she said, "you can't keep people safe by worrying." She snuggled him under her other arm.

He pulled away from her. "What do you mean?"

"I used to do it, too. I'd worry myself sick when your father was twenty minutes late or when either of you had a sniffle. I knew it was crazy, but I figured that if I made myself miserable enough, the sniffles wouldn't turn into pneumonia and your father wouldn't wind up in a ditch somewhere. And that if anything bad really did happen, I had already made myself so unhappy worrying that I wouldn't feel so much pain afterward. That's complicated. Do you understand?''

Rachel pulled away. ''You're both nuts. I'm going to my room.''

The old Rachel was back with a vengeance. Tala knew she'd pay for having seen this gentler side of her daughter. Tala let her go. She'd talk to her after she finished with Cody.

Cody sat up and wrapped his arms around his knees.

''It didn't work,'' Tala said. ''Because as your sister aptly put it, it's nuts. I couldn't worry enough to keep your father from being killed, and it hurt every bit as much afterward.''

''But the elephants are so big...and dangerous.''

Tala took his hand. ''The next time you meet them, I'll to be there to introduce you to them properly so that you can see how dear and kind they really are.''

''But they're so big,'' he repeated.

''Rattlesnakes are small. Does that make them any less dangerous?''

''Oh, Mom!''

He flopped back onto the bed, obviously worn out. ''I don't want any dinner,'' he said. ''Am I too old to take a nap?''

''Not at all.'' She took off his sneakers and pulled the quilt at the foot of his bed over him. When she looked up, he was already asleep, cradling his pillow like a teddy bear. She bent and kissed him, then turned out his light and closed the door behind her.

Across the hall, she knocked softly at Rachel's room.

"Yeah?"

"May I come in?"

"Do you have to?"

"Yes."

Rachel sprawled on her beanbag chair nodding her head in time to the music coming over her headphones.

"Off," Tala said, pointing to the headphones.

"Whatever." Rachel clicked off the sound system and pulled the headphones off her ears.

"Thank you for looking after Cody."

"Yeah, whatever."

"I didn't know you worried about me, too."

Rachel looked away. "Hey, you're a big girl now. You can take care of yourself."

"Actually, I can. And I can take care of you and Cody as well. Even under the same roof."

"Not out at the farm!"

"Maybe not. But somewhere. I'm working on it."

"Right. As though you'd ever sell 'Daddy's little dream preserve.'"

Tala sat down on the end of Rachel's bed. "You blame me for his death, don't you?"

Rachel glanced at her mother. "If he'd never met you he'd have gone to work in the bank the way he was supposed to, and he'd be alive today and we'd be rich!"

"He'd have been miserable. And neither you nor Cody would exist."

"We didn't ask to be born."

"Nobody ever does. But once we're here we better make the best of it and the best of us."

"Goody Two-Shoes rides again."

Tala took a deep breath. "Okay, that's it. I know there's a human being inside there someplace because you just gave me a fleeting glimpse. This snippy little cynic routine is getting old. Everybody is sick of walking on eggs around you. You are a thirteen-year-old girl. And I, whether you like it or not, am your mother. From here on in you're going to treat me and everybody else with respect."

"You want me to live a lie."

"If that's what it takes. Being ill-tempered doesn't make people feel sorry for you—they just don't like to be around you. I love you, and I really believe you love me and Cody as well."

"If you loved me, you'd sell that place and move into town."

"Into what? One of Oxley's twelve-hundred-square-foot condos? Your bed wouldn't even fit in the bedroom."

"A house like Ashley's."

"Ashley's father is a doctor. I can't afford one-twentieth of their house payment."

"Then make more money."

Tala began to laugh. "You're absolutely right. I have dedicated my life to staying poor and living in the country just so I could make your life a living hell. It's my one true goal." She couldn't stop laughing. She felt the tears start, and held her sides while she rocked back and forth on the bed.

"Mom?" Rachel sounded scared. "Mom? Mama?"

Suddenly Rachel flew across the room and into her mother's arms. A moment later they were both laughing and crying so hard that Tala was afraid they'd never stop.

But finally they hiccuped into silence. Rachel still held on tight. "I do love you, Mama," she whispered.

"And I love you. Somehow we'll get through this and make it better. I promise."

ONCE SHE WAS CERTAIN Cody was asleep and that Rachel was at peace—or as much at peace as she could be these days, Tala found that Irene had taken to her bed with a headache and Vertie was in her room with the door shut. Tala knocked, and stuck her head in to tell Vertie the status of the children. "Can you keep an eye out for a while? I really need to go talk to Pete about what happened this afternoon."

"I think that's an excellent idea. I'll call you out there if we need you."

"Cody will probably sleep through the night. He generally does after one of these bouts. And Rachel can fix herself a sandwich if she gets hungry."

"Don't worry about us. Go see the man."

CHAPTER FOURTEEN

FOR THE FIRST TIME, Tala used the key Mace had given her to unlock the front gate so that she could drive through without calling on the intercom first. After she drove through, she locked the gate behind her and parked her truck at the front door of Pete's building. There were no lights showing either from his living room or bedroom, although the Land Rover sat outside.

At eight-fifteen in the evening, he couldn't possibly be in bed asleep.

To be certain, she bent her ear to the front door and heard music. Something low-down and bluesy, but she couldn't recognize the artist. Pretty sad, whatever it was.

She raised her hand to knock, then dropped it, and fumbled with the big key ring until she found the key to Pete's front door.

She'd never done anything this bold in her life, but she was afraid that Pete might not want to see her or talk to her about the debacle this afternoon.

She felt the lock click and turned the knob. The door opened silently onto a dark living room. The computer was dark as well.

The music came from Pete's bedroom and spilled

out through the half-open door. She walked over to it and stopped with her hand on the door frame. "Pete?" she called tentatively.

She heard a grunt from inside and a rustling sound.

"Go away."

She pushed the door open. She could see from the light outside his windows that he lay fully dressed on his bed, arm across his eyes. His feet were aimed at the headboard.

He opened his eyes and tilted his head back so that he could see her upside down. "How'd you get in?"

"Used my keys." She walked to the foot of the bed and around to the far side. "Are you drunk?"

"Sober as a judge. I plan to remedy that situation as soon as possible."

She walked around and sat on the other side of the bed.

"Want to talk about it?"

He turned his head away. "About what? I'm having an early night."

She sighed and took a deep breath. "I know something happened this afternoon, and that it was pretty traumatic. But I don't know exactly what."

He started to sit up, thought better of it and slumped back. "There's a bottle of bad bourbon in the refrigerator. How about bringing it to me with a tall glass full of ice?"

"Tall glasses get you drunk faster?"

"You got it."

"No, you want to get drunk, you get it yourself."

"Great employee you are. Refuse a direct order.

Ought to fire you for insubordination.'' He looked up at her. ''Actually, that's an excellent idea. You're fired.''

''Fine. Mace will rehire me in the morning. In the meantime, what did you do to my kids?''

''What did I do to *them?*'' He sat up quickly. ''First off, that Ashley, the girl who came with Rachel—did you know that girl is incapable of shutting up even for one minute?'' He began to flutter his hands over his chest, and his voice went high. ''‘Oh, aren't they just the cutest things! And my, aren't they big! And you must be really big and strong to look after them.'''

''What about Rachel? Cody?''

He drove his hand through his hair and flopped back down on the bed. ''Okay. At first I thought it was going great. Once Ashley put her stamp of approval on the expedition, Rachel seemed to think it was okay for her to show a little enthusiasm. I could see she liked the girls and they liked her. They've been known to take off for the boonies when strangers appear, but they stuck around in their enclosure and waved their trunks around.''

''Great. So what went wrong?''

He continued as though she hadn't spoken. ''Mace was great. He always is with other people's kids. I was explaining about the differences between African and Indian elephants. Rachel seemed interested.''

''And?''

''The girls were standing close to the bars chirping and dancing. Rachel was rubbing Sophie's trunk. I didn't realize Cody wasn't with us until I heard this kind of moan from behind us. I turned around and he was standing by the door as though he'd been frozen. His face was so green I was sure he was going to throw up. I started over to him, and Sophie picked that moment to lift her trunk and trumpet. Cody was out the door before I could take two steps. The next thing I knew, he'd locked himself in Irene's car and was lying on the floor of the back seat yelling his head off.''

"You're exaggerating." But Tala felt cold. She remembered that one night at the farmhouse, when Cody had come very close to full-blown hysterics. But he'd been having nightmares. He'd been asleep. This was awake.

"Exaggerating, hell! Irene tried to talk him out, so did Mace. Even that Ashley gave it a go. Hell, if I'd been Cody I'd have come out just to shut her up. But nothing.''

"Where were you?"

"Standing there gawking like a fool, I imagine. The girls were very upset. They didn't understand what was happening a damn bit more than I did. They wanted to help, and came flying around the corner of the building, and started milling around the car.''

"Oh, my."

"Yeah. The minute Cody raised his head and saw them walking around outside, he really freaked.''

"How'd you get him out?"

He sat up. "I've got to hand it to Rachel. She walked to the car right between the girls. She even patted Belle on her way. It was like she'd been with elephants her whole life. I was damned impressed. No fear at all.''

"And Cody?''

"She leaned over and started talking very quietly to him through the window. After a while I could see he'd calmed down some—his shoulders weren't shaking. And then he sat up and flicked the button for the locks.''

"And got out?''

"No. Irene started to open the front door, but Vertie stopped her and told her to let Rachel handle it.''

"And did Rachel handle it?''

"Like a trouper. You know, every time I've seen those kids together it's been trench warfare, but she climbed into the back seat of that car, put her arms around Cody and talked to him for a good ten minutes. By that time he'd calmed down completely, but he still wouldn't come out of the car. When Rachel said it was all right, Irene, Vertie and Ashley all piled in and drove off. A great outing that turned out to be.''

"Pete, I'm so sorry.''

"I was sure I'd have them all eating out of my hand before this afternoon was over.'' He ran his hands through his hair. "I'm not cut out for this crap.''

"What crap?''

"This fatherhood crap.''

"They had a father, Pete. So far as they're concerned, you're simply a nice man who offered them a chance to see elephants at close range.''

"The hell I am. I should 'a' known it wouldn't work. I'm no good with kids."

For a moment she looked down at him, then she bent over him and kissed him. Her lips touched his gently, the tip of her tongue teasing his. For a moment he resisted, then with a groan he opened his mouth and met her kiss and deepened it.

She broke away first and slid out of his reach. "It's not you. My children are having a hard time getting used to life without their father. At bottom they're good kids."

"Like I said, I don't know anything about kids."

"Who does? Parenthood doesn't come with a guidebook, worse luck. This afternoon may have been a good thing in the long run. They came closer to opening up than they have for a long time."

He stared at her, then without a word he rolled off the bed and padded into the kitchen. Tala heard the refrigerator door open and shut, the tinkle of ice cubes and the sound of liquid—a lot of liquid—being poured. She followed him, still not turning on any lights in the darkened apartment. "Put that down. My granddaddy used to drink when he got worn-out with farming and worrying about money. He was a bad drunk."

He lowered the glass and looked at her, his eyes narrowing in the gloom. "He abuse you?"

She laughed. "Sakari didn't allow anyone to smack me around except her. And I think even drunk he knew that if he ever raised a hand to *her* he was a dead man." She propped a hip onto the computer desk. "He always woke up with the same problems and a hangover to boot. So will you, if you drink that."

"But I'll have a few hours of blessed oblivion."

"You'll have nightmares. Put it down, Pete," she said quietly.

He stared at her mulishly, raised the glass to his lips, then sighed and poured the contents down the sink.

Tala let out a breath she hadn't known she was holding.

"Hate the taste anyway," Pete said.

"So do I."

He stared out the window over the sink with his hands in his pockets. For a long moment neither said anything, then he said, "You know, I acted as midwife to the first female gorilla born in the zoo where I interned."

Confused, Tala said, "Uh-huh."

"The mama had been captured as a baby and raised completely alone in a small roadside menagerie. When the zoo acquired her, she wasn't socialized. Unfortunately, she got pregnant almost immediately. The baby was a beautiful little female."

"Wonderful," Tala responded, wondering where the story was going.

He turned. "The point is that Millie damn near killed the baby before we could rescue it. She didn't see a beautiful newborn baby to nurture, she saw something alien."

"Oh, Pete, did you get to the baby in time?"

"Yeah. As a matter of fact, she swung it at me by

one leg. I caught it in midair. And once it was out of her sight, she was her sweet old self again.''

"What did you do?''

''The zoo raised the baby by hand, of course. There's nothing sweeter than a baby gorilla. And as soon as they dared, they introduced her to the group, who took her in and babied her like a bunch of maiden aunts—the way elephants all gather round to mother a newborn.''

"How did her mother act?''

''Like it was a strange new intruder. She had no recollection that this youngster was hers.'' He leaned back and closed his eyes. ''By that time several of the others had conceived and born babies success-fully. And the second time Millie gave birth, she was a great mother.''

"What made the difference?''

''Gorillas don't have instincts about that sort of thing any more than human beings do, Tala. They have to learn how to be good mothers and fathers from watching the way other members of the group function. And they have to learn young, or they may never pick up the knack.''

"And?''

"And I didn't.''

"Mace is a wonderful father.''

''Oh, right. By the time I was twelve I'd been through half a dozen housekeepers. My father worked night and day. He never came to Little League games or coached my soccer team. My mother wasn't around to bake cookies and drag me to church on Sunday. Occasionally, I'd spend the night over at one of my friends' houses and be awe-struck.''

''Your mother didn't choose to die.''

''I'm not blaming her. I used to blame my father, but I know now he was so eaten up by grief he didn't know I was alive.''

''But you were going to marry Val, weren't you? Start your own family?''

''Only because it seemed the best solution at the time.''

''I didn't exactly come from the Cleaver house-hold either, Pete. My granddaddy died when I was ten and left Sakari and me scrambling for every penny and trying to run the farm alone. At least you didn't have poverty to deal with.''

''No, I didn't. I had bikes and roller skates and my own telephone line. I just didn't have a parent. So now I don't know how to be one.''

''You don't have to. They're my kids.''

''And you're still leaving those kids with Irene and Vertie?''

Talk about blindsided. That was the last straw. An-ger welled up in her and overflowed. She actually shook her finger at him. ''You have just finished spinning me a great long tale about how gorillas have to learn to be parents from other gorillas, and Mace told me about how every time a baby elephant is born the whole herd nurtures it. And what's that saying about it taking a village to raise a child?''

''Now, wait, Tala.''

''Wait, nothing. You spend your days dumping guilt on me because I've got a support group of nurturers to help me when Lord knows I need it. The kids are better because of it and so am I.''

''I didn't mean…''

''Yes, you did. I hate my living arrangements, but they're the best I can do with what I've got.'' She turned on her heel and strode toward the front door.

He reached it a step ahead of her and held it closed. ''I love you, Tala.''

''What?''

''I said I love you.''

''Oh, Pete,'' Tala said, reaching for his hands. ''What on earth are we going to do?''

He wrapped his arms around her and held her close. ''Hang on and pray for the best.''

ALL TALA'S DOUBTS about Pete's tenderness vanished as his big fingers fumbled with the buttons of her blouse. They undressed one another slowly, shyly, as though this were the first time, savoring the discovery, until at last they faced one another naked.

They caressed each other languorously, kissed gently and deeply, ran fingers and tongues across one another's skin. Pete circled her nipple with his tongue, and Tala felt as though she were being stroked with the warmth of a million candles. Her loins were already aching for him, pulsing, as his mouth sought out the curve of her ribs, the hollow beside her hipbones.

So tantalizingly slow, yet not tentative. She felt possessed and possessing at the same time. His fingers slid between her legs and found the point that caused instant waves of pleasure to wash over her.

She held him, stroked and pleasured him, taught her fingers the silken feel of him, her nostrils the musky scent of his body. He rolled over on his back and pulled her on top of him. She arched her back and began to move against him slowly as he entered her.

The buildup of pressure in her loins was slow but inexorable as though she were being carried higher and higher on wings that were not her own. He watched her from half-closed eyes and parted lips. She controlled the pace, or thought she did, until rational thought became impossible, and every nerve in her body centered where she felt him inside her.

"Yes," he whispered, and began to move faster.

And then they reached the crest together. She thought she screamed. Certainly she heard him yell.

The waves seemed to go on and on, longer and higher than she'd ever known was possible.

When at last they began to subside, she folded onto his chest, not ever wanting to let his body or this moment go.

He held her against him and kissed her hair.

She whispered something against his chest.

"What?" he asked.

"Fingers trailing in the stream," she whispered.

"You're not making sense."

"Yes, I am. Hold me."

"My pleasure."

CHAPTER FIFTEEN

"I HAVE TO GO," Tala said into Pete's chest. He groaned and held her tighter. "I'll have to drive out to the house and pick up some clothes for tomorrow, but I want to sleep in town tonight in case the children wake up and need me, and I definitely want to have breakfast with them and take them to school."

Pete didn't say anything for a minute, then he sat up. "Right. I'll drive you."

Tala slid off his chest and braced herself on her arms. "Not necessary. I'll be fine."

He rolled a short strand of hair around his fingers. "You haven't had any dinner, have you?"

She shook her head.

"Neither have I, and unlike you, I can't live on air." His rumbling stomach accompanied him.

"What's that got to do with anything?"

"We'll stop in town, pick up some fast food, eat it at your kitchen table, feed the cats and the deer, then I'll follow you back to the Newsomes and make sure you're safe."

"Oh, Pete."

"Don't give me any of that's-not-necessary stuff. The only time bad things happen to you is when you're either at home or going there. Nothing seems to happen to the place when you're not there. Which is a pretty good reason for spending the nights at the Newsomes until further notice.''

She flopped onto her back. ''You sound like Vince Oxley.''

''Vince? He's Vince now?''

''I couldn't keep calling him Mr. Oxley all afternoon. He also said I ought to spend the nights in town.''

''He's right.'' He stroked her back. ''Let's go.''

In the end they split a pizza in public. Tala knew word of that would get back to Irene Newsome probably before she did, but it was time to start acting like a grown woman.

''Tala,'' Pete said over the last piece of pepperoni, ''I have something to tell you.''

Her heart froze. What now?

He looked up at her, set down the pizza and took her hand.

''I had a call from Mary Ann and Jim Hildebrand this afternoon. The people with the big-cat sanctuary.''

Tala caught her breath and held it.

''They want to pick up Baby tomorrow afternoon.''

''No!'' She felt her eyes begin to tear. ''So soon?''

''They wanted to come this afternoon, but I convinced them that you needed some time with her before she left. She's well enough to leave, Tala. And she's a danger to the sanctuary.''

''I know.'' She held his fingers tight. ''It's just

that I hate endings. I've had so many of them.'' She looked up at him. ''Tomorrow afternoon?''

''They'll be here for lunch, load her up and take her afterward.''

''How? Tranquilize her?''

''Not unless absolutely necessary. They have a special van, secure, well ventilated, padded inside. She'll probably sleep all the way.''

Tala nodded.

''You okay with this?''

''I have to be.''

''Sorry to add this to the day you've already had.''

''Parts of it were very nice.'' She smiled at him.

''Come on, let's get out of here. Maybe there'll be time for another nice part before you have to go to the Newsomes.''

But there wasn't time for more than a kiss or two before Tala gathered up her overnight case and walked out onto the back porch of her house to help Pete feed the deer. The night was cold and clear. No moon, but so many stars that the Milky Way really looked like skim milk poured from a jug.

Suddenly Tala moved. ''There. You hear it?''

''What?''

''Baby. Sometimes at night when the wind is right I can hear her roar all the way from the sanctuary.''

''Not possible.''

''Be still. Listen.''

Pete listened. Faintly, carried on the breeze, he heard a roar and the chuffing cough that followed it.

''You hear? It's Baby.''

He smiled, picked up her bag and kissed her

soundly before he closed the door of her truck on her.

As he followed her taillights up the hill to the highway, he opened the window of the Land Rover and heard another series of coughs. Tala was wrong. Definitely a big cat—bigger than a cougar. But not Baby.

THE NEXT MORNING, Vertie took the children to school because Irene asked Tala to have breakfast with her. As she poured her second cup of green tea, Irene asked, "Did you have a nice time yesterday afternoon?"

"I could lie and say I did, but I really didn't."

"Mr. Oxley is a very fine man. He's quite well-off, educated, a gentleman…"

"Probably true, but he's not my type. Sorry, Irene."

Irene looked up, then dropped her eyes and began to stir her cup in small circles. "And Dr. Jacobi? Is he your type?"

Tala sighed and closed her eyes. "We shared a pizza."

"He held your hand."

"Man, do you have a grapevine going. Better than I guessed. Yes, he held my hand."

"Is that all?"

Tala set her cup down. "Why on earth would you ask a question like that?"

Irene turned away, put her napkin to her mouth and whispered, "Because I'm frightened."

"Frightened? Why?"

"I've lost Adam, and Hollis, and in a few years the children will be up and grown, and Vertie is no spring chicken, not that she's any consolation. Oh, well, of course she is, but I'm afraid I'm losing you, too."

Tala was out of her chair and on her knees beside Irene in an instant. "You'll never lose me! You're my family, my children's grandmother, the mother of my husband..."

"Your first husband."

"Irene, stop that. You and I are Ruth and Naomi. Ruth got married again, and she never lost Naomi. As a matter of fact, Ruth made Naomi's life much happier."

Irene stared at her. "Married?"

"Oh, Irene, that's just a figure of speech! Good grief, Pete Jacobi lives in two grubby rooms in front of an examining room."

"If you married, you could live in town. I'd be so happy to buy you a house as a wedding present."

Tala knew how much that cost Irene. Her heart turned over. "You are so dear to me, Irene. From that first Thanksgiving when Adam brought me home to dinner. I was sure it was a setup to embarrass me, but you put me at ease and made me feel a part of the family in the first five minutes."

Irene bolted up from the table so quickly she turned over her cup and spilled tea on the white damask cloth. Tala grabbed the fragile cup to keep it from rolling off the table. Irene stood at the French windows and held on to the sheer curtains as though she needed the support.

For a moment Tala was afraid her mother-in-law was sick. Then she saw Irene's shoulders heave. She was crying. Tala sat on her heels, dumbfounded.

After a few moments Irene pulled a tiny square of white lace-edged linen from the sleeve of her sweater, blew her nose and said without turning around, "You shouldn't thank me."

"I don't understand."

Irene turned and braced herself on the edge of the credenza. "That dinner *was* an ambush. But it certainly didn't turn out the way I thought it would. When Adam told us he loved you and wanted to marry you the minute he graduated from Princeton, and go to work for the Wildlife people instead of going to business school, I thought his father was going to have a stroke right then and there."

Tala felt suddenly cold. She'd known Adam's father hadn't approved of her, but Irene had never shown any sign of disapproval.

"I knew that if we forbade him to see you," Irene continued, "Adam would turn your relationship into some Romeo and Juliet thing and he'd never give you up. So I invited you to Thanksgiving dinner, and I did everything I could to make it so fancy and formal he'd see for himself how unsuitable you were." She tried to smile. "All those forks! Even Vertie didn't know what to do with them."

Tala smiled back. "I got an old copy of *Emily Post* out of the library the week before Thanksgiving and practically memorized it." She stood up and began to blot the tea from the cloth.

Irene stared at her openmouthed, then laughed

softly. "Now that's why I love you. Who would think you'd do something like that?"

"I wanted Adam to be proud of me. I didn't even know how to *pronounce* demitasse. I was sure I'd pour giblet gravy all over my new dress. But you were so sweet. I never guessed…"

"Don't you look at me like that, Tala Newsome." Irene strode to the table, took Tala by the shoulders and shook her. "I knew in the first five minutes you were the daughter I'd never had and always wanted, and the perfect wife for Adam. I've loved you ever since, and don't you doubt that for one tiny little moment or I swear I will—I don't know what I'll do, but it will be something awful."

Tala relaxed. "Was it because I knew which fork to use?"

Irene began to crumble a triangle of toast with her fingers onto the tablecloth. "I was jealous as the dickens the first time I saw the way Adam looked at you. You wait until Cody brings home his first girl. You'll see."

"Was Vertie in on it?"

"Lord, no! By the time the turkey came out of the kitchen, I was so ashamed of myself I wanted to die." She moved around to the other side of the table and sank into her chair again. She didn't even appear to notice the stained cloth.

She reached for Tala's hand and pulled her back into her chair. "I knew that day you were what Adam needed to make him happy, give him the courage to live his own life, and not the life his father planned for him. You were his anchor and his sail."

Tala felt her own eyes begin to smart as she closed her fingers around Irene's.

"I know you're a young woman," Irene said, "that you have to get on with your life, find someone else to love. But why, oh why, does it have to be that Dr. Jacobi? Why couldn't you find someone more…" She hesitated.

Tala said gently, "Someone more like Adam?"

"I know that's not possible. It's just that Dr. Jacobi is so, so…"

"Big?"

Irene sniffed, then giggled. "That's part of it. But he's so rough, and the children don't like him. I don't think he likes them, either."

"Pete has a very hard time showing his emotions," Tala said, then remembering his actions the night before, "A very hard time. But that doesn't mean he doesn't feel."

Irene withdrew her hand and began to dab at the tea stain. "He seems so cold and, I don't know, angry. Bitter."

"I know. But Rachel isn't going to win any Miss Congeniality awards right now, and Cody… Irene, I worry about him."

"So do I. But I think he'll be fine if his life stays simple and on an even keel for a while. He needs to feel safe, not physically safe so much as emotionally safe."

"He was terrified of poor Sophie, Belle and Sweetiepie," Tala said. "This is the kid who thinks nothing of tackling a sixth-grader who outweighs him by fifty pounds, or sliding into home plate and knocking the catcher ass over teakettle.''

"Those are familiar things. The elephants, Dr. Jacobi, it's all so new. I think he's afraid to lose anybody, anything else in his young life. Maybe you should take him home to Bryson's Hollow next weekend.''

"I never told you this, but the last time he spent the night there, he had horrible nightmares all night until I finally sat up in his room in the rocking chair and held his hand all night.''

"Oh, dear.''

"I didn't want to worry you. That's why I haven't pushed. I know why Rachel wants to stay here. It fits her life-style at the moment. She can show her friends that she lives in the finest house in town, not in an old farmhouse in the middle of nowhere. But Cody, my tough little Cody, is scared to come home.''

"The way I'm scared I'll lose you. And the children, too, for that matter. It's not like I have any real rights in their lives.''

"Rights? You're their only grandparent, their caregiver, the person they come to when they don't talk to me about something. I know Rachel had sex education in school, but you're the one who got stuck with answering all her questions about menstruating, aren't you?''

Irene blushed. "Actually, Vertie is.''

"I think my kids are very lucky to have someone they can pour out their problems to. I never had anybody like that. Heaven knows I could never talk to

Sakari. The only time I tried, she flew off the handle and said I was going to turn out no good just like my mother.'' Tala ducked her head.

"Oh, my dear.''

Tala lifted her face and said practically, "I never learned to communicate properly with other people. Until Adam. And then you and Vertie. You'll always be dear to me. Remember Ruth and Naomi?''

Irene sniffled. "I'll bet Naomi never set Ruth up the way I set you up that Thanksgiving. Can you forgive me?''

"For what? Wanting the best for your son? I must have looked like the very worst. Trashy little bastard girl who didn't even know who her daddy was? Raised by dirt farmers in Bryson's Hollow and never been out of Tennessee? I'd probably have acted like Adam's daddy and forbidden my son to see me.''

Irene laughed, then suddenly serious, caught Tala's hand. "Do you love this Pete Jacobi?''

"As long as he and the kids hate each other, it doesn't matter what I feel for him.'' She leaned back in her chair. "I wish with all my heart he was somebody safe, somebody quiet and gentle like Adam. Instead…''

"Nothing and nobody is safe, Tala.''

Tala came around the table and hugged Irene.

"Well, this is a pretty picture, I must say. Y'all been sipping on the bourbon with breakfast?'' Vertie said from the doorway.

"No, but I wish I approved of bourbon before lunch,'' Irene said, raising her chin and dragging her fingers under her eyes to clear away the tears without smudging her mascara.

"Somebody die?"

"We are alive," Tala said. "And getting livelier by the minute." She stood up, leaned down and kissed Irene on the cheek. "Now, I've got to get to work. Can't afford to be late. It ticks off the girls."

MARY ANN HILDEBRAND was a solid rectangle nearly six feet tall with cropped graying hair, skin that had seen too much sun and bright blue eyes that crinkled at the corners when she smiled, which was often.

Her husband was whipcord thin, closer to fifty than forty, and had a full bushy beard that went from brown at the corners to gray around his mouth. As they climbed out of their van in their wrinkled safari clothes and heavy boots, Tala thought of Jack Sprat and his wife.

The way they put away heaps of Mace's roast-beef grilled sandwiches reinforced the image. Tala sat quietly beside Pete on Mace's couch and listened to zoo talk and vet talk and safari talk and sanctuary talk.

"Oh, yes," Mary Ann said to Tala, "there's a network of sanctuaries across the country. Someone has to take the abandoned and abused castoffs of man's vanity. Might as well be us." She grinned at Tala. "Now, since we've got a trip ahead of us, maybe we'd better meet our passenger."

"You check her out, pet," Jim said, "while I finish this excellent coffee. My God, Dr. Mace, I'd forgotten what a terrific cook you are."

Baby sat in her cage and watched Tala and Mary Ann from narrow golden eyes.

Mary Ann dropped onto her haunches in front of the cage. "How's my girl? Ready for a ride to your new home?" Baby leaned over to get her ears scratched. "She's a young one. Probably no more than two." She bent to look at Baby's shoulder. "Wound looks clean. Pete's a fine surgeon. Jim worked with him before..." She glanced around at Tala.

"I know about what happened."

"Good, because I am no good at keeping secrets." She laughed, and Baby jumped. "See? Jim says I laugh like a lion. Probably right. Never thought I'd spend my life around big cats." She rubbed Baby's ears. "Got a master's in art history. Wanted to work in a nice, clean museum."

"What changed your mind?"

"Not what. Who. Jim Hildebrand with his dimples and his dreams." She stood. "Now I wouldn't have it any other way. Come on, let's move that van back here and get the princess loaded."

"We call her Baby."

"Fine. Baby, come with Mommy."

Baby loaded as though she were walking up the ramp to her coronation. Tala stood in the circle of Pete's arms and tried not to cry.

Then they loaded the zoo food and the rest of Tala's leftover venison into the storage portion of their van, which was set up with refrigeration to keep everything fresh.

As the Hildebrands were ready to move out, Jim

leaned out the window. "What we were talking about? If you find out anything, anything at all, you call me. We'll mobilize the troops. It's not going to happen if we can stop it." He waved and drove off.

"What was he talking about?" Tala asked.

"I'll tell you later when I'm sure of my facts."

"Tell me now."

He kissed her nose. "Give me until tomorrow. Meanwhile, would you indulge me and spend tonight at the Newsomes again?"

"Pete…"

"I think I may have a line on what's been happening to you. I want to check it out."

Tala froze. "Pete, please, don't do anything dangerous."

"No danger. Promise. Just stay at the Newsomes tonight. I'd rather you stayed here with me, but I don't think Irene would like it."

"She knows I've been seeing you."

"Seeing? Is that what you've been doing?" He looked down at her with an innocent grin.

She hit him. "Come on, we've got elephants to feed."

"WHAT ARE YOU going to do about Tala?" Mace asked Pete as they sat in Mace's trailer eating Denver omelets that evening.

Pete ran his hand over his head. "Nothing I can do at the moment, is there?"

"Quite a lot, I'd say."

Pete stood and began to pace. "We've got some problems."

Mace peered at him over his glasses. "You're not still worrying about Sunday afternoon's disaster?"

Pete dropped onto the sofa, spread his legs in front of him and leaned back to close his eyes. "Sunday was only part of it. Say what you like about Irene Newsome, she understands the realities of life. She wants somebody who can give Tala what she deserves. I live in two rooms attached to an elephant enclosure, and I'm perfectly happy with the arrangement. But I can't ask Tala to share them with me. She wants her family back under one roof. A decent one." He pointed toward the enclosure across the way. "That ain't it."

"If you're actively searching for a reason to screw up both your lives, I'm certain I could come up with better excuses than that."

"How's this for an excuse? Her kids don't like me. One of them is scared to death of elephants, which, you may have noticed, is what I do. And that is not negotiable. The girls are as much a part of my life as her family is of hers."

"Granted. But opinions of small boys can be changed with time and effort."

"Opinions of mothers-in-law can't."

"Of course they can. Irene wants to see that family happy as much as you do."

"Just not with me. Besides, I know nothing about kids. I definitely do not want to screw up somebody else's, especially a pair who have been jacked around by life the way those two have."

"You survived."

"Yeah, right. Dr. Normal at your service."

Mace picked up the dirty plate from Pete's place, scraped it into the sink, rinsed it and set it into the dishwasher. For a long moment neither man spoke, then Mace said, "We all do the best we can with the hand we're dealt. Many of us never know the love of a woman, but you have been granted the love of two. Unless you really want to lose the love of the second, I would suggest you figure out a way to enhance and preserve the experience." Without another word he picked up his jacket and walked out the door of the trailer.

Pete surged to his feet, ready to follow his father. How dare the old man preach to him?

Then he sank back on the sofa. If Val hadn't died, would he have been able to keep her? She was carrying his child. If she'd told him, he would have married her in a heartbeat.

But would any woman marry him knowing that he was "doing the right thing"? Val wouldn't have. She would have walked out and taken that job in Los Angeles. He'd always told himself he loved her. Now finally he admitted that he hadn't loved her *enough*. She knew it instinctively. That was why they had fought that last day. He had protested, and she'd been hurt, but she'd known in her heart.

What about Tala? Did he love her enough to marry her, kids, in-laws and all? Or did he want to spend the rest of his life alone?

No, he did not. He'd better find some way to make a decent life for all of them—and that included Rachel and Cody. They were as much a package deal as Mace and the girls.

He stood and went to find his father. He needed to apologize to him.

And then he needed to ask his advice, something he'd never done in all his years.

CHAPTER SIXTEEN

"WHY ARE YOU still out there?" Pete asked when Tala answered the phone at the farmhouse.

"Not hello? Gee, I miss you?"

"I want you out of there."

"Pete, you're starting to frighten me. What is this about?"

"Just go. I'll call you later."

"Fine." When Tala put down the telephone, she felt a stab of fear. He was right that nobody seemed to bother the farmhouse when she wasn't around, but that could change.

This time she packed a suitcase—a worn, old one that Adam had taken to college with him. The weather had begun to warm up slightly. It was still cold, but the skies were clear. The deer would feed early tonight.

As she opened the door of her truck and began to climb in, she heard a sound and froze.

She was obviously losing her mind. Baby was a hundred miles away by now, safe in her new home. So how could she be hearing what she was hearing?

Tala sat behind the wheel, locked the doors and turned on the headlights. What if Baby had not been alone? Was that what Pete was worried about? Had the Hildebrands told him they'd had reports of another big cat in the area?

The deer could not escape a hunting lion. Nor would a human being.

She was safe enough in her truck, and surely there would be no way a big cat could stray into Hollendale, or even into the suburbs, without being spotted.

She longed to stop at the sanctuary, but she'd missed dinner at Irene's, and she wanted to be there to tuck Rachel and Cody in. She'd call Pete from there.

At ten o'clock when she finally got to the phone, Mace answered. "Not here at the moment, m'dear."

The short hair at the back of her neck lifted. "Where is he, Dr. Mace?" She tried to keep her voice level.

"Gone off on some errand or other. Very secret. Some sort of mission for Jim Hildebrand."

"Please, please, ask him to call me when he gets in. No matter what time it is."

She climbed into bed and lay there unable to sleep. Surely Pete wouldn't be crazy enough to try to track a big cat in the woods at night. The odds were all on the cat's side.

She flung back the covers and began to get dressed. She had to find him.

As she reached for her sweater, the telephone on her bedside table rang. She grabbed it quickly before it could wake the household. "Yes?" she said breathlessly.

She collapsed on her bed when she heard his

voice. "Pete, where have you been? I've been worried sick."

"Why?"

"I heard the roar again. It can't possibly be Baby. You've been tracking it, haven't you?"

She heard his sharp intake of breath. "I've been driving, stopping, rolling down my window and listening."

"I'm right, aren't I? That's what Jim Hildebrand told you. There's another big cat loose out there in the woods, isn't there?"

"Not to my knowledge," he said carefully.

"Then what is it?"

"Don't come to work tomorrow. Mace and I will come to Irene's to talk to you all."

"I hate this cloak-and-dagger stuff, Pete."

"I think we're going to need Irene's help in her official capacity with the county. Better to talk face-to-face. I'm ninety-nine percent certain that no one's in any danger tonight." Then he took a deep breath. "I love you more than life."

The line went dead.

She flung herself down on her bed fully clothed. Didn't Pete understand that loving someone meant trusting that person? Didn't he realize how much worse she worried when she didn't know what was happening?

How could he love her and not know that?

"I'LL TAKE THE CHILDREN to school and be back before they get here," Tala said the next morning after she'd warned Irene and Vertie to expect visitors.

"Not today you won't," Irene told her. "Teacher's in-service today. I hope you didn't try to wake them."

Tala sank onto the nearest chair. "I don't even know their school schedules any longer."

She looked up at Irene, who stood smiling at her sadly.

"Maybe you're right. Maybe it is time for me to start looking for a house to rent in town. It may be ratty, but Rachel will just have to put up with it. And I'll look for a tenant for the farm, somebody who'll take care of it until I know what to do about it."

Irene sat across from Tala. "Oh, dear, you sound so sad! It's the right thing to do. I'll help you find a house to *buy,* and I'll give you the down payment and the closing costs. It's the least I can do."

Tala sighed. "If I have to borrow money from you, I will. But borrow, not take."

"Whatever you say. What changed your mind?"

"I can't do it alone any longer. I kept trying to convince myself I could be true to Adam's wishes, and do what Rachel and Cody and you and Vertie all wanted and still manage to be my own person."

"What do *you* want?" Irene sounded more and more concerned.

Tala slumped in her chair. "I don't know anymore." She looked up at Irene. "Maybe I just want to matter."

Before Irene could answer, the doorbell rang.

Vertie walked in ahead of Pete and Mace. "Look what the cat dragged in." She pointed toward the table. "Y'all want some coffee? Breakfast?"

"No, thank you." Pete's eyes were fixed on Tala's face. He'd always looked serious, but now he looked formidable, like a knight ready to go into battle. "Sit down, please, everyone," he said. "We have some serious talking to do."

"What on earth?" Vertie said, but she sat nonetheless.

"First off, I'd better give you some background," Pete said. "Unless you want to, Tala?"

She shook her head.

Pete nodded and started his story with Tala's finding of the wounded lioness in the road on her way home. Vertie was fascinated, Irene appalled, but when they tried to interrupt, Pete stopped them.

"Baby's been moved now to a sanctuary outside of Knoxville."

"Thank God," Irene said. "A lion? In Hollandale County? Did you tell the sheriff?"

"Not yet."

"Well, he sure doesn't need to know now she's gone," Vertie said, crossing her ankles. "Just make a bunch of to-do in the newspapers and maybe get people riled up about your elephants. Take my advice, keep your mouth shut."

"I'm afraid that won't be possible," Mace said. "I think Tala's lion had company."

So there *was* another lion. Tala closed her eyes. They'd have to bring in the sheriff, maybe the Fish and Game people, hunt the poor thing down and probably some trigger-happy deputy would kill it. If it didn't kill somebody first.

"I don't know how much you know about game laws in Tennessee," Pete said.

Vertie raised an eyebrow at him. "Hunted all my life. And my grandson was a game warden."

"Certainly no one has come before the county council seeking approval to keep a lion," Irene said. "I may sleep through those things occasionally, but *that* I would have remembered."

"Nobody got permission."

"So someone owns a lion illegally?" Irene's hand flew to her chest. "You're saying it's *escaped?*"

"No, I don't think it's escaped. And I don't think it's alone."

"What?" Tala jumped up. "More than one?"

Pete's hand reached for her instinctively. Then he dropped it and turned back to Vertie and Irene. "There's a network of sanctuaries for wild animals that stretches across the country. They keep their ears pretty close to the ground to locate animals that are being abused or have been abandoned. Or worse."

"Worse? What could be worse?" Vertie asked.

"When Jim and Mary Ann Hildebrand came to pick up our lioness on Monday, Jim told Mace and me that there's been rumblings across the sanctuary system in the last couple of months about a private exotic animal hunt. Illegal in Tennessee."

Irene gasped. Tala covered her mouth with her napkin. Vertie merely narrowed her eyes.

"Pete and I had no reason to think our lioness was anything other than an aberration. But Jim Hilde-brand thinks she may have been one of several big cats illegally acquired for this hunt, and that she may have been shot when she escaped.''

Vertie and Irene sat openmouthed and stunned.

''After what I heard last night, I think Jim may be right.''

Seemingly unaware that Irene and Vertie watched him, he put his arm around Tala's waist and held her against his side. ''That's where I was last night,'' he told her softly. ''I didn't want to worry you until I was a lot surer. I think that's why someone tried to keep you away from home at night. Big cats tend to roar after dark. With the night breeze and no traffic, the sound would carry farther. Someone was afraid you'd hear them. And you did, only you assumed you were hearing Baby.''

''So they ran me off the road and set my barn on fire.''

''My guess is that the organizers probably hired a few men to look after the animals until the hunt. Those lowlifes wanted you far away.''

''And those same goons shot Baby?''

''I think so. Only before they could find her to finish her off, she wandered onto the road where you picked her up. They probably have no idea whether or not she's still alive. I hope they're looking over their shoulders every time they go into the woods wondering whether she's ready to pounce on them from a tree.''

''Young man, this is all very interesting, but what proof do you have?'' Irene asked.

''Last night I heard the cats.''

''Coming from where, precisely?''

"I'm only certain of the general area. But I'm sure enough of what I heard so that I called the Hilde-brands this morning. They're on their way, but they won't get here for a couple of hours at least."

"Sound follows the streambed and the valleys, Irene," Vertie said. "You'd know that if you'd ever been on a coon hunt. You can hear the blasted hounds baying, but you don't have any idea which direction they're calling from. Darned irritating at two in the morning."

"I cannot regret I have never been coon hunting, Vertie," Irene said. "Pete, maybe what you heard was a cougar."

"Cougars are solitary except at breeding season. The sounds I heard came from more than one big cat. And I saw lights in the woods. Just a couple of lanterns, and just a flash, but I saw what I saw. They're up there, all right, the cats and the men who are looking after them until the hunters arrive to shoot them down like fish in a barrel."

"Where did you see the lights?" Vertie asked quietly.

Something in her voice made Pete look at her. She had leaned forward with her elbows on her knees. "All I can tell you is that I was about twenty miles past Tala's place by road, but the road twists and turns so much, I can't say for sure. It's pretty confusing up there at night. It could only be a couple of hollows over from her place as the crow flies."

Vertie leaned back and closed her eyes. "I am a foolish old woman."

"What?" Irene jerked around to stare at her. "You are nothing of the sort."

"Oh, yes, I am. That could be my land they're on."

Vertie glanced at Mace. "I said I was planning to log that land in a couple of years, but for the last two years I've rented it out. There's an old cabin on it that my daddy built with his own hands. Not fancy, but it's shelter."

"And someone's using it?"

"I didn't think anybody'd been there except for the occasional weekend deer hunt during the season. I don't drive up there. Should 'a' known. They paid me a darn sight too much money for it."

"Who?" Mace asked.

Vertie waved a hand. "Some consortium of hunters out of Charlotte and Richmond. They got some fancy name. I haven't looked at the lease in a while. It's at my lawyer's office."

"Who do the checks come from?"

"Direct deposit twice a year from the corporation."

"Then you better go roust that lawyer out and have him fax us a copy of that lease right now," Irene said. She turned to Pete. "Luckily, I have a separate line to the fax because of county council business."

Vertie nodded and pulled herself up. Suddenly she seemed like an old woman.

"Vertilene Martindale Newsome, you get the lead out of those jeans," Irene said, grabbing her by the arm. "This is not your fault, do you hear me? We are going to fix this."

"Oh, Irene, all those poor animals…"

"Were alive last night. At least Pete thinks they were. They may not be alive long if you don't call your lawyer for those papers." Irene turned to Pete. "And you and I, young man, are going to use the other line in the den to call Sheriff Craig and tell him to deputize the entire county if he has to. We are going to stop those bastards!"

"What bastards, Gram?" Cody said from the doorway of the living room.

"You weren't supposed to hear that." Irene blushed. "But in this case it's apt." She grabbed Pete's arm. "Come on. Time's a-wastin'."

"Rach still asleep?" Tala asked.

"Yes'm, as usual."

"Go get her up and dressed, and the both of you come down here."

He grumbled, but he went. Tala turned to Mace. "Maybe you're right. Maybe they're all caged. But if even one of them is wandering around loose, I'd prefer to have my children behind ten-foot fences with razor wire on the top of them and an armed man with experience looking after them."

"Good thinking," Mace said. "But what about Cody's fear of elephants?"

Tala looked at him a moment. "Let me talk to him."

"Of course."

"The lawyer's faxing the lease," Vertie said as she came back into the room. "The organization calls itself Stateside Safaris.'' She raised an eyebrow. ''Isn't that sweet? The checks come from a bank in Charlotte. The sheriff can probably trace the members, but it's going to take some time.''

''Time's what we don't have,'' Pete said.

''The sheriff is on his way,'' Irene said.

''What can we do in the meantime?'' Tala asked.

''Mom? Why'd you make the dork get me up?'' Rachel stood in the doorway with her hands on her hips and her feet apart. She wore jeans, a sweater that hung to her knees and a look of pure annoyance.

''Rachel, Cody,'' Tala said. ''Come into the den. I have to talk to you.'' She pulled the sliding doors that separated the den from the living room closed behind her and faced her children. ''We have a problem, and we need your help.''

''What kind of help?'' Cody said, his eyes wide and frightened.

She sank to her knees and took his hands. ''I want you and Rachel to be in the safest place possible, so you have to go with Dr. Mace and the others to the elephant sanctuary just for a few hours.''

''You promised you'd come with me next time,'' Cody said.

''You don't have to see the elephants, Cody bear. You'll be inside Dr. Mace's trailer. And before you know it, I'll be right there and then we can go meet the girls together, just the way I promised.''

''Where will you be?''

''I have to stay here for a little while, but I'll be perfectly okay. If I know you're both safe, I'll have one less thing to worry about.'' She turned to look at Rachel, whose eyes were wide and serious.

"What is the danger, Mom?'' she asked. "Is it some kind of deadly virus or something?''

Tala shook her head. "Actually, it may be nothing at all. We're just taking precautions. So, Cody bear, will you be okay?''

Cody looked at her for a moment without speaking, then he said, "Can Gram come with us?''

"If you ask her nicely, I'll bet she will.''

He sighed. "Well, okay. But you still have to keep your promise.''

She hugged him tight. "That's my Cody. Come on, guys.''

Five minutes later Tala stood on the front step and waved as Mace drove Cody, Rachel and Irene away.

SHERIFF CRAIG'S SQUAD CAR pulled up ten minutes after Mace drove out.

"Would you like to tell me what the Sam Hill's going on here?'' he asked as he came into the living area.

Pete and Vertie told him. "Hell, if there's any chance of this being true we got to check it out.'' He looked out the front window. "Where is Billie Joe anyway? He was supposed to be right on my tail.'' He hit a button on his radio. "Billie Joe? You lost?''

Only static answered him. "Dadgummit, the fool's turned off his radio.''

The sheriff called his office. "Y'all heard from Billie Joe since I left?'' He listened a moment, then raised his head. "Nothing. Where the hell is that boy? See if you can raise him. Tell him to get over here pronto."

Vertie spoke up. "We can't wait. Time's wasting. We got to go out there and check it out."

"And walk into half of the state of North Carolina carrying elephant guns?" the sheriff said. "No, Miss Vertie, you stay here."

"Hell, no." Vertie dragged her car keys out of the front pocket of her jeans. "There's an old logging trail into the place that nobody knows about. We'll be on top of them before they know we're there." She arched an eyebrow. "You'll never find it without me."

The telephone rang. Tala picked it up, listened, and handed it to Craig. "Yeah, Mabel?" He listened a moment, then said, "You call every deputy we got, and stay off the police band. Tell 'em to use their cell phones. Tell 'em to meet us at..." He looked a question at Vertie.

"Hoskins Crossing out by Miller's Hollow."

"You get that, Mabel? Good. Quick, now. Bye."

He dropped the phone in the cradle. "After Irene called, I asked Mabel to see if there was any big influx at the hotel or the motels. Not families—just men in groups or by themselves."

"And?" Pete asked.

"Last couple of days we got us maybe twenty middle-aged men driving fancy new SUV's and carrying enough armament to start World War Three. I'd say whatever's happening is happening pretty soon."

"Let's go," Pete said.

"Wait a minute," Craig said. "How does this hunt work, Dr. Jacobi? If they turn loose lions and tigers and chase 'em through the woods, we could be in big trouble. I'm not having my men facing tigers."

Pete shook his head. "The hunters group around one of the cages with their rifles already loaded and cocked. At a given signal, somebody opens the cage door. As the cat runs out, everybody shoots. Only one cat at a time."

"That ain't huntin'! That's murder."

"Not if I can help it." Vertie started for the door. Tala followed her.

"Where do you think you're going?" Pete asked.

"I'll ride with Vertie, of course."

"No," Pete said. "You go to the sanctuary."

"The children are safe, and Vertie and I will be even safer. We'll have half the sheriff's department looking after us."

"Then stay here out of the way."

"I've spent my life out of the way. Sitting by the phone and worrying about what was happening to the people I loved." She stuck out her chin and blinked back the tears. "Don't you understand that waiting alone to hear whether your man is safe is much worse than being there and seeing for yourself?"

He wrapped his arms around her and kissed her. After a moment she pulled away, picked up her purse and ran toward the door. "Come on, Vertie, we'll take my truck. It's got four-wheel drive."

FOUR SHERIFF'S PATROL CARS blocked the road at Miller's Hollow. Tala passed them slowly while Vertie pointed to the nearly overgrown opening to a small side road.

Tala lowered the windows on the truck. She couldn't hear anything that didn't belong in the woods—no lions, no tigers, and so far, no gunshots.

The truck crept through the brush that threatened to obliterate the road. It bucked and bounced over the ruts. Behind her, the string of cars, lights now off, sirens silent, followed sedately. There was no way to drive this terrible excuse for a road fast.

"Around this bend we come out on the far side of a little valley," Vertie said. "If we stay under the trees, we ought to be able to see without being seen."

Tala parked, climbed out of the car, shut the door silently and crept through the brush. A moment later she felt Pete's hand on her arm—none too lightly.

"Get back in that truck," he said as he looked past her.

She nodded and was turning back when she saw his eyes widen. "Good God," he whispered.

The sight stopped her in her tracks. Through the trees stood a small meadow surrounded by freshly felled pine and oak trees. At least fifteen metal cages and enclosures were scattered over the area. Inside these confined spaces, lions and tigers paced and snarled.

Beyond them, across the same small stream that wound through Bryson's Hollow, a half-dozen large camouflage tents had been set up. Fifteen or twenty men, most in camouflage gear, lounged in camp chairs outside the tents. And stacked against them were rifles and shotguns. An arsenal.

"Holy hell!" Sheriff Craig whispered. "We better take 'em by surprise and hope they cave in. They may have planned to shoot animals, but I don't think any of 'em got into this to shoot lawmen. At least I hope they didn't, because if they fight we are sure outgunned."

"Shouldn't we call the Staties and wait for them?" one of the deputies whispered.

"No," Pete snapped. "Any minute they may decide to start shooting the first lion."

"Yeah," Craig said. "Pretty things, aren't they? I'd hate to have to shoot one myself."

"I've brought my pistol loaded with tranquilizer darts," Pete said. "If one gets let out, I can immobilize it with one good shot. The Hildebrands are bringing heavy-duty guns so we can tranquilize the rest, and in the meantime, Dad's loading up everything we've got and standing by just in case."

"I'll pass the word to the boys not to shoot unless they have to. Vertie, you and Tala go back to your truck and get out of here."

Vertie nodded and started back up the trail.

Tala was following when a shout from the camp stopped her. Billie Joe was running down the other side, waving his hands and yelling. "Break camp, break camp! The sheriff's on his way!"

At that point a man came out from under the nearest tent flap and stood with a rifle across his chest.

"Oxley!" Pete said.

"Yeah, and that's a Purdey double rifle he's carrying in his hands," the sheriff finished.

The camp below was a madhouse. Oxley shouted. "Let 'em loose!" he shouted and broke for the woods.

"Damnation! You men are under arrest!" Craig yelled and fired a shot into the air.

"Don't shoot at the cats!" Pete shouted as he raced down the track.

Tala took Vertie's arm and hurried back to the truck. She had to get the elderly woman to safety.

As she stumbled through the brush, she could hear panicky shouts, car engines revving behind her as the frightened hunters tried to escape.

The running deputies had raised a swirl of dust on the trail. She could barely see. This must be what warfare was like.

People shouted, guns popped.

Above the din came the screams and roars of terrified animals.

The blow knocked her onto her knees.

"Where's your truck?"

She blinked up at the furious face of Vince Oxley.

"Vertie!" she shouted. "Get out of here!"

"Tala?"

Oxley whirled at the sound.

"Go! Now!" Tala grabbed Oxley's calf with both hands and bit him.

"Goddamn!" He kicked; she held on. Any minute now he'd either shoot her or bring that rifle butt down on her head.

She rolled away from him and heard her truck accelerating up the hill. For once, Vertie had listened to her.

He hauled her to her feet. "I need a car *now*."

"I'm fresh out. Try a squad car."

He glanced over his shoulder. "Yeah." He began to drag her with him.

Back in the clearing the noise was beginning to die down. He glanced over her shoulder and then back at her. No more smarmy charm. What she saw in his eyes was pure hatred.

"Please don't shoot me," she whispered. "My children need me. I'll come with you."

"The hell you will," he snarled.

CHAPTER SEVENTEEN

ONE MOMENT she was cowering beside Oxley, the next she was flying through the air to land with a thud that knocked the breath out of her and left her gasping.

She was alive! He'd tossed her into the brush like a rag doll, but he hadn't shot her or clubbed her.

She heard his running footsteps and then the growl of a heavy engine. Hadn't they left even one deputy to guard the squad cars?

She struggled to her feet. Her shoulder hurt, her back hurt. But she had to tell the sheriff about Oxley's escape. She bent over to get the breath back into her lungs and then hobbled toward the camp. She kept to the trees where she could hide if any of the other hunters tried to escape her way.

As she broke through the trees, she could see a circle of deputies around the hunters, all of whom were on their knees with their hands in the air. Even from this distance, she could hear them shouting angrily for their lawyers.

Pete stood beside the open door to one of the cages. She prayed the hunters hadn't had time to release any of the animals.

She cupped her hands around her mouth. ''Pete!

Pete! Sheriff Craig!'' She pointed over her shoulder. ''Oxley's gone that way. I think he's stolen a squad car.''

Pete saw her and ran up the hill. ''Tala! What are you doing here?''

''I bumped into Oxley.'' She rubbed her shoulder.

''Damn!'' Craig snarled something unintelligible to one of his deputies, who began to walk toward her.

He was twenty yards closer than Pete when he slid to a stop.

''Oh, man.'' His eyes were huge.

Pete froze, the deputies froze, the prisoners froze. All eyes turned toward her.

''What?'' she said.

''Stand very still,'' Pete said. ''Whatever you do, do not turn around.''

''What is it?'' she whispered.

''Can't get a clear shot,'' the deputy whispered.

''Is it Oxley?''

''No, ma'am,'' the deputy whispered. ''Behind you is the biggest, blackest, meanest-looking sum'bitch I have ever seen, and if I can get a clear shot at it, I will kill it deader than a doornail.''

''No, you will not,'' Pete snapped. ''You might hit Tala.''

Her knees began to shake. ''Pete? What do I do?''

''I've got a better angle than this guy has,'' Pete said. ''I am going to draw my pistol very slowly, and when I say 'go,' I want you to throw yourself as far to your left as you can and roll away as fast as possible.''

"What's he doing?" she asked in a small voice.

"Crouching behind you lashing his tail. He's scared."

"He's not the only one."

"I'll get you out of this, Tala. Trust me."

Pete knelt slowly, cradled the pistol in both hands. She looked straight down its long, black barrel. "Get ready," he said. "Go!"

She heard the pop of the pistol and felt the wind from the dart as she rolled away.

She heard the animal scream and wrapped her arms across her head, expecting to feel claws or crushing jaws against her neck. A moment later, Craig yelled, "Okay—run."

She sprang to her feet and ran down the hill, afraid to look behind her.

Strong arms grabbed her.

For an instant she buried her face against Craig's chest, then broke free and ran to Pete.

A deputy was pulling him to his feet. In front of him, tongue lolling, eyes rolling, lay the panting leopard.

"He'll be out like a light in a couple of minutes," Pete said. She threw her arms around him.

Her hand came away wet and covered with blood. "Pete, you're hurt."

Pete looked at the ripped sleeve of his jacket. "He grazed me with a paw when he fell." He held her away from him. "Are you all right? Did Oxley hurt you?"

"I'm fine."

"You may need a shot," Craig said to Pete. "Jackson, how soon'll the ambulances be here?"

"Not for me," Pete said.

"We got us one case of angina, two possible heart attacks and a broken ankle. One of our fearless hunters fell down the hill in his haste to get away. All the others we're shoe-horning into the squad cars. Except for that fool, Billie Joe." The sheriff smiled grimly. "The Staties just showed up to give him a private ride. I'm leaving half-a-dozen deputies here and the others will come back once the prisoners are locked up. I'll follow you in one of the cars, Frank," he called to the young deputy who'd faced down the leopard. "You follow me. That way, if we run into Oxley, we'll deal with him. He's a smart one. Started a panic and then ducked into the woods." The sheriff shook his head. "I can't believe he stole one of my squad cars. Don't that beat all?"

"Is Vertie all right?"

"She drove around to the front, stopped one of the two squad cars I left on the road and sent 'em back to get you where she'd left you and Oxley. By the time they got there, Oxley was long gone. But we'll catch him. I've already alerted the Staties."

"He's got your police scanner, Sheriff," Pete said. "He'll be able to monitor your calls."

"We'll still get him. At the moment we got us a bigger problem."

"Like him?" Tala said, pointing to the slumbering leopard.

"We managed to stop 'em from turning most of the cats loose, but those hoods who were working for Oxley say we got us three full-grown male lions, at least two tigers and one leopard loose in these woods.''

Pete groaned.

"Well at least we got the leopard. I'll get a couple of my boys to drag him into an empty cage before he wakes up," Craig continued. "I sure hate to notify the public, but we got to. Tell 'em to stay indoors and bring in the children and the pets until we recover the rest of the cats.''

"Wait!" Pete said. "The only inhabited farm within miles is Tala's. I think we can get those cats back into their cages before we have to tell anybody about them.''

"How the hell we gonna do that?"

"Open their cages and put fresh meat in them. They're scared and confused. They want a familiar den and I doubt if these bozos have been feeding them much. They should come back in a couple of hours if they feel safe.''

"And if they don't?"

"Mace will bring our tranquilizer guns. I had to guess at the dose in the darts I'm carrying, but Mace has had time to check the weights and load our rifles with the proper dosages. And the Hildebrands ought to be here soon with extra rifles. We'll arm your best sharpshooters and let your other deputies back them up. Hopefully, we'll have all the loose animals tranquilized and back in their cages before the public finds out about this.''

Tala caught her breath. "Pete, you need to have your arm looked after.''

"Time enough for that after we save those cats."
He touched her cheek. "Just think how'd you feel if
it was Baby."

"You said human beings came first, remember."

"These cats haven't done anything wrong. If
there's a chance to save them, then I've got to take
it. Can you see that?"

Of course she could. But she could also see that
he was walking into danger, risking his life. It was
his to risk, just as Adam's had been. But the ones
left behind were the ones who suffered.

He watched her. "If anything had happened to you
back there, I don't think I could have survived. So I
know how you feel. I love you, so it's got to be your
choice. Do I go or stay?"

The deputies didn't know or understand big cats.
They'd be on edge in the woods and would shoot
first and ask questions later. They might even shoot
one another.

If Pete were with them, that wouldn't happen. If
someone had to make a life-or-death decision about
one of those cats, Pete should be the one to make it.

She sighed. "Okay," she said. "Here's the deal.
You have to promise to be extra careful. And if it
comes to a choice between you and the animal, you'd
better put your own safety first and come back to me
in one piece."

"I promise."

She smiled up at Pete and nodded, although her
heart lurched so painfully against her chest she wondered whether she'd cracked a rib when she fell.

"Good." Pete held out his hand to the sheriff.

"Lend me your cell phone. I'll call Dad. Irene can watch the kids."

"Vertie and I will drive there right now," Tala said.

"Hey, folks, looks like the marines landed just in time," came a cheerful voice. Down the hill from the parking area trotted Jim Hildebrand, a heavy rifle slung over his shoulder.

"Jim, thank God." Pete clasped his hand. "We've got six hours of daylight left and five cats to capture in these woods."

"Whoa!"

"Had six," the sheriff said, pointing to the sleeping leopard. "Doc took care of that one."

"Just in time," Tala added.

"Those guys kill any?" Jim asked.

"All safe except for the five they turned loose."

"Think we can get 'em back?" Craig asked.

"Piece of cake." Jim laughed and unslung his rifle. "I'll tell Mary Ann to bring some bait, then we'll organize your guys, Sheriff, if that's all right."

"Fine." The sheriff sounded relieved. "I've got a fugitive to catch."

Pete walked up the hill toward the parking area with his arm around Tala. She leaned against him and wished she could change her mind about his joining the hunt.

"Maybe Jim doesn't need you," she said quietly.

"He needs us all. Mace included. Believe me."

At the top of the hill, Pete used the sheriff's cell phone to call the sanctuary. After five rings the answering machine picked up. "Dad? If you're there, pick up.'' A moment later, Pete said, ''He must still be in the workroom loading darts.'' He spoke to the machine, ''Jim and Mary Ann are here. We're missing five big ones. We'll meet you at the sanctuary or along the road to pick up our equipment.''

Tala put an arm around Pete's waist. ''Please, at least stop at the sanctuary long enough to let your dad bandage that arm.''

''I'm fine. Bleeding's just about stopped. I've had worse than this. My patients often don't appreciate my help.''

She looked over at a deputy standing beside a state police car. ''Is that Billie Joe in the back seat? I can't believe he'd be a party to this.''

The sheriff walked up beside them. ''Young idiot's feeling real sorry for himself. Talking his fool head off to anybody who'll listen.'' Craig looked pointedly at Tala. ''And he's got some interesting things to say.''

''Why would he do something like this?''

''Money. He told us that a pair of the heavies Oxley hired to baby-sit the cats were the ones trying to get you off your place at night. Oxley told 'em they couldn't take the chance you'd hear the cats.''

''I didn't like Oxley much, but he seemed like a decent enough person.''

Craig looked from Pete to Tala, then said quietly, ''Honey, I don't know how to say this, and I sure don't know how to tell Irene, but Oxley tossed that fancy Purdey double rifle of his in the bushes when he took off in my squad car and...''

She felt her knees begin to shake. The sheriff looked so serious.

Pete held her up with his good arm.

"I been keeping this between me and the state crime lab," the sheriff continued. "The rifle that killed Adam used a .577 nitro express shell. So far as I know, the Purdey is the only one that does."

The world spun. Pete held her. Barely registering, she saw Vertie climb out of the front seat of Tala's truck and run to her. "Tala, honey, thank God you're safe. I didn't want to leave you, but I thought if—"

"You did the right thing," Tala said softly.

She couldn't take in what the sheriff said. Oxley? With the same kind of rifle that killed Adam? She had spent an entire afternoon with him. He'd been out to her land, her house...

Tala took a deep breath and turned back to the sheriff. "The day we went house-hunting, Vince told me he'd never seen the farm, but before he got there he said there was a wonderful location for a house on the rise across the stream. I didn't think anything of it at the time, but how could he know if he'd never been there?"

CHAPTER EIGHTEEN

PETE DROVE Tala's truck with Tala and Vertie squeezed in beside him. Sheriff Craig and another deputy followed in the only two squad cars not transporting prisoners. So far there had been no sightings of Oxley or the sheriff's car, but Sheriff Craig was certain Oxley wouldn't make it out of the state.

"I'll drop you and Vertie at the sanctuary, then Dad and I can go back to the woods in the Land Rover," Pete said. "By the time we get there, Mary Ann and Jim will probably already have all the animals under lock and key."

"You're saying that to make me feel better," Tala said.

"I know Jim. He thinks like a big cat."

The truck was running beside the tall fence that marked the start of the sanctuary. Pete turned a corner and jammed on his brakes. The sheriff skidded to a halt behind him and jumped out of his car.

Twenty feet in front of them stood Sweetiepie.

"She's out!" Pete said as he opened the truck door. "Somebody left the gate open."

Sweetiepie raised her trunk and began to trumpet, then sank to her knees. Tala jumped out and ran toward her. "She's hurt."

"No, that's what she was taught to do to let somebody get on her. She wants me up there," Pete said. He climbed onto her massive thigh, grabbed her ear and hauled himself up. The moment he settled on her back, she levered herself up on her front feet and stood up. Pete dug his toes behind her ears and hung on.

"She looks bigger out here," Vertie said.

Sweetiepie swung around and headed back toward the front gate of the sanctuary like an Olympic race walker.

"She can really move, can't she?" Sheriff Craig said.

"She came to find Pete. Something's wrong at the sanctuary." Tala climbed back into her truck and followed. Her hands were shaking.

Sweetiepie slid to a halt inside the gate of the compound so quickly that Pete nearly sailed over her head, while Tala missed slamming into her rear end only by a couple of feet. She climbed out of the truck and tried to make sense of what she was seeing.

"Sweetiepie, leg!" Pete said. The moment Sweetiepie lifted her foreleg, Pete slid off and held on to her tush as she lowered him to the ground, then she shoved him behind her.

Sophie stood to the left of the gate with her head toward the road, but her body angled away.

"Mama! Stay there!"

Rachel's voice seemed to have come from somewhere behind Sophie.

"Rachel? Cody?" Tala called.

Vertie stood behind her. "Where are they? And where's Irene?"

Rachel's hand waved from behind Sophie's right foreleg. "We're back here, Mom. We're fine."

The same could not be said for Sheriff Craig's squad car. It faced the gate, but at the moment it was poised precariously on the passenger side with Belle's tushes rammed under it.

Tala could hear Belle grunt and strain as she rocked back and forth. Her heavy forehead was braced against the side of the car. The car lifted slowly, teetered for a moment, then crashed onto its roof and lay there with all four wheels spinning, like some giant beetle that had fallen onto its back.

"Get her off me," a voice screamed from inside. "Make her stop!"

"Dr. Pete," Rachel shouted, "he's got a gun."

Tala ducked and dragged Vertie down beside her.

"Hell," Craig snarled, "he must have found my backup under the seat."

Belle screamed in fury, pulled back her head and drove her forehead full force into the metal of the squad car.

Oxley howled. "Oh, God, she's gonna kill me. Get her off me."

"Throw out your weapon, Oxley, and maybe Dr. Jacobi'll be able to call her off," Craig shouted from behind the open door of his squad car. "It's all over, fool. She *will* kill you if you don't come out with your hands up."

"I can't come out. She won't let me."

"Dr. Jacobi, can you call her off if he surrenders?'' the sheriff asked loud enough for Oxley to hear.

Pete replied just as loudly, ''Not sure I can. She's pretty pissed off.''

''Might help if you told us about Adam Newsome,'' the sheriff said.

''I don't know anything about that.''

''Billie Joe tells a different story. He's already given us his side of the story.''

Belle punctuated the sheriff's words with a solid bang.

Oxley screamed again. ''All right, all right! I'll tell you what happened. But it was an accident. I never meant to hurt anybody. Just get me out of here.''

''I haven't seen a gun yet, Oxley. Toss it out.''

A moment later an arm lobbed the sheriff's spare automatic through the open space where the windshield had been. ''Now, for the love of God call her off.''

Pete took a deep breath, stuck his hands in his pockets and sauntered toward Belle. ''You've made your point, girl,'' he said evenly. ''Back off now, so we can drag the bastard out.''

Belle stared him down, stubborn belligerence in every line of her body and the slant of her narrow little eyes.

''Now, Belle,'' Pete continued reasonably, ''it's not going to do a bit of good to crush him, although I'd admit I wish we could. We need to talk to him, hear what he has to say.''

She stood swaying, lining up her tushes for another attack.

Pete took his hands out of his pockets. "*Now,* Belle. Back off right this minute."

Belle took her time making up her mind. She swayed and stamped, swung her trunk in obvious frustration, then backed off a few steps. She never took her eyes off Pete.

A moment later Oxley was dragged out of the car and into the arms of the waiting deputy. He was crying. Shards of glass fell from his disheveled hair.

"Those damn elephants…"

Pete turned to him. "Can it, Oxley. One more word and I'll turn all three of them loose on you."

Oxley shrank against the deputy.

As the sheriff pushed Oxley toward the second squad car, Rachel slid slowly out from behind Sophie's right front leg.

Tala ran toward her and swept her into her arms. Pete was right behind her. "Rachel, where's Cody?"

"He's back there," Rachel said, pointing over her shoulder. "He won't let go."

Cody's small body was nearly hidden behind Sophie's gray column of a leg. His arms were wrapped around her and his forehead pressed against the folds of her skin. His eyes were closed. Sophie swayed gently almost as though she were rocking a cradle.

Tala dropped on her knees beside him and wrapped her arms around his body. "Cody, Cody bear. It's okay."

His face still pressed against Sophie's leg, Cody whispered, "She saved us. I kicked him and he shot at us and she saved us."

Sophie chirped gently, and reached around to caress the child with her trunk. Pete knelt beside Tala and laid his hand on Cody's shoulder. "Hey, guy," he said. "You're safe."

Vertie leaned against Pete. "Is your grandmother okay?"

Rachel nodded. "She's inside with Dr. Mace." She began to sob. "Mom, he tried to take us with him. He said we'd buy him time. He was going to let the elephants loose on the road and drive off, but Sweetiepie stood in the gate and wouldn't let him out. I thought he was going to shoot her, but then Belle bashed him so he couldn't. And then she bashed him again, and we got out of the car and ran."

Cody looked at Pete. "He nearly grabbed me when we ran," Cody said. "But Sophie got between us and hid us behind her." He lifted his face to his mother. His look was seraphic. "I love her."

"Then Sweetiepie took off," Rachel continued, "and I think he tried to shoot us, and Belle kept bashing him and bashing him."

"We hid behind Sophie," Cody said. "She wouldn't let us go."

"Pretty fancy cavalry," the sheriff said. "Got to say it's damned effective."

Pete looked around. "Where's Dad? And Irene?"

"When Dr. Mace first saw the squad car, he opened the gates, but it wasn't Sheriff Craig, Mom," Cody said. "It was that man. He locked Dr. Mace and Gram in that building."

"I'll get them, Pete. You stay here," Sheriff Craig said.

"I'm coming with you," Vertie said. "If that man hurt Irene, I'll brain him."

Pete nodded. The sheriff called to his deputy, "Get the bolt cutters out of the trunk of my car." He looked ruefully at his battered squad car. "Better try yours. I don't think my trunk'll open from that position."

Cody sighed deeply and finally released his grip on Sophie's leg to turn and wrap his arms around Pete's neck. "I'm sorry, Dr. Pete," he whispered.

"Sorry, guy?" Pete asked. "What for?"

Cody mumbled something into Pete's neck. Pete smiled and patted him awkwardly. "Hey, it was okay to be scared of them. You didn't know them then."

Cody raised his head. "I'm not scared of Sophie. She looked after us."

Tala hugged both of them. "You won't be scared of Belle and Sweetiepie either when you get to know them."

Sophie sighed and moved a few feet away.

That's when Pete saw the drops of blood pooled beside her left foot. "She's hurt!" he said.

Cody wailed and grabbed the elephant's leg again. "He shot at her. I thought he missed."

Tala moved Cody and Rachel out of Pete's way as he walked to Sophie's other side. Blood poured down the side of her head from a six-inch gash in her ear. She flapped it in irritation and pain as he tried to get her to lower her head.

"Oh, please," Cody wailed. "Don't let her be hurt."

"I think he just clipped her ear," Pete said. "From

down here I don't see any blood in the flesh underneath. Must not have pierced the hide over her skull, but ear wounds bleed heavily. It must hurt like the dickens, though.''

Cody looked up at his mother with tears streaming down his face. ''She didn't run away, not even when he shot her. Mom, he could have killed her, but she didn't run away. She saved us.''

At that moment Irene stumbled out of the workroom and into Vertie's arms. Mace was right behind her. Pete ran to his father. ''Dad, are you all right?''

Mace ran his hand down the back of his head. ''I'm fine, son. Great baby-sitter I turned out to be.''

''Are the children all right?'' Irene caught Pete's arm.

''Here, Gram,'' Rachel called.

Irene ran to hug them. ''I have never been angrier in my life. The nerve of that man!'' She glanced at the car, then looked more closely. ''My word, how did that happen?''

''It is a long story,'' Tala said dryly.

Pete started back toward the little group, but the elephants blocked his path. Belle and Sweetiepie advanced on Sophie to voice their concern and to touch her wounded ear tenderly. Then, as one, they turned to Pete. First Sophie, then Belle and finally Sweetiepie all ran their trunks over him and lowered their big heads in greeting.

Tala had never before seen them treat him that way. She stood transfixed and watched the joy in his face as he rubbed first one trunk, then another.

''Well, I'll be damned,'' Mace whispered. Then,

"Come on in the trailer, everybody, we could all use some hot chocolate with lots of sugar."

"I'll help," Tala said.

Now that the crisis was over, Cody's energy came back with a vengeance. He grabbed Irene's hand and began to pull her toward the trailer. "I kicked him, Gram. I was scared, but I kicked him anyway, and then Sophie came and got us and…"

"He is never going to shut up about this," Rachel said. "What a dork." The affectionate look on her face belied her words. "Are you coming, Mom?" She smiled at Tala.

"I'll be there in a minute," Tala said.

"Don't bother. We have plenty of baby-sitters." Rachel looked over her shoulder and actually grinned. "Really *big* ones."

The moment Mace's door closed, Pete grabbed Tala and swung her around so that she dangled a foot above the ground. "If anything had happened to them…"

"It didn't, thanks to the girls. They did it for you, you know," she whispered. "They love you."

"I think they finally approve of me. And you're a big part of the reason. You and those kids of yours. Even Vertie and, God help me, Irene. Because of you I've finally got enough love for the whole world." He kissed her deeply, set her down and held her shoulders. "Okay, you better let me say this before I lose my nerve."

"What on earth?"

"Just listen. I don't know the first thing about kids."

"Your gorilla didn't either until she learned."

He grinned. "Yeah, but I'm older than Millie and I'm a man. If I can convince Rachel and Cody I'm not an ogre, and if I provide Irene proof that I can give you all a decent home, will you please marry me?"

Tala gaped. "Are you serious? Do you have a clue what you're getting into?"

"Not a clue. But when I thought Oxley had Rachel and Cody, I was darned near as scared as I was when I saw that leopard behind you. I'll never be their father, but I'd like to be a part of their lives. And yours, if you'll let me."

She threw her arms around his neck. "Then yes, yes, yes!"

He kissed her long and hard, then pulled away from her as though he'd suddenly remembered something. "Damn and blast." He grabbed her hand and began to pull her toward the trailer. "The heck with hot chocolate, Dad and I have some big cats to catch."

CHAPTER NINETEEN

A WEEK LATER Sheriff Craig sat at Irene's morning-room table, put another of Lucinda's lemon tarts on his plate and brushed the crumbs from the last three off his uniform shirt. "I thought you folks deserved to hear the details about Adam's death from me."

Vertie, Irene and Tala sat across from him. Pete lounged beside Tala with his arm across the back of her chair.

"There won't be a trial," the sheriff continued. "Oxley's pleading guilty to second-degree murder. His lawyer advised him there wasn't a jury in America that wouldn't lift up the jail and drop him under once they heard about that hunt."

"Smart lawyer," Irene said.

"Oxley swears he shot Adam by accident, but an accident with a firearm that occurs in the commission of a felony, which is what he and Billie Joe were committing at the time by poaching deer, is murder, pure and simple. Mr. Oxley won't be seeing the light of day for about twenty years, give or take."

Tala grabbed Irene's hand. She wanted the sheriff to finish before Mrs. Lippincott brought Rachel and Cody home from their practices. Whatever they needed to hear, she would tell them.

Craig waved away another cup of tea.

"Plus all the other charges—illegal hunting, possession of illegal arms, kidnapping. Lord—I don't have time or energy to go into all the details." The sheriff took another bite of lemon tart.

"Why'd he do it?" Vertie asked. "That's what I want to know. The man was rich. His daddy and granddaddy both used to go on safari in Africa at least once a year."

"Used up quite a bit of the family fortune doing just that," Craig said. "Didn't leave nearly as much as Oxley thought he'd get. But he did inherit his grandfather's Purdey double rifle, the one he'd used to shoot elephant and rhino in Africa. Oxley wanted to hunt big game, too, but he wanted to make money doing it, and he didn't want to have to go to Africa. Neither did his buddies in that Stateside Safaris crowd. So Oxley told 'em he'd give 'em a trophy hunt for twenty thousand dollars each."

"That much?" Irene asked.

"I'd guess you could call this his pilot program. He's been working on it now for at least two years, setting things up while he was working on those condos. And by the way, his construction loans are way past due. He's facing foreclosure. That's why he staged the hunt now to pick up some quick cash."

"And he picked me and my land," Vertie said.

"Because it was isolated. He didn't think Tala would matter much. Billie Joe told him she worked nights, and he didn't expect to have those cats around more than a couple of weeks. Then those bozos he hired let a lion get loose."

"Baby," Tala said softly.

"They chased her, and one of them thought he shot her, but they couldn't find her, and apparently those two couldn't track a polar bear's prints through snow."

"But how did Adam come to get shot?" Vertie asked.

"Oxley started those condos over two years ago, remember. And apparently Billie Joe has been on his payroll most of that time. Billie Joe was with him way back in the woods..."

"On my property?" Vertie whispered.

The sheriff looked at her and nodded. "Afraid so, Miss Vertie."

"I wish I'd never inherited the place." Vertie sniffed and blew her nose loudly into a tissue.

"It could have happened anywhere," Tala said gently.

"Anyway," Craig hurried on, "he and Billie Joe were sighting in that fancy antique rifle on a few out-of-season deer. Oxley didn't even have a hunting license. Doesn't believe in 'em. He'd been caught before in North Carolina. Adam walked up on 'em. Billie Joe says he must have recognized him, because Adam didn't draw his weapon."

Tala closed her eyes. She didn't want to hear this part, but she needed to. She gritted her teeth. "Go on."

"Oxley swears he was so startled he swung around with the rifle and bang, the hair trigger went off and Adam went down."

Pete began to knead Tala's shoulder. She clutched Irene's hand even tighter.

"Oxley pretty well blackmailed Billie Joe into helping him move Adam, and then to keep him up-to-date on the investigation. But I didn't let anybody in on everything we found out—not even my own folks. Everybody's connected too tight around here. After all this time, Oxley thought he was safe."

"I invited him to dinner," Vertie said.

"I tried to fix him up with Tala, Vertilene," Irene said tartly. "Stop this mully-grubbing. I won't have it. We didn't do anything wrong. That man did."

Vertie sighed.

"She's right, Miss Vertie," Pete added. "And we'd never have saved the rest of the cats if it hadn't been for you."

"Got to hand it to your deputies, Sheriff," Pete said. "It's not easy to keep your nerve with lions and tigers in deep cover, but nobody panicked."

"You were right about not notifying the media. Now that would have been panic, let me tell you. Luckily those cats made a bee-line for those cages the minute they smelled the meat you and Hildebrand put in them. Acted like they hadn't had a bite in a week."

"Probably hadn't," Vertie said. "That's another thing I hold against those people." She sighed. "Lord, I hope I can start to feel better about this sometime."

"You'd can start this minute," Irene said. She turned to the sheriff. "Thank you for telling us."

Craig stood, and Irene followed him to the front

hall, then came back after he left. She stood straight in the doorway. "I need you back the way you were, Vertie—irritating. Not some hangdog feeling sorry for herself. I've gotten used to the real you."

Vertie raised her head. "Used to me? I was mistress of this house long before you were."

Irene smiled. "That's a start." She sat down at the table and laid her hand on Tala's. "Are you all right?"

Tala nodded. "Better than I have any right to be."

"Good, because the way you and Dr. Jacobi have been carrying on, I sincerely hope you're planning a wedding."

EPILOGUE

"THAT IS CERTAINLY the most outrageous trio of bridesmaids I ever saw," Irene sniffed, and waved the antique lace fan she carried in her kid-gloved hands. "Lord knows what the town will say. Elephants in the retinue indeed."

"Come on, Gram," Cody said as his mother tried to hold him still long enough to finish tying his bow tie. "They'll be back behind the new fence. It's not like they'll be walking up the aisle in front of Mom." He scuffed his feet and rolled his eyes.

"I wish they could," Rachel said. "I don't know why Pete wouldn't let me tie ribbons around their trunks," Rachel said. "Ashley and I thought they'd really look pretty."

"Too much like the circus," Tala said. "Pete would never allow it. Besides, they'd have taken approximately six seconds each to untie them and trample them in the mud."

Cody wriggled.

"Stand still or I'll never get this straight. And I may strangle you." Tala tucked the ends of his bow tie neatly behind and gave it one final tug. "There. You clean up pretty well, Cody, if I do say so myself."

"I hate it," he mumbled. "Why do I have to dress up? It's your wedding."

"I don't know why Pete couldn't make this one teeny little exception and let us ride the girls to the altar," Rachel said. "Ashley would never have gotten over it. I'd be the coolest person in school."

"Rachel, you're messing up your dress lying on the bed that way," Tala said. "Get up and sit in a chair like a lady. And the girls wouldn't fit in the house. It's too hot outside for an outdoor wedding."

Rachel rolled her eyes. "At least I don't have ruffles. I'd die if anybody saw me in ruffles."

"Well, you got your first heels out of it and no ruffles. So you've got nothing to complain about."

Rachel sniffed, but looked at the satin pumps with the one-inch heel as though they were the ruby slippers. "At least we got a nice house out of this, even if it is in an elephant sanctuary," Rachel said.

"And at least Pete has fenced off the area in front of the enclosure so those creatures can't wander all the way to the front gate and run over the guests," Irene said.

"If they hadn't wandered to the front gate, Cody and Rachel would have been stuck in that car with Oxley, Irene," Tala said reasonably. She slipped the second pearl stud in her ear and slid the back onto it.

"I suppose so." Irene looked around. "It *is* a nice house, Tala, I must admit. Pleasant, roomy, lots of light."

Tala looked around the big bedroom with satisfaction. Big, open rooms, post-and-beam construction, windows everywhere. And separate bedrooms and baths for Rachel and Cody, as well as a guest room and bath, should Dr. Mace ever decide to abandon his trailer. At the moment, Jim and Mary Ann Hildebrand were occupying it for the wedding and reception.

The furnishings were a combination of antiques from Irene and Vertie, leftovers from the farm and new, modern pieces she and Pete had chosen.

Rachel slept once more in the Shaker bed her father had built for her, and Cody rocked in the rocker that had been Adam's third birthday present to his son.

Tala smiled at her mother-in-law. "You know, I feel that Adam is finally at peace now that he finally has his preserve."

"I can hardly wait for the first interns to arrive next summer," Irene said. "I'm planning to volunteer, you know. Just a bit of record-keeping, but I do want to be a part of it. I know you're happy your farmhouse will actually be used as dormitory space and not simply torn down or abandoned. And with Vertie's land added to yours, the preserve is really quite large." Irene glowed. "The Adam Newsome Nature Reserve," she said, wiping away a tear. "He would be so proud that you managed to accomplish what he couldn't."

"Eventually he would have."

"You never told me how much the state paid for your farm, but if you and Pete need money, you know…"

Tala shook her head and smiled at Irene. "You are

bound and determined to give me money. I promise you we don't need it, although the kids will probably keep conning you out of things we can't afford. Now that Pete's taking over Dr. Wiskowski's practice, we'll do fine. Come fall, I'm going back to college.''

''Who's going to look after...'' Irene waved a hand. ''The girls?''

Tala glanced at her offspring. ''Actually, we figured Cody and Rachel could do all that, plus big Bertha, who arrives a couple of weeks after we get back from our honeymoon. I hear she's very shy.''

''Mom!'' Both children wailed simultaneously.

Tala chuckled. ''All right, all right. Mace will be here, and both Pete and I will work here as much as we can, then we're going to hire a couple of interns from the college this fall. It'll work out.''

''You're taking on too much as usual,'' Irene said.

''No, I'm not. Now, scat, you two. Wait downstairs for Irene and me. Where's Vertie?''

''She's already sitting in the front row,'' Rachel said and closed the door behind her.

''Do you mind so much?'' Tala said, taking Irene's hand.

Irene smiled at her. ''No, dear. He's very different from Adam, but he is a kind man, and we have all grown very fond of him these last six months.'' She waved her fan. ''And he did build you this lovely house.'' She began to sniffle. ''I'll miss having you at *my* house.''

''You'll have Rachel and Cody for two weeks while we're in Thailand, and weekends and sleepovers after that.''

"Are you sure you want to spend the rest of your life with elephants?"

"Not only with elephants, Irene, with Pete and the children. And Mace. And you and Vertie. *And* elephants."

The strains of a harp came from the floor below.

Tala took a deep breath. "Time to give away the bride, Irene."

Irene sniffled again, blew her nose on her lace handkerchief, clicked her fan shut and dropped it on the bed. "Never. You'll always belong to me."

Tala moved through her wedding in a sort of dream, only concentrating on Pete's huge hands as he gently slid the gold band on her finger, and then as she worked his gold band onto his. Everything felt right.

The last six months they'd built a house together, gotten the park set up, worked out ground rules for stepfatherdom, and helped Jim and Mary Ann Hildebrand build enclosures for the new big cats they'd taken in after Oxley's little fiasco. Baby now had her very own pride.

They had argued, laughed, made wild love and gentle love, and learned the sheer pleasure of sleeping like spoons.

She stood on tiptoe to lift her face for Pete's kiss.

As their lips met, the walls began to reverberate with the trumpeting of three elephants. Tala broke the kiss and began to laugh. She heard chairs scrape and murmurs as the wedding guests moved uneasily.

"Stampede?" she whispered to Pete.

He pulled her back into his arms. "Nope. That's my side of the family. I'd say they approve."

HARLEQUIN® SUPERROMANCE®

HOME ON THE RANCH

Welcome to cowboy country!

MONTANA LEGACY by **Roxanne Rustand**
(Superromance #895)
Minneapolis cop Kate Rawlins has her own reasons
for wanting to sell her inheritance—half of the
Lone Tree Ranch, Montana. Then she meets
co-owner Seth Hayward and suddenly splitting the property
doesn't seem like a good idea....
On sale February 2000

COWBOY COME HOME by **Eve Gaddy**
(Superromance #903)
After years on the saddle circuit, champion bronco
rider Jake Rollins returns home—determined to find
out whether his ex-lover's daughter is *his* child.
On sale March 2000

Available at your favorite retail outlet.

HARLEQUIN®
Makes any time special ™

Visit us at www.romance.net

HSRRANCH

HEART OF THE WEST

Every Man Has His Price!

Lost Springs Ranch was famous for turning young mavericks into good men. So word that the ranch was in financial trouble sent a herd of loyal bachelors stampeding back to Wyoming to put themselves on the auction block!

July 1999	*Husband for Hire* Susan Wiggs	January 2000	*The Rancher and the Rich Girl* Heather MacAllister
August	*Courting Callie* Lynn Erickson	February	*Shane's Last Stand* Ruth Jean Dale
September	*Bachelor Father* Vicki Lewis Thompson	March	*A Baby by Chance* Cathy Gillen Thacker
October	*His Bodyguard* Muriel Jensen	April	*The Perfect Solution* Day Leclaire
November	*It Takes a Cowboy* Gina Wilkins	May	*Rent-a-Dad* Judy Christenberry
December	*Hitched by Christmas* Jule McBride	June	*Best Man in Wyoming* Margot Dalton

HARLEQUIN®

Makes any time special™

Visit us at www.romance.net

PHHOWGEN